SPECIAL MESSAGE TO READERS

THE ULVERSCROFT FOUNDATION
(registered UK charity number 264873)
was established in 1972 to provide funds for
research, diagnosis and treatment of eye diseases.
Examples of major projects funded by
the Ulverscroft Foundation are:-

- The Children's Eye Unit at Moorfields Eye Hospital, London
- The Ulverscroft Children's Eye Unit at Great Ormond Street Hospital for Sick Children
- Funding research into eye diseases and treatment at the Department of Ophthalmology, University of Leicester
- The Ulverscroft Vision Research Group, Institute of Child Health
- Twin operating theatres at the Western Ophthalmic Hospital, London
- The Chair of Ophthalmology at the Royal Australian College of Ophthalmologists

You can help further the work of the Foundation
by making a donation or leaving a legacy.
Every contribution is gratefully received. If you
would like to help support the Foundation or
require further information, please contact:

THE ULVERSCROFT FOUNDATION
The Green, Bradgate Road, Anstey
Leicester LE7 7FU, England
Tel: (0116) 236 4325

website: www.fou᠁**lverscro**᠁**.com**

D1065905

Wendy Soliman was brought up on the Isle of Wight in southern England, but now divides her time between Andorra and western Florida. She lives with her husband Andre and a rescued dog, of indeterminate pedigree, named Jake Bentley after the hunky hero in one of her books. When not writing she enjoys reading other people's books, walking miles with her dog whilst plotting her next scene, dining out and generally making the most out of life.

TO DEFY A DUKE

Elias Shelton, the Duke of Winsdale, has a duty to produce an heir. Completely indifferent, he leaves his mother to invite the most suitable candidates to a house party at Winsdale Park, promising to choose one of them as his duchess. Returning home after several days of pre-nuptial carousing, he falls from his horse and badly injures his head. His life is saved by a mysterious woman who fascinates and enthrals him: Athena Defoe, who along with her young twin sisters is hiding from her past in a tumbledown cottage on Eli's estate. Can Eli help his new love escape her pursuers before it is too late?

Books by Wendy Soliman
Published by The House of Ulverscroft:

LADY HARTLEY'S INHERITANCE
DUTY'S DESTINY
THE SOCIAL OUTCAST
THE CARSTAIRS CONSPIRACY
A BITTERSWEET PROPOSAL

WENDY SOLIMAN

◆

TO DEFY A DUKE

Complete and Unabridged

ULVERSCROFT
Leicester

First published in Great Britain in 2013

First Large Print Edition
published 2015

A catalogue record for this book is available
from the British Library.

ISBN 978–1–4448–2256–4

Published by
F. A. Thorpe (Publishing)
Anstey, Leicestershire

Set by Words & Graphics Ltd.
Anstey, Leicestershire
Printed and bound in Great Britain by
T. J. International Ltd., Padstow, Cornwall

This book is printed on acid-free paper

1

Southern England, September 1816

As Athena walked briskly through the wooded slopes of Whispers' Hollow, the hem of her gown became soaked with dew. She pulled her thick shawl more closely about her to ward off the chill. Weak sunshine broke through the early morning mist, dappling the fallen leaves beneath her feet with its sporadic rays. She breathed deeply of clean, fresh air that smelled of damp, loamy earth and changing seasons.

Keen to reach the spot where she hoped to find a crop of common field mushrooms, Athena didn't linger to appreciate the beauty of her surroundings. She thought wistfully of the cosy bed she had just vacated, leaving her twin sisters sleeping peacefully in it, glad not to have disturbed them. She stifled a yawn, perpetually tired these days, but sleep was a luxury she could no longer afford to indulge in.

'We should count our blessings,' she said aloud. 'Hard work never hurt anyone.'

Her companion, to whom this remark was

addressed, cocked his head to one side and then wagged in enthusiastic agreement. Athena smiled, something she'd had precious little occasion to do since her circumstances had taken such a dramatic downward turn. Consumed by feelings of great affection, she ruffled Boris's scruffy ears.

Boris was a rather unfortunate looking dog, but that was hardly his fault. Gangly-legged, uncoordinated, and with a shaggy coat the colour of the autumn leaves, he was neither one thing nor another. Even the most prejudiced eye, which Athena's most decidedly was, couldn't describe him as handsome, or pedigreed. But he was a good hunting dog, ensuring Athena's current abode remained rodent-free, and a faithful companion as well as a ferocious guardian. Athena shuddered, hoping that quality wouldn't be called into action in the immediate future.

'Here we are, Boris,' she said, striding into a clearing and having the satisfaction of seeing a fine crop of mushrooms flourishing beneath the shade of a tree. 'Just as I had hoped. They will make a tasty addition to our rabbit stew this evening.'

'Woof.'

'I'm glad you agree . . . Boris, come back. What is it?'

Athena straightened up from examining the

mushrooms, having just assured herself they were the non-poisonous variety she'd been hoping to find. Immediately suspicious of Boris's abrupt disappearance, she tried to convince herself he was merely tormenting squirrels. Surely, her whereabouts hadn't been discovered already? Her heart quailed at the very thought. Would her uncle never leave her in peace?

'Boris!' Her dog came bounding back into the clearing, almost flattening the precious mushrooms in his enthusiasm. 'Ah, there you are. Did you catch the squirrel? Careful of the mushrooms.'

'Woof!' Boris bounded off again, and then came back, wagging. It was obvious he expected her to follow him.

'Oh, all right.' She placed her basket to one side, straightened her skirts, and trailed after Boris. 'What are you so anxious for me to see?'

She followed Boris for a full minute before they came to a track. At first, she couldn't see anything remarkable about it. Then she did and gasped. To one side of it stood the most magnificent horse she had ever seen — a grey stallion of impeccable pedigree, if she was any judge. It looked up from the patch of grass it was cropping when Athena appeared, whinnied, and then continued with its breakfast. It was complete with saddle and bridle, but lacked a rider.

'What the devil?'

Athena cast her gaze around the clearing, expecting the horse's owner to appear at any moment. The thought alarmed her. Anyone in these woods this early in the day couldn't be up to any good, and she had only Boris for protection. Fierce as he was, he was no match for a bullet or rapier.

'Stop being so fanciful,' she chided, speaking aloud to herself as she always did when she was anxious, which meant she held perpetual one-sided conversations with herself nowadays. 'Mr. Moncrieff doesn't possess such a fine animal.'

Boris barked again, bounding ahead of her and leading Athena to the owner of the beautiful horse. He was flat out on the ground, blood pouring from a nasty gash on the side of his head. Unsurprisingly, he was unconscious. Athena knelt beside him and felt for a pulse. It was strong and regular, which reassured her, but his wound definitely needed dressing. With a wistful sigh, she lifted her skirts and tore a strip from her one remaining respectable petticoat.

Balling up her makeshift bandage, she placed it firmly against the side of the man's head to stem the flow of blood, and held it there. That was all well and good, but it meant she could neither move, nor go to fetch help. The moment she released the pressure, the bleeding would start up again. What to do? She had no idea how long the man had been there. Surely, not long? Only an idiot would ride through these woods during the hours of darkness. Just as well he hadn't been here long, and she was the one to have found him, or he would have bled to death. Athena knew a thing or two about injuries, and was absolutely sure of that.

'Go and fetch Millie,' Athena told Boris, hoping against hope he would understand her.

The dog obediently loped off in the direction of their cottage but, even if Millie returned with him, it would be at least ten minutes before she got here. Millie only had one speed.

Athena sat on the ground beside the injured man and placed a hand on his forehead. He was burning up. Lord have mercy, did he have a fever? Panic gripped her. Is that why he'd fallen from his horse and hit his head? If it was contagious, it could place her entire family at risk because, of course, Athena would take him back to the cottage and nurse him back to health. The fact that she barely had the means to feed her existing family didn't signify. It was her Christian duty to help a fellow human being in his hour of need, and somehow they would manage. Besides, once she was at home, with her precious collection of herbs to hand, she would soon make him better. It was simply a matter of deciding how best to get him there. In his unconscious state, he wouldn't be able to walk, or ride, either.

Athena looked at him properly for the first time, blinked rapidly, and gasped. He was quite simply the most beautiful male she had ever set eyes upon. He was dressed simply in the style of a man from the middle classes in old breeches that displayed toned, muscular thighs. Athena probably wasn't supposed to notice such things, but since she'd never been one to conform to the conventions, and given that she was saving his life, she felt justified in noticing. His upper body was covered by a grubby white shirt open at the neck, no neckcloth or coat in evidence.

She wondered about the quality of his horse, which was too fine for a man of his status. Perhaps he was a horse dealer, delivering this fabulous beast to one of the many great houses in the locality. Yes, that could be it. She would have delved into his saddlebags, looking for clues as to his identity, but she needed to keep pressure on his wound, and so couldn't move from his side.

That provided her with a legitimate excuse to look at him while she waited for help to arrive. She had never felt the slightest desire to ogle a man before, but then she had never encountered one quite as compelling as the individual who held her complete and absolute attention. He had thick black hair, coated in his own blood, and the longest eyelashes she had ever seen on a man's face. That hardly seemed fair. What need did a man have for glamorous lashes? They curled back on themselves, protecting eyes, which were firmly closed. Athena wondered what colour those eyes might be. Brown, she thought. Yes, definitely, they ought to be brown. A deep, rich shade of brown.

'Stop being so ridiculous!' she chided.

But still, as she continued to look at the man, absorbing the perfect symmetry of his features, a strange feeling consumed her — a warning or a premonition — it was difficult to know which. She was supposed to find this man. She didn't know how she could be so sure about that — she just was. She also knew, since she had found him, her circumstances would never be quite the same again. Well, that was one good thing, because she had hit rock bottom, and they could only change for the better.

Her unnamed horse dealer had a strong, square jaw decorated with several days' worth of stubble, a straight, almost aristocratic nose. His face was all fascinating planes and angles, and his mouth . . . oh his beautiful, sensual mouth. Athena leaned towards it, quite overcome by the symmetry of his lovely sculpted lips, until his breath hit her face and she almost gagged. If she hadn't been holding her sacrificed petticoat to his injury, she would have jumped to her feet in outrage. The man smelt like a brewery. Well, presumably that explained why he had fallen from his horse. Athena wrinkled her nose in disgust, feeling she would be totally justified in leaving him where he was.

But, of course, she would not.

'What's happening, pet?' Millie asked, puffing along behind Boris. 'This creature came back alone and gave me such a fright. I thought you'd been found again, and I . . . hey up, what have we here?'

'He's drunk,' Athena said, laughing in spite of her disapproval. 'And out cold. I would leave him, but for this injury.'

'We need to get him on his horse. He's too big for us to carry.'

Yes, that was certainly true, Athena thought. He was far taller than average, and his large body appeared to be made up of solid muscle.

'It will take us both to lift him up, and I'm worried about the bleeding.' Athena lifted her make-shift dressing, gratified to notice that

8

the flow of blood had slowed significantly, but hadn't stopped all together. 'I need to secure this bandage in place,' she said, sighing as she tore another strip from her ravaged petticoat and bound it tightly around the man's head. He groaned, but didn't open his eyes.

'Right we are, Millie. We shall have to try and push him over his saddle, face down. It's the only way we can manage this. If we grab one shoulder each to get him upright, we can then try and boost him up from behind.'

'It might be easier if I went back for the pony and trap,' Millie said dubiously.

'That will take too long. By the time you've woken Meg up, which you will most assuredly have to do because that pony is the laziest creature on God's earth, got her into her harness and persuaded her to come out here, half the morning will be gone. I don't have time to waste on intoxicated fools.'

'Very well, lass. Let's try and move him.'

It was like trying to move a mountain, but Athena refused to be defeated. On the third attempt, they managed to get him to his feet, and leaned him against a sturdy tree. Athena felt mildly elated.

'Hold him up, Millie, while I get his horse.'

'Do you think such a fine animal will agree to stand still?' Millie asked dubiously. 'Them types tend to be pretty skittish.'

9

'We shall just have to see.'

The horse was still cropping the grass, looking up every so often to see what was happening, but showing no inclination to take to his heels. He made no objection when Athena took hold of his bridle and walked him towards the man who'd so carelessly tumbled from his back.

'This is going to be very undignified for you,' she told the horse, stroking his soft muzzle. 'I'm very sorry about that, but I'd be greatly obliged if you would stand still, and not cause us further difficulties.'

Athena halted the horse as close to the tree the man was snoring against as she could manage, and tied his reins securely to a stout lower branch. Despite her annoyance with her unwelcome visitor, she still took a moment to admire his physique. Now that he was upright, he was even more impressive. Or would have been, except Athena was out of charity with him for ruining her day and refused to be impressed by broad shoulders and a muscular chest that tapered to a narrow waist and slim hips. He was taller than average and even in an intoxicated state he exuded a rather intimidating aura of authority, as though he was accustomed to being obeyed. Athena looked at him, determined *she* would not be intimidated by an unconscious person whom she didn't even know. But again, she felt anew the wakening of a deeply disturbing dormant feeling inside of her. This annoying intruder affected her on a level she appeared unable to control, and she wasn't the least bit happy about it.

'I've never seen anyone snoring in an upright position before,' Athena remarked, thinking it might be a useful habit to acquire, provided it didn't require one to become intoxicated in order to achieve it. 'Right, Millie, let's drag him to the horse and endeavour to get him aboard.'

'It looks an awful long way up,' Millie replied dubiously. 'And this fellow's no lightweight.'

'Yes, but nevertheless.'

The two of them struggled, puffing and straining, to no avail.

'It ain't no good.' Millie leaned against the tree, panting, looking hot and bothered. 'Perhaps we should wait until he wakes up. Or you could go back to the cottage for your herbs, if you're worried about his wound.'

'No, I can't treat him properly here. Besides, I need to get back to the twins before they wake up and wonder where I am. They will only become anxious otherwise. We need to do something.' Athena frowned. 'You're right, I definitely don't like the look of that wound. Blood is still seeping, and I think he must be unconscious, in spite of the snoring, which is a concern.'

'Wonder who he is? Perhaps one of us can run for help.'

'There is no one close enough to help. That's why we chose this isolated situation.' Athena sighed, thinking frantically. 'At least the horse is co-operating. He hasn't tried to back away, which makes me think we should trade on his goodwill.'

'All right. But how?'

'Millie, go the other side of the horse, if you please. I shall throw this aggravating man's arms over the saddle. If you would kindly grab his hands when I tell you to, I'll then endeavour to push him up from his . . . er, backside.'

'You can't be touching a man's unmentionables, Athena.' Millie sounded quite shocked. 'You have your reputation to consider. Best let me do it.'

Athena smothered a smile. 'No, Millie, you have a weak heart.'

'Nonsense, I'm as strong as an ox.'

'A weak heart, and I'm stronger than you are. Besides, there's no one here to see us except this ungrateful drunkard. I don't care what he thinks, and don't give two figs for my reputation.'

'Hmm, all right, if there's no other way, I suppose we must.'

'Come, we're wasting time.'

It took far longer than Athena expected just to get the unconscious man at the horse's side and his arms thrown across the saddle. He would keep dropping one and wrapping it around Athena's person. Really, if she hadn't been absolutely sure he was unconscious she would have said he was doing it on purpose, just to aggravate her.

Finally, they managed it.

'Now for the tricky part,' Athena said, breathing hard. 'Are you ready, Millie?'

'As I ever will be.'

'Right, take his hands and I shall boost his posterior.'

Athena bent her knees, placing her shoulder beneath the man's buttocks. Her strength was dwindling, and time was getting on. She couldn't afford to waste any more of either, so she was determined this would work on the first attempt. His legs dangled against her side, the heels of his boots hitting her painfully on the arm. They were very fine boots, she noticed, albeit muddy and dusty, made of the best leather.

'Must be good money in the horseflesh business,' she muttered mutinously.

She took a deep breath, then straightened

her knees and pushed as hard as she could, straining every sinew. Millie pulled from the other side and, by some miracle, they moved the man far enough off the ground for him to finish half way across the saddle. Athena was both surprised and elated. She really hadn't thought it would happen quite so easily, and glanced suspiciously at the inert figure dangling inelegantly over the horse. She could have sworn he had given her a helping hand, and was certain he had groaned when she placed her hands on his backside. She peered at his face, almost relieved to find he was still dead to the world. She must have imagined it.

'Well done, Millie!' Athena clapped her hands together in triumph. 'One more push from this side, and I think he will be secure.'

Millie joined Athena and they managed to manipulate the man so his stomach rested on the seat of the saddle, his legs dangling to one side, his torso to the other.

'Lead the horse, Millie, and I'll walk beside his accident-prone rider to keep an eye on his wound.'

'Very well.'

'Come along, Boris, we're leaving.'

2

Who was Boris, damn his eyes?

Elias Shelton remained cooperatively draped across Byron's saddle as his rescuing angel spirited him off to wherever it was she planned to take him. His head hurt like the devil, his entire body ached, and his gut protested at the astronomical amount of brandy he'd forced upon it the night before. Death would be a happy release, except he had no wish to die, at least not until he had discovered the identity of his fair saviour.

Eli had difficulty remembering precisely how matters had come to this rather humiliating, yet immensely entertaining pass. He recalled being with Franklin and Johnson, drinking and wenching in their usual competitive manner in the taverns that littered the dockside in Portsmouth. He was supposed to be back at Winsdale Hall by now. That much he did know. His mother would be displeased by his continued absence, although he wasn't precisely sure why. Elias tended to do as he pleased, and it was many a long year since his mother had dictated his movements. Even so, there was something important nagging away

15

at the back of his aching head, something he'd agree to do against his better judgement — hence the carousing, which had proven an effective way of taking his mind off things.

He'd been taking a shortcut through the woods. Then he must have fallen asleep and slithered from Byron's back. The next thing he knew an angel with the most remarkable eyes, a soft yet scorching touch, and a face to inspire the most taciturn of artists, had placed her gentle hands on him, rousing him from his stupor. He'd taken a peep at her, dazed and disorientated, but ready to tell her there was nothing wrong with him that dousing himself in cold water and sleeping for a sennight wouldn't put right.

Unfortunately, he chose the wrong moment to open his eyes. She happened to lift her skirts just as he did so, muttered something uncomplimentary about him, and tore her petticoat to shreds. The glimpse of shapely limb coincidentally afforded him was reason enough to pretend continued delirium. Perhaps the snoring had been a little too much, but he'd done it to cover the surprised gasp of approval that slipped past his lips at the sight of her, and thought he'd be best advised to keep it up. He was surprised it didn't make her suspicious. As far as he was aware, unconscious persons weren't given to snoring.

Who was she? Was she real? Was he even more intoxicated than he'd realised, and his subconscious had conjured up an image of his ideal woman? Very likely, because it was a lady, or perhaps ladies, responsible for his aching head. That much he did know. There was something about a female he very much wished to avoid — except, he wouldn't want to avoid her if the woman in question was this guardian angel.

She placed something against his aching head. He'd obviously split it open when he fell, and even her assured yet gentle touch was torture. She had spoken to him incessantly in a soothing, melodic voice that enchanted him, as did the feel of her cool fingers against his heated skin when she brushed his hair clear of the wound. She had rested his head in her lap, pressing firmly against his wound, and Eli had no longer felt any pain. Instead, he had selfishly remained insensible. He had been enjoying himself far too much to bring the entertaining interlude to a premature end.

His rescuing angel had been treating him like a normal person, until she caught a waft of the brandy on his breath. She then upbraided him quite violently for his drunkenness. When had anyone last dared to upbraid His Grace, the Duke of Winsdale, for

17

inappropriate behaviour? It was a refreshing change and entirely deserved.

Someone else had approached. His rescuer had called her Millie, and they fell into a discussion about the best way to transport Eli somewhere more convenient to treat his wound. Ah, things had become really interesting, then. His lovely companion would have to man-handle him in order to achieve that ambition. Eli resisted the urge to smile at the prospect.

Athena. Millie had called her Athena. A lovely name for a beautiful lady. The goddess of wisdom, if he remembered his Greek mythology a'right. How appropriate. The two women had agreed upon their strategy and made several attempts to get him to his feet. Eli didn't want them to strain themselves, but couldn't very well bring himself to help, either. It would be over too quickly if he did. Aching head and complaining stomach notwithstanding, Eli couldn't remember the last time he'd enjoyed himself so much. Besides, standing up would bring back the dizziness that had been partly responsible for his fall in the first place, wouldn't it?

Thus vindicated, he had remained a dead, unmoving weight on the ground. His goddess had complained vociferously as she draped one of his arms across her narrow shoulders and struggled to elevate him from his prone position. Eli had obliging left his arm where she had placed it, enticingly close to her left breast, and chanced a quick peep down at her body while she was preoccupied. He had sucked in a sharp breath when he was treated to a close, intriguing glimpse of enticing curves hidden beneath a hideous worsted gown. A body that had matched the lovely face, but that body ought to be clad in satins and silks. And so it would be, if Eli had his way.

He had quickly closed his eyes again before she caught him awake. His eyes were bound to be horribly bloodshot, anyway. They probably resembled a map of Jamaica, definitely not a sight fit for a lady. Eli tried not to lean too much of his weight against his lovely Athena's delicate shoulders as his rescuers had dragged him towards a sturdy tree. Leaning against the tree in question — Eli had decided it was time to be a little more cooperative when he found himself guarded by the older, much stouter, Millie. He had wondered what relation she was to his goddess. Not a mother, obviously, since Athena addressed her by her Christian name and appeared to be the one in charge. A faithful retainer, perhaps? Yes, most likely.

Eli briefly had opened one eye again, keeping his head bowed as he admired the elegant sway of Athena's hips when she moved away from him. He groaned, a different sort of pain gripping him as she reached Byron and caressed the horse's muzzle. The only living creature Athena ought to be caressing was him, damn it! Athena had led Byron across to Eli's position, and he listened as the two women laid plans to boost him across Byron's back, arguing about which of them should touch Eli's backside.

Please, sweet goddess, have mercy on a humble duke.

She had won the argument, but the moment he felt her small hands on his posterior he had reason to regret her victory. He had sucked in another sharp breath as his groin constricted in response to her touch. God's beard, it had been pure torture being thrust against a horse's flank with a raging erection *and* a pounding head. His discomfort turned to amusement when Athena had let forth with a string of the most unladylike curses. When the devil had she learned to swear like a sailor?

Finally, after he was laid across Byron's saddle to their satisfaction and his acute frustration, Millie led the stallion forward. Athena walked beside him, her delicate, flowery fragrance assailing his nostrils as she pressed her shredded petticoat firmly against his wound. Boris, he could now see as he briefly opened an eye again, was the most uncoordinated excuse for a dog he'd ever encountered. Still, at least he seemed dedicated to Eli's goddess, which reassured him to some degree. He didn't like the idea of her living around these parts unprotected, which was presumably the case. Were there any men beneath her roof, presumably they would have been summoned to help rouse Eli. Had that been the case, he would have regained his senses long before now.

The journey was slow. Every one of Byron's steps jolted through Eli's body like a bad debt, making his head hurt even more. He was so curious about Athena he barely noticed the discomfort. They were on Eli's land. He didn't know all of his tenants — not even by sight. There were far too many of them for that, but one as beautiful as Athena would surely have been noticed by one of his servants by now, which meant she would have been brought to his notice, albeit by a circuitous route.

'Here we are, Millie.' Byron came to a halt, and Eli quickly closed his eye again. 'Damnation, he's still unconscious. He should have woken up by now. I don't like it. I hope he hasn't permanently damaged himself.'

'Athena, where have you been?'

'We were worried about you.'

Perdition, Eli must have a concussion. He opened his eyes and saw double. Two children — young ladies of no more than fourteen — ran out of a tumbledown cottage to meet Athena, frowning with anxiety. They were identical in all respects, as far as Eli could tell, given that he was observing them upside down. Both wore worsted pinafores of an unidentifiable colour — plain and service-able, yet neat and clean. They had blonde hair tumbling down their backs and, unlike Athena, were pretty rather than striking. Eli preferred the colour of Athena's hair, which was also loose, hanging almost to her waist in a mutiny of curls, a ribbon holding a few strands off her face. It reminded him of the colour the leaves would soon turn at this time of year — a riotous array of deep russet, golden brown, red and orange, too. Oh, what he would give to run his fingers through that tangled mass! How many hours would he happily wile away, trying to identify all the colours?

Athena was a most unusual lady, and Eli would know her better or die on the attempt.

'There's no cause for concern,' Athena said, speaking gently.

'But who's this?'

'And where did this lovely horse come from?'

'I found this gentleman in the woods. He fell from his horse and hurt his head.'

'Will he die?'

'Of course not, Lyssa.'

'Athena will use her herbs to make him better, I expect.'

'Which is more than he deserves,' Athena replied with asperity.

'Why does he not deserve to be made better? I don't suppose he would have fallen from his horse if he could have helped it.'

'He's intoxicated, Selene. That's why he fell.'

'Oh.'

Lyssa? Selene? It was a relief to know there were actually two of them. Twins also named after Greek goddesses. Well, at least he wasn't seeing double, and he'd learned more about his lovely Athena into the bargain. She had to be related to the twins in some way. What were the chances of unrelated women all being named after Greeks, and living in the same establishment? That was one puzzle resolved, but a far greater one remained. What the devil were they doing on his land? Eli was unlikely to discover the answer unless he opened his eyes. Besides, it was deuced uncomfortable, being laid across a saddle like a sack of corn.

It was time to wake up.

'What shall you do with him?'

'How shall you get him off the horse?'

Deuce take it, did those twins always talk in tandem?

'I shall have to pull him down, I suppose.'

Oh, sweet Athena, don't make it sound like such a chore. The thought of Athena's delicate hands once again assaulting his person occasioned a change of heart. Perhaps he'd remain insensible for just a little longer.

'No, lamb,' Millie said. 'I expect you want to make up some herbs for his cut head. The girls and I will get him down.'

I think not! 'Argh, wh-where am I?'

'You're awake.' Athena came into his line of vision, her expression both anxious and relieved. 'How do you feel?'

'Upside down.'

'Here, let me help you. You're lying over your horse's saddle. If I guide you, do you think you can get down?'

Touch me and you'll be lying down, too. 'I'll try. What happened to me?'

'I found you in the woods.'

'Lucky for you she did, my good man, otherwise you would have bled to death by now,' Millie said emphatically.

'Here, Millie and I have got you.' One pair of heavy hands clutched his waist on the left. A much softer pair took his opposite flank.

'Slide down slowly and we will catch you.'

Eli pushed his hands against the saddle, and slithered to the ground. His knees conveniently buckled beneath his weight, and he just happened to lurch towards Athena. She reached out to steady him, and somehow it was *she* who finished up in *his* arms, and he was supporting her. He could feel heat coruscating between their bodies and, just for one divine moment, the gentle pressure of her breasts pressed against his chest. His hands slid to her slender waist, their gazes clashed, and locked. Her eyes widened, as though she didn't quite understand what had just passed between them. A deeply disturbing jolt rocked Eli's battered body, one which he had no difficulty recognising. Passion, lust, and desire all bundled into one neat package. Perdition, but he wanted this fiery vixen!

'Oh!' she said, recovering first, and seeming genuinely concerned by his contrived *accidental* contact with her. 'Are you going to swoon?'

'Enough of those liberties, you oaf,' Millie said at the same time. 'Unhand Mrs. Defoe at once.'

Mrs. Defoe? Damnation, she was married. That shouldn't have surprised Eli. Such a jewel would have been snapped up by any man with eyes in his head the moment she left the schoolroom. She clearly wasn't a lady of his class, but she *was* educated. He could tell that much from her voice, her poise, the quick thinking that might well have saved his life, and . . . well, her every action gave the impression of elegance, intelligence and deep rooted common sense. The fact he couldn't seem to think too coherently when anywhere near her had nothing to do with the bash he had incurred to his head, and everything to do with the pure animal attraction he felt for her. Eli suspected she was a middle-class woman who had fallen on hard times. But where the devil was her husband?

'It's all right, Millie. Our guest is just a little woozy. Lean on me, sir, and we'll get you inside.'

'Thank you.'

Eli did feel woozy, and parched, and every damned thing. But all his discomforts paled in insignificance when set against the quite violent attraction he felt towards his lovely tenant. Eli had lost count of the number of women he'd dallied with during his adult years, some of whom had actually lived beneath his protection for a while. Every one of them had been a lively, witty, attractive, intelligent woman from the upper-echelons of society. None had come close to claiming his affections, or moving him in any significant way, other than the obvious.

Athena Defoe, did she but know it, had a lot to answer for.

'What is this place?' Eli tried not to show his concern when he was led towards a building that looked like a tumbled down stable.

'It's a woodsman's cottage on the Duke of Winsdale's estate,' Athena replied.

'Is it fit for human habitation?' he asked dubiously.

'It's adequate,' she replied tartly. 'Or would you prefer us to return you to the woods and let you bleed to death?'

'I haven't thanked you for saving me,' he said, trying for his most charming smile, which failed to make any discernible impression upon his lovely rescuer. Strange, it had never let him down before, but then she didn't yet know his identity. Everything would change once she did, which was why he didn't plan to tell her quite yet.

'Come, it's this way.'

Athena and Millie supported him through a warm yet dilapidated kitchen. The aroma of something simmering over the fire made Eli's stomach growl. There was an alcove off the kitchen with a cot set up in it.

'Lay down on here,' Athena said. 'Raise your feet and I will remove your boots. You will be more comfortable that way.'

I'll be more comfortable if you remove my breeches and lay with me.

'What should we call you?' Athena asked.

'The name's Franklin,' he said, thinking quickly and borrowing his drinking partner's name. Since he was largely responsible for Eli's condition, the very least he could do was lend him his identity. The moment she knew who he really was, word would be sent to Winsdale, Athena would lose her sparkle and become subservient, and his pleasure in her company would be at an end.

'Well, Mr. Franklin, it's very fortunate for you I decided to go out at dawn and pick mushrooms.' She peeled back the dressing on his head, and tutted. 'If I hadn't found you, you really would have bled to death.'

'Thank you,' he said solemnly, picking up her free hand and recklessly kissing the back of it.

She blushed to the roots of her colourful hair and snatched her hand back. 'You're entirely welcome.' She turned towards the door. 'Lyssa,' she said.

'Yes, said two voices at once. The twins had, he realised, been watching proceedings from the curtained doorway with eyes the size of saucers.

'Unsaddle Mr. Franklin's horse and turn

him out to pasture with Meg. I'm sure your horse is used to oats, Mr. Franklin, but I'm afraid we don't have any. Grass will just have to serve.'

'Byron won't mind in the least.'

'Selene, bring Mr. Franklin's saddle and bridle into the house, along with his saddlebags. They look expensive and ought not to be left outside.'

The twins dashed off to do as Athena asked.

'Are they your sisters?'

'Yes.' Athena stood up. 'Rest there. I shall heat up a herbal concoction and will be back directly. Is there anything you need?'

Yes, you. 'Water would be appreciated. I'm parched.'

'That's hardly to be wondered at.' She stood up, sent him a reproving look, and shook out her skirts. 'Millie will bring you some.'

He watched her go, feeling more content than he had for months, years even. Then in a blinding rush, he recalled what it was he'd been drinking to forget, and his heart lurched. His mother had lost patience with him. He was thirty years old, the current titleholder of a rich and noble duchy and, scandalously, still unmarried. He had skilfully managed to avoid the matchmaking mamas

29

for years now, but his own mother had finally had enough of his procrastinating. She had lectured him without let up until he agreed it was time to alter that situation. He'd known as much for years, of course. It *was* his duty to produce an heir and ensure the continuance of the Winsdale dynasty. And so his mother, with his reluctant agreement, was holding a house party this coming week, to which all the most eligible and suitable young ladies had been invited. Eli had promised to select a wife from within their ranks before the final day.

Suddenly, he wanted to send word to his mother telling her to call the whole thing off. His life had just been saved by the ideal woman. A woman who fired his passions, and overwhelmed him with a torrent of protective feelings he had never thought to experience.

Unfortunately, she also lived in a near-derelict cottage, was already married and, in spite of her exotic name, clearly wasn't duchess material anyway.

3

Athena moved aside the curtain that closed off Millie's sleeping quarters from the main body of the kitchen. Those quarters were currently occupied by their very large, very attractive uninvited guest, whose presence Athena found disturbing, and yet oddly stimulating. Her entire person had been in a heightened state of cautious awareness since first setting eyes upon him, almost as though her subconscious was trying to tell her their meeting had been more than a case of mere happenstance.

Athena shook her head, mentally upbraiding herself for her foolishness. Lack of sleep must be making her fanciful, she supposed.

Mr. Franklin's body spilled over the edges of the cot, causing it to bow beneath his weight. He didn't look at all comfortable, but that hadn't prevented him from falling into a deep sleep. Well, she hoped he was merely asleep, and he hadn't lost consciousness again. She stood stock still and continued to gaze at him, not bothering to conceal her admiration since there was no one there to take her to task for it.

No man had any right to be so beautiful, she thought mutinously. She tried to ignore the profound effect he had on her and concentrate on the best way to treat his injury. The unfamiliar feeling tugging at Athena's heart made that an impossible ambition to achieve, and her mind would insist upon taking unfamiliar, if rather stimulating, detours.

It was desire that had her thoughts running out of control, she realised, widening her eyes in surprise. She desired him. At last, she knew how it felt to be attracted to a member of the opposite sex, even if the attraction was nothing more than a flight of fancy. It was most inconvenient that desire chose to come calling at a time when she must concentrate all her energies on keeping her family's heads above water. She would have liked to examine the emotion at greater length, albeit vicariously, just to satisfy her curiosity on the matter, but she had no time to waste on daydreams.

She continued to look down at Mr. Franklin, resisting the urge to pull the coverlet higher for fear of waking him. Besides, if she did, it would deny her the view of his rather impressive torso, visible thanks to the thin fabric of his shirt. God forbid he should wake up and catch her gawping. Such thoughts renewed her determination to make him well again and send him on his way. If it was desire muddling her thinking, then she could live quite happily without it, thank you very much.

Athena felt a violent urge to place a kiss on the sleeping man's lips. Such uncharacteristic whimsy brought her to her senses. She leaned over him, satisfied herself he was still breathing, and hastily left his alcove. Once she had returned the curtain to its rightful place, she busied herself in the kitchen. The concoction of herbs she had set to boil would speed his recovery, and his departure, after which she would be quite herself again.

'We will have to feed him when he wakes up, Millie,' she said.

'I don't see why.' Millie puffed indignantly. 'It's not as though we asked him to come here and disrupt us.'

'We can't let him starve. Besides, if he eats and I treat his wound, he will recover his strength more quickly and be fit enough to leave us.' Athena ignored the sinking feeling this prospect engendered. 'Then things will return to normal.'

'Well, all right,' Millie said reluctantly. 'I suppose I can summon up some broth and bread.'

'Thank you, Millie. You do that, and I'll see to his injury.'

'What about you, lamb? You've had no breakfast.'

'I'm fine.'

'You have to eat,' Millie replied, a mutinous set to her jaw. 'You're far too thin as it is, and you'll be no good to anyone if you wilt for want of sustenance.'

'I can't afford the luxury of wilting,' Athena said briskly. 'Have the girls had their breakfast?'

Millie rolled her eyes. 'Try stopping those two gannets from consuming everything placed in front of them.'

'They *do* have healthy appetites, it's true, but they work so hard, Millie.' Athena sighed. 'Far harder than they should have to at their age.'

'Aye, true enough.' Millie's expression softened. 'They're good girls, for all their high spirits.'

'I will deal with Mr. Franklin's wounds, after which he'll probably sleep again,' Athena said. 'Then I shall go into the village as planned and try my luck in the haberdashery stores.'

'Our visitor certainly knows how to choose his moments.' Millie placed her hands on her ample hips, her stance radiating disapproval. 'He's disrupted everything.'

'Not really.' Athena felt a fierce desire to defend Mr. Franklin, even though Millie spoke the truth. 'All it means is we shall be without mushrooms in our stew this evening, and that's hardly the end of the world.'

'Harrumph. You just take care, Athena. There's more to Mr. Franklin than meets the eye. Take my word for it.'

Athena gasped. 'Whatever do you mean? Surely you don't think he's here to — '

'No, don't alarm yourself. I don't think we actually have anything to fear from him. If he was sent to look for us, he would hardly have thrown himself from his horse to get our attention.'

'No, I suppose not.' Athena released the breath she was unaware she had been holding. 'I would much prefer not to have to move again. I like this district. There are plenty of grand establishments in the area, full of fine ladies to enjoy our wares. I have a feeling our fortunes are about to change for the better.'

'Well, they could hardly get worse.'

'Oh, Millie, what would I do without you?' Athena threw her arms around the older woman and gave her a fierce hug. 'You are my rock.'

'There, there, child.' Millie patted her back. 'Don't go getting all tearful. Things will work out. You just see if they don't.'

'Did I do the right thing, Millie?' Athena scowled, filled with dismay as she recalled her reckless actions. 'Dragging the girls away from the only home they ever knew, and

35

forcing them to live in places like this?'

'Think of the alternative.' Millie shook her head repeatedly. 'Oh no, there was nothing else you could have done. Besides, the girls are happier than they've been for a long while because they're free to be themselves. Country living agrees with them, too.'

'Even in this hovel?'

'They are young, well able to cope with a little damp and discomfort. You're the only one I worry about. You're so busy caring about the rest of us you neglect your own needs.'

'Well, if I do well in the village today, we ought to be able to move somewhere better before winter sets in.'

'I'm sure you will prevail. How can anyone resist such exquisite handmade lace, even if you can't trade on its rightful name? It's still unique and will be much sought-after once word spreads. You just wait and see.'

'If I could explain its true history, then I would agree with you. But, of course, that's impossible.'

'Your handiwork will call to any lady with an eye for quality.' Millie wiped her hands on her pinafore. 'Now, I've brushed your best gown for you.'

Athena rolled her eyes. 'You mean my *only* other gown.'

'Don't say that!'

'Why not? It's true.'

'When I think of what you gave up — '

'Then don't think about it, Millie,' Athena replied assertively. 'I've trained myself not to regret that which can't be changed. Besides, if I had my time over, I would do exactly the same thing again. Although,' she added with an impish smile. 'I might have sacrificed a few of the herbs that took up so much space and squeezed another gown or two into my valise instead.'

Millie laughed. 'You're wearing your best petticoat?'

'Oh lord!' Athena's hand flew to her mouth as she lifted her skirts and revealed her torn petticoat.

'What the devil happened to that?'

'I used it as a dressing to stem Mr. Franklin's bleeding.'

'Your lovely petticoat.' Millie groaned. 'What did you do that for? I despair of you sometimes.'

'Well, it was that or let him die. What would you have done?'

'Let him die,' Millie replied with asperity, making them both laugh. 'I washed your only other petticoat, but it's so thin and darned it's not fit to be seen.'

'Just as well no one will see it then.' Athena sighed. 'Don't fret, Millie. As soon as we're established, I will purchase the fabric for ten new petticoats, I promise you. And at least one new gown,' she added, smiling.

'Aye well, I'd best go and wake our visitor and feed him.'

'Good, and when you've done that, I'll treat his wound. It will give me an opportunity to test a new idea I have regarding the prevention of scarring.'

'Don't you be worrying about that rogue having a scar to mar his beauty, young lady. I'm sure it's less than he deserves after behaving so irresponsibly.'

'Very likely, Millie, but this experiment is for my benefit as much as for his. Look upon it as a scientific research, if you like.'

'Huh, I look upon it as tomfoolery.'

Millie went off, muttering about ungrateful drunkards, making Athena smile as she vigorously stirred her pot of herbs. It was almost the right consistency, and now just needed to cool. She used tongs to remove the pot from over the fire and set it down on the slate hearth.

The girls burst into the room, struggling beneath the weight of Mr. Franklin's saddle.

'It's very fine,' Selene said, reverently stroking the soft leather.

'So is the bridle,' added Lyssa. 'The stitching is so ornate. I've never seen anything like it before. Mr. Franklin must be very rich.'

'Shush.' Athena placed a finger against her lips. 'He'll hear you. It's very rude to speculate in such a manner.'

'He'll probably think our cottage is beneath him,' Selene said.

'Well, if he does, he's welcome to leave any time he wishes.'

'Meg is showing off for his horse. She keeps trying to kick him,' Lyssa said, giggling.

'Oh dear!' Athena poured her cooled herbal mixture into a basin and stood up. 'Now get back to work, girls. I shall be with you directly.'

★   ★   ★

Much as he would have preferred to sit up and have a good, long conversation with her, Eli had become proficient at feigning sleep in Athena's presence. He sensed her standing over him and kept his eyes closed, his breathing even. He knew it was her. Her floral fragrance, evident even above the smell of damp and mould that prevailed in this miserable hovel, gave her away. How could his steward have allowed tenants to move in with the place in this condition? He would have strong words to say to Bairstowe on the matter.

Ways in which he could repay Athena for

saving his life whirled around his aching head, but first he needed to understand what the devil she was doing, hidden away here in his woods. That would require earning her trust, and he didn't have long in which to achieve that ambition. If he didn't return to Winsdale Hall soon then a search would be instigated, if it hadn't been already. His valet had returned ahead of him, and Eli was supposed to be close on his heels. It could only be a matter of time before he was found here. Since Salter knew he often saved himself a long ride by cutting through the woods, it would be the first place he looked for him.

Athena was hiding from something or someone, he was absolutely sure of it. If his tenure here became common knowledge, she would be plagued by locals curious to know how it came about. At the very best, her reputation would be ruined. She *was* a married woman, but even so . . . At worst it could give away her location to whoever she was hiding from, which would be a sorry way indeed to thank her.

The rustle of her clothing and a soft sigh told him she was leaving his bedside. *Don't go!*

She went.

As soon as he heard the curtain that divided off this uncomfortable alcove from the kitchen being pulled back into place, he leaned up on one elbow and pressed his ear to the curtain in question. It was old, but smelt of fresh air and was scrupulously clean. Athena was trying to maintain standards, in spite of the obstacles set in her path. Eli admired her pluck and determination. His own determination to help her, even if she wouldn't welcome his help, grew by the second.

She was in the kitchen, talking quietly to Millie, but not so quietly he couldn't hear what she said. Millie resented having to feed him. Why the devil should she be so begrudging of a little broth and bread?

Perdition, they couldn't afford it! Spoiled fool that he was, he hadn't stopped to consider that possibility. Well, he would go hungry rather than deprive his goddess of food. She had just declined breakfast, and Eli's fall meant they would be without the treat of mushrooms to accompany their evening meal, apparently. Never had such nugatory concerns . . . well, concerned Eli before. He was being a wretched nuisance, but salved his conscience by reminding himself just how much help he could actually give Athena just as soon as he returned to the Park and put arrangements in hand.

If she would accept it.

He hardly knew her at all, but already suspected she had fierce pride and an

41

independent spirit.

So did Eli.

They were in conversation again. Millie was to feed him, and Athena would then treat his wound. God love her, she hoped to avoid him being scarred! Eli wanted to leap out of this lumpy cot, burst through that curtain, pull her into his arms and kiss her witless for being so considerate. Hopefully, she would attend to his cuts and bruises alone. Eli would then be able to question Athena about her circumstances without Millie, who'd just admitted to her suspicions about him not being whom he said he was, coming between them.

Lost in the depths of his own thoughts, he only just caught their conversation about Athena's gown. She only had one other beside the drab one she was wearing. Eli frowned, ignoring the strain it put upon his injury when he furrowed his brow. She really had fallen upon hard times. Worse yet, she appeared to have sacrificed her only good petticoat to save his life. Eli was filled with deep feelings of awe and gratitude. He could buy her a hundred petticoats and not notice the cost. He might very well do precisely that before he was much older. The fact that he was on the brink of matrimony certainly wouldn't stop him.

Lace? What was that about lace? She was going into Winsdale to try and place home-made lace in the haberdashers' establishments situated there. Neither shop would take it. Both proprietors were very particular about their suppliers, but Athena sounded desperate. Now, if he could just jump on Byron and get into town ahead of her, he could change that situation in a heartbeat.

Someone was coming. The rich aroma of broth and freshly baked bread preceded Millie, even before the curtain was jerked open. Eli sat up and blinked.

'Bread and broth,' Millie said curtly, placing a tray across his legs.

'Thank you. It smells delicious.'

And it was. He broke off a piece of bread and dunked it into vegetable broth, eating hungrily. He was sharp-set, which seemed rather disobliging of him, given the residents of this dwelling were struggling to put enough food on their table.

'You must let me pay for this,' he said.

'I would let you without a second thought, but Mrs. Defoe wouldn't hear of it.'

'Does she need to know?'

'We have no secrets,' Millie said, sounding just a little less severe.

'Sometimes secrets work to the greater good. Mrs. Defoe has a fierce sense of pride

43

and duty, it seems to me.'

Millie flexed a brow. 'You see a lot for a man who's been out of his senses the entire morning.'

Eli treated her to a wry smile. 'I have a very hard head.'

'Just as well.' Millie turned towards the curtain. 'Well, I can't stand around here, wasting time. I have work to do in the vegetable garden.'

And she was gone. Eli finished his meal quickly, feeling a lot better with it inside him. He was wondering what to do with the empty bowl when Athena appeared, smiling like the angel she was.

'You're looking better,' she said.

'I feel it, thanks to you. The broth was delicious, as was the bread. Did you make it?'

'Lord no, I wouldn't know where to begin.'

Interesting. She'd never had anything to do in a kitchen. Who the devil was she? Athena took the bowl from him and returned it to the kitchen. When she came back, she had a bowl of clean water and another with something that smelled of fragrant herbs.

'I'm going to clean your cut,' she told him, leaning over him to examine it. 'I ought to warn you, it will hurt.'

He looked into her eyes. They were enormous, the most fascinating shade of brown. 'If you were to hold my hand, I'm sure it will help me to bear the pain.'

'Mr. Franklin, please!'

'Sorry,' Eli said, not feeling sorry at all. 'Go ahead, then. Do your worst.'

She dipped a cloth into warm water and gently washed away dried blood. Eli flinched.

'Stop being such a baby. I've barely touched you.'

Oh, sweet lady. If only you knew.

'It's as clean as I can make it. I'm going to apply this concoction of herbs I've made up for you. They will help to fight infection, reduce any swelling and, with luck, avoid scarring.'

'What's in them?'

'A combination of comfry and goldenseal roots, amongst other things.'

'Hmm, isn't comfry likened to turnip?'

She paused and sent him a searching look. 'You're very well informed.'

'I have the type of mind that retains useless knowledge.' He shrugged. 'It's a blessing and a curse.'

'I'm sure it must be.' She applied her herbs with a firm touch, causing him to suck in a sharp breath. They stung like the devil. 'Where do you find such ingredients in these woods? I don't think they're native to these parts.'

'I travel with certain potted herbs wherever I go.'

But not with adequate clothing, he thought.

'I almost always need to use them.'

'And you know what you're doing, presumably?'

She appeared amused rather than offended by the question. 'You're not the first person to doubt my abilities, but you're still alive, aren't you?'

'Thanks to you.'

'All plants produce chemical compounds that are beneficial to us humans, provided one gets the mix right, of course.'

He sent her a wicked smile that caused her to blush. 'I'm sure you know how to agitate the mix.' She was doing a damned fine job of agitating his blood.

She looked as though she wanted to take him to task, but wisely refrained from doing so. If she tried to bandy words with him, she would definitely come out on the losing side.

'There, that's all done.' She fashioned a gauze bandage around his head, pulling it tight enough to make him wince. He wondered where it had come from, since he didn't think it had formed part of her petticoat. Presumably, she travelled with such supplies, along with her herbs. If she took such a keen interest in medicine then that was the most likely explanation. 'You'll feel tired again now, I expect. Sleep some more. I have to go into

46

the village, but when I return I'll see how things are progressing.'

'Where's Mr. Defoe?' he asked abruptly.

She dealt him a sharp look. 'Not here.'

'What are your sisters doing?'

'Why do you ask so many questions?'

'I already told you. I have an enquiring mind.'

'My sisters are in the other room, making lace.'

'Lace. Is that what takes you into the village?'

'Yes. I hope to sell it to the haberdashers. There is a wealthy duke who lives near here. Do you know of him?'

'I've not had the pleasure.'

'No, I don't suppose you have.'

'Did it not occur to you I might be delivering the stallion I was riding to him in my capacity as a horse dealer?'

'I . . . just a minute.' She scowled at him, her flawless complexion stained with a touch of colour. She had such beautiful, soft skin. Eli yearned to reach out and run his fingers down her cheek, but resisted only because he thought the gesture would be unwelcome, to say nothing of inappropriate. 'I didn't say I thought you were a horse dealer.'

Perdition, so she hadn't. Eli was so keen to keep her talking he had become incautious. 'I must have heard you speculating with Millie while I was sleeping just now.'

'I didn't say anything to Millie about your occupation.' She stood up and glowered at him. 'Were you awake all the time in the woods?'

'No, on my life, I do assure you I was not.' Eli crossed his fingers beneath the thin cover. 'If you said something like along those lines, perhaps my mind absorbed it in my unconscious state without my being aware of it. They do say, you know, that hearing is the last sense to desert one in such circumstances.'

She flexed a brow. 'Another snippet of useless information retained by your enquiring mind, no doubt.'

'Quite so.' He sent her his most charming smile. She absorbed it without appearing the least disturbed by it. 'Tell me more about the local duke.'

'Apparently, he's having a house party in a few days' time, and it occurred to me our products might appeal to some of his guests.' She briefly closed her eyes, as though willing that to be the case. 'A lot of grand ladies have taken against machine-produced lace. We, on the other hand, retain all the old skills and never produce two articles that are the same.'

'What do you make?'

'Why would you care?'

Their gazes duelled. Her eyes widened and were shot through with the most fascinating shards of silver, intoxicating Eli with their scorching lustre. He fell captive to her breath-taking beauty and touching vulnerability, unable to remember when a woman from any walk of life had last intrigued him more.

'You fail to make allowance for my enquiring mind,' he said softly.

'We make fans, shawls, fischus, doilies, purses . . . all manner of things.' She stood up abruptly. 'And now I must leave you. Try to sleep.'

Eli reached out and caught her hand. Taken unawares, she gasped and sent him a look of curiosity rather than outrage.

'Thank you, Mrs. Defoe,' he said with great formality. 'You saved my life, and I shall now be eternally in your debt.'

Before she could respond, he raised her hand to his lips and placed a firm kiss in the centre of her palm.

4

Eli waited patiently until he heard Athena depart before leaving his damnably uncomfortable cot. There was a tiny window above his head that looked out over the paddock. He knelt up to watch his goddess as she caught the pony that had so captivated Byron, and swiftly harnessed it to an ancient cart.

'Surely, she's not going to drive that rattletrap into the village,' he muttered, frowning at the prospect. 'It will never make it.'

Byron was still taking an active interest in the pony. He leaned over the railings, whinnying pathetically, and then trotted up and down, tail raised, showing off. The pony ignored him, causing Eli to smile. It looked as if they had both fallen victim to the charms of the females resident at this tumbledown cottage, with equally discouraging results.

Athena had changed into a dark blue gown that did look slightly more presentable than her previous garment. Well, almost anything would have. She had, to his disappointment, pulled her hair up and placed a straw bonnet on top of the resulting style. She looked tidy and respectable. She looked adorable, and the desire to replace her ancient clothing with silks and satins grew ever more desperate.

The twins came tumbling out to join their sister and passed parcels to Athena — lace presumably — which she laid carefully in the bed of the cart. One of them handed her a delicate shawl in blues and silvers, which she draped across her shoulders. Even Eli, who knew little about such matters, could see it was exquisite. It transformed her entire appearance and would, he suspected, make any lady who saw it anxious to own one similar. Very clever!

The sisters exchanged a few words, but Eli couldn't hear what was said. Athena then climbed up onto the box seat and encouraged the pony forward with a slap of the reins against its rump. Byron protested loudly, looking as if he was contemplating jumping the fence in order to join his lady love. Eli empathised. The girls waved Athena off and returned inside, heads together, chatting and laughing.

Eli ventured out into the kitchen. It was still full of the enticing aroma of vegetable broth, but even that delectable smell failed to mute the even stronger tang of mould. At his leisure to examine the cottage, Eli was frankly appalled. It seemed the entire upper floor was unusable since the staircase had rotted clean through. He could see daylight through parts of the upper floor where receptacles had been placed, presumably because the roof leaked.

Where the devil did Athena and the girls sleep if they couldn't go upstairs? There was only one other room downstairs, which was presumably where the twins were now. Not ready to face them yet, Eli wandered outside, careful to keep clear of the garden where Millie was hard at work. If she saw he was up and about, he wouldn't put it past her to send him packing. Eli's lips twitched. A duke being evicted from his own derelict cottage by a maidservant would make an amusing change from the sycophantic behaviour he was normally obliged to endure.

Eli glanced up at the outside of the building and could see why there were so many pots on the upper floor. There were numerous holes in the thatch and, where it was still intact, the straw was rapidly rotting away. He tutted as he made his way to the downstairs room window. He wanted to see what the twins were up to without their being aware of it.

Peering cautiously over the rotted sill, he found them seated together in front of a dwindling fire, industriously making lace, chatting incessantly to one another, laughing frequently. Golden thread spooled from bobbins as their industrious fingers moved with swift efficiently back and forth. They didn't even appear to look at what they were doing. It was quite astonishing, and Eli remained where he was for several minutes, admiring their skill and discipline. Left to their own devices at such an age, Eli's sisters most definitely wouldn't have applied themselves to their work, but then they had never had to earn their own living or worry about where the money for their next meal would come from.

Aware Millie might discover him missing at any moment, Eli couldn't afford to be caught spying on the twins. But still he took a moment to peer around the room, curious to know where the three sisters slept. Craning his neck, he caught sight of a large cot, pushed into one corner of the room, out of the way of the lace industry. Presumably, it was pulled in front of the fire when they were ready to retire. Eli took comfort from the fact at least they would be warm. Unless it rained, of course. They would never be able to prevent rain and damp penetrating the thatch if there was a heavy downpour.

'That, at least, is something I can rectify,' he muttered to himself, moving away from the window.

53

As he did so, he noticed the most incredible arrangement, as out of place perched on the window ledge in this ruined cottage as the beautiful lace the girls were producing was. Eli squinted, trying to figure out what it was. It appeared to be a wild artichoke decorated with dried corn, fir cones and forest fruits. It was stunning in its simplicity, a testament to the creativity of its designer, and her determination to turn this hovel into a home with deft touches.

Eli had no doubt it was Athena's work.

Such talent, he thought, walking away, wishing his mother could have seen it. She would have been enchanted.

Eli was about to continue with his exploring when he heard hooves on the nearby track. Presumably, it was a search party on the lookout for a missing duke. Not wanting Millie to intercept the rider, Eli stepped into the track in a place where he wouldn't be seen from the cottage and waved the rider down. It was Salter, his valet.

'God in heaven, what happened to you, your grace?' Salter dismounted, looking suitably concerned, presumably because of the bandage circling Eli's head, and the scrapes to his cheek not covered by it. 'We were that worried when you didn't return home.'

'Nothing of consequence. It's just a scratch.'

'Where's Byron? We need to get your grace back to Winsdale Park. Her grace will wish to call a physician.'

'No, Salter, no physician. But I'm glad you're here. Make yourself useful, and ride into the village as fast as you can. Call at Miss Dawson's haberdashery — '

'Haberdashery, your grace?' Salter blinked, presumably thinking the bash to his head had robbed Eli of his senses. 'Are you quite sure?'

'Never more so.' Miss Dawson's was the superior establishment, guaranteed to attract a better class of trade. 'Tell Miss Dawson that a lady by the name of Mrs. Defoe is on her way to offer them handmade lace for sale. Make it clear it would please me if she accepted her merchandise. But she must not, on any account, allow the lady to know I've interfered.'

'Yes, your grace, but — '

'Miss Dawson is to offer her a generous price. Are we clear?'

'Yes, your grace, but begging your pardon, perhaps I should escort your grace back to Winsdale Park first.'

'Just go! Cut through the woods, and you will arrive before the lady. Then return to Winsdale Park. Tell them I've been delayed, and will be back by nightfall. Say nothing about this,' he added, pointing to his head.

Salter pursed his lips. 'As your grace wishes.'
'I *do* wish.'

Salter remounted with apparent reluctance, turned his horse and cantered away.

Eli watched until Salter disappeared from view then continued exploring the outside of the cottage. He could see Millie, bent over in the vegetable garden, pulling what looked to be potatoes and placing them in a basket. He didn't think Athena's family had been here for long, so how had they managed to grow such an impressive array of vegetables so quickly? Presumably, the woodsman's garden had been left to go wild when Eli had moved him to another location on the estate and decided to abandon this one indefinitely. Millie must have reclaimed it. Eli admired her ingenuity.

Around the next side of the cottage, Eli found himself confronted with an array of potted herbs, their pungent fragrance intoxicating. He recognised one or two. Most, he did not. This was clearly Athena's collection, so precious she would rather have them with her rather than additional gowns. Several scrawny chickens clucked to themselves as they pecked away at the ground in a wire run nearby.

Athena's dog appeared out of nowhere, sat down, and observed him impassively, head cocked to one side. Why hadn't Athena taken him with her? The answer was as obvious as it was infuriating. She would prefer for the creature to protect her family rather than herself. Damnation, Athena wouldn't be safe alone. Her looks, if nothing else, would ensure she received all sorts of unwelcome attentions. Eli was sorely tempted to ride after her, and protect her himself.

He knew he couldn't do that because it would create more difficulties for her than it would solve. He sighed, never having resented his elevated rank more.

'Come along then, Boris,' he said, holding out his hand. 'I don't think we've been formally introduced.'

The dog deigned to get up and thoroughly inspected Eli's hand. Appearing to find nothing to object to, he wagged his tail against Eli's boots and then found a patch of sun in which to curl up, still watching Eli intently. Eli laughed and leaned down to ruffle his scruffy ears, wishing his own life could be as uncomplicated.

Next to them was a pile of wood, Eli noticed a block with an axe leaning against it. Logs waiting to be cut for their fire, he supposed. Eli blanched at the thought of Athena taking on such a task, but it must be one that fell to her. Millie was too old, the twins too young, to manage it.

A smile flirted with Eli's lips as he picked up a thick log and placed it on the block. He swung the axe over his shoulder a couple of times to get the feel for it, then brought it down again with considerable force and spliced the log cleanly in two. Eli had never chopped logs before, and he was pleased to discover he actually knew how. The exertion made his head pound, but it was also very satisfying, if warm work. He pulled his shirt over his head and, naked to the waist, put his back into the task, smiling with satisfaction at the thought of being useful to his goddess.

His Grace, the Duke of Winsdale, was enjoying himself.

★ ★ ★

Athena dismissed the distraction of Mr. Franklin from her thoughts as Meg plodded along at her usual frustratingly slow pace. She knew better than to try and hurry the pony. If she did, the wretchedly stubborn creature would simply stop moving all together. With nothing better to do than to give Meg the occasional direction with a twitch of the reins, Athena focused her mind on her purpose for this excursion, brought about by her perilous situation, both pecuniary and personal.

She had been into Winsdale village just

twice since moving to the locality. Athena was cautious of showing herself unless it was absolutely necessary. Those seeking her whereabouts appeared to have eyes and ears everywhere, and it was becoming increasingly difficult to outwit them. During those two visits, she had checked out the haberdashers' stores, pleased with what she saw in them. They were modern and elegant, but also a trifle intimidating.

The duke's establishment, and all the other grand houses in the district, were what had attracted Athena to the area, convinced their presence would secure her a market for her goods. The ladies frequenting those houses would surely appreciate their quality and individuality. However, the haberdashers' stores proved to be very well stocked indeed — far better than Athena had anticipated. There were only so many shawls, and purses, and the like that a lady could possibly require. Only so many fripperies the shops could afford to stock.

But she and the twins were here, living on the outskirts of Winsdale with neither the means nor the will to move on yet again.

Athena would just have to be at her most convincing.

'Oh, botheration!' Athena threw back her head and sighed, aware that their meagre

59

amount of cash was almost exhausted. 'What if they say *no?* What shall we do then?'

A rider came hurtling down the track in the opposite direction, spooking Meg, unsettling Athena. This track only led to the cottage, and they weren't expecting visitors. Athena's scalp prickled. The twins! She didn't recognise the man riding the horse, but even so . . . He slowed when he saw Athena, took a close look at her, doffed his cap, then resumed his canter without saying a word. She expelled a relieved breath. It was her whom the pursuers most particularly wanted to find. It was her description that would have been widely circulated. Had the man been set to look for her, he would have stopped her then and there. Besides, Boris wouldn't let anyone get close to her sisters.

The twins were safe, at least for now.

Athena straightened her bonnet and encouraged Meg forward again, still wondering what the man had been doing on the track. She dismissed his purpose from her mind when she saw chimney smoke in the distance, and the first of the village cottages came into view. There was more traffic now, and she was obliged to concentrate on keeping Meg on the track. She halted the cart outside the first of the haberdasher's establishment, the one with a well-maintained façade and enticing window display, and tied off the reins. She noticed one or two curious glances being sent in her direction and tried not to panic. Two men stopped dead in their tracks on the opposite side of the road and watched her with unbridled curiosity. Athena ignored them. Men tended to gawp at her, for reasons she'd never properly understood. That's all this was. No one knew she was here, she reminded herself for the thousandth time. If she scampered off like a frightened rabbit every time someone looked at her, she would achieve nothing.

Clambering down from the box seat, Athena reached for her parcel of goods, squared her shoulders, and entered the shop. She saw a few ladies inside it glance admiringly at her shawl, which gave her the courage she needed to go ahead with her task.

'May I help you?' a severe looking lady enquired.

'I'd like to see the proprietor, please.'

'You are speaking with her. I'm Miss Dawson. How may I be of help?'

Athena launched into a description of her handmade lace, holding up her shawl as an example. She expected to be turned away by this rather aloof woman but, to her utter astonishment, she smiled at Athena and took a closer look at her wares.

'This is quite exceptional,' she said,

fingering a delicate fan. 'And so unusual. I think we might easily find a market for such pretty things.'

'You do?' Delight and relief spiralled through Athena.

'Absolutely. The Duke of Winsdale is having a house party next week. The ladies always come into the village during the proceedings, looking for trinkets they don't find in the larger establishments in London. I think your beautiful things will take their fancy the moment they lay eyes on them.'

'Well, that's most encouraging. It's hand-made, you see.'

'Indeed I do. I hear many complaints about the inferior quality of machine-made lace nowadays.'

Athena could have kissed her. 'Quite so,' she replied, managing to control her satisfied smile. She wished Mr. Moncrieff could have heard Miss Dawson's comment. It vindicated her strongly-held belief that was partly responsible for Athena's current predicament.

'How much can you offer me, and what prices do you expect them to fetch?' Miss Dawson asked.

Negotiations were undertaken, and Athena could scarce hide her relief when Miss Dawson offered to take everything Athena had in the cart. The amount she was prepared to pay literally took Athena's breath away, far exceeding her most optimistic expectations, even though it was far less than she could have charged, had she been free to call the lace by its proper, better known name. Better yet, Miss Dawson paid her on the spot, when Athena had supposed she would have to wait until her items were sold before she actually saw any money.

'I shall take as much as you can offer me, Mrs. Defoe,' Miss Dawson said. 'But I must insist you offer it only to me.' She sent a scathing glance through the shop window, towards a competing haberdashery store directly across the road. 'Exclusivity is my bye-word. It will lower the tone, and the value of your merchandise, if it's available just anywhere.'

Athena suppressed a smile. It suited her very well to only deal with one establishment. 'I understand perfectly.'

'Then we are agreed.'

Miss Dawson sent a lad out to the cart to collect the rest of the parcels. Athena shook the lady's hand, and left the establishment with a far lighter step than the one that had propelled her into it. She failed to suppress a smile when she noticed two assistants scurry to rearrange the window so some of Athena's items could be prominently displayed there.

With a heavier purse than she had known for many a long day, Athena stopped at a butcher's cart to purchase a treat for their supper. She would have liked to delay and buy a few things for the girls, but she had been here for long enough, attracting far too much attention. Miss Dawson hadn't asked where Athena lived, but had enquired if more merchandise could be made available. Athena had promised to call upon her again in a few days' time with additional stock.

Since now they didn't have to worry about finding enough money for food, she and the girls would work their fingers to the bone, if necessary. Opportunities like this were few and far between, and Athena couldn't afford to waste this one. It might provide them with enough funds to see them through the coming winter.

As she drove home, she finally allowed herself to think about Mr. Franklin, hoping her herbs were already taking effect. Byron whinnied a frantic greeting to Meg when she reached the cottage. Athena laughed as she jumped down from the cart, and the girls came dashing up to her.

'How did you get on?' Lyssa asked.

Selene looked anxious. 'Did you manage to sell anything at all?'

'Everything,' Athena replied, patting her

heavy reticule and being rewarded by the satisfying sound of rattling coin.

'All of it?' the girls asked together, mouths hanging open.

'Yes, and they might very well want more. Miss Dawson, the owner of the shop, looked very severe, but she was actually quite charming. She said she had seldom seen such exquisite work, and whoever made the lace possessed a rare gift.'

Millie trudged over, a heavy basket of potatoes in hand. 'Well done, lass,' she said, smiling. 'I knew things would pick up.'

'It seems almost too good to be true,' Athena said. 'I can still barely credit it myself.'

'Well, we'd best get these potatoes washed and prepared.' Millie nodded towards the basket. 'Come along, you two. You can help.'

'We possess a rare gift,' Selene said giggling.

'That's right,' Lyssa added with an impish smile. 'We couldn't possibly lower ourselves.'

Laughing, Millie aimed her hand at Selene's ear and shooed the girls inside ahead of her.

Athena released Meg from her harness and, much to the delight of the prancing Byron, turned her back out in the paddock. As she did so, she sensed a presence behind her, turned slowly, and gasped. Mr. Franklin was standing, shirtless, beside the block, a neat pile of logs stacked beside it. She tried to speak, but her mouth had gone dry and the words stuck in her throat. Just for a moment, she allowed her eyes to linger on his impressive torso. It wasn't every day a woman was treated to such a fine sight. Then she pulled herself together and frowned at him.

'What on earth do you think you're doing?'

'Helping you by chopping a few logs.'

'A few? You've done almost the whole pile. You will have done your head no end of harm. That's far too heavy work for a man in your condition.'

'And what condition would that be?' He leaned on the axe, muscles flexing as he sent her an annoyingly smug smile that had a most disconcerting affect upon her.

She ignored the question, mainly because she had no idea how to answer it, and focused her attention on his bandaged head instead. There was no blood showing on the gauze, implying the herbs had done a good enough job already to withstand the pressure he'd just so foolishly put himself under.

'You've been exceedingly rash,' she said with asperity. 'But, I thank you for the logs.'

'I could hardly leave the task to you.' He picked up one of her hands.

Dear God, don't let him kiss it again!

'I couldn't bear to think of you damaging your delicate hands.'

'I don't chop the wood myself.'

'Oh, then whom — '

'I have an arrangement with a lad from the nearest farm. He comes once a week to do it, and I pay him a few pennies for his trouble.'

'Well then, at least I've saved you a few pennies.'

'And deprived the lad of his income.'

'Ah, I didn't stop to consider.'

'No, you did not.'

They walked around the cottage, to the front door. Mercifully, Mr. Franklin put his shirt back on before they did so. It was very hard to string coherent thoughts together when a half-naked man with a mocking smile and plethora of hard muscles stood beside her, showing off every bit as much as his wretched horse.

'How went it in the village?'

Athena couldn't help smiling. 'I managed to sell everything I took with me, *and* Miss Dawson is anxious for more.'

'I'm very pleased to hear it. Are you able to supply more in time?'

She blinked at him. 'In time for what?'

'Why, in time to meet her needs, of course. What else?'

'We're very resourceful.'

67

'Surely Mr. Defoe provides for you all?'

'I need to take another look at your head,' Athena replied.

Mr. Franklin shot her a knowing look. 'Very well.'

She sat him on a kitchen stool, unwound the bandage, and gently probed at his wound. 'Yes, it's doing well. I shall apply some more herbs to it now and another lot in the morning. You will have a nasty bruise and a scar, at least initially, but if you persevere with my treatment, I believe it will fade quite quickly.'

'Much as I would like to stay, I must be on my way again within the hour.'

'Oh, but — '

'Even if I wished to stay, there's nowhere for me to sleep without inconveniencing you. Besides, I don't imagine Mr. Defoe would approve.'

'Mr. Defoe isn't here.' Athena sighed, surprised at just how much she didn't want him to leave. But he was right, of course, he couldn't stay. Besides, if he was strong enough to chop wood, he could certainly ride to wherever he was going. Athena didn't want to know where that was. It would be easier to put him out of her mind that way. 'Very well. I shall do another poultice now, and then make up a jar of herbs for you to take with you. Apply them

68

twice a day for a week.'

'Will you allow me to pay you for your kindness?' Mr. Franklin asked when Athena had applied the new poultice and re-bandaged his head. 'After all, without you I would most likely be dead.'

'No, that's out of the question. I didn't do anything anyone wouldn't have done in the same circumstances.'

'I disagree.' Mr. Franklin's eyes shimmered with an elusive emotion that made Athena feel quite warm all over. It was very difficult not to react to his lazy, persuasive charm, but Athena couldn't afford that luxury. She turned away from him and busied herself with her pot of simmering herbs.

'This should be ready momentarily,' she said hastily.

'Very well.'

She didn't look at him but could hear amusement in his voice, as though he knew perfectly well what effect he was having on her, the wretched man.

'We'll say no more about it.' He paused. 'For now.'

For now? 'Should you pass this way again, I would be interested to know how well the cure works.' Athena blushed, wondering what had made her say that. She *was* curious to know how the herbal treatment went, but knew deep in her heart that wasn't the only reason why she wished to see Mr. Franklin again.

'I think I can safely promise you of that satisfaction, at least.'

Mr. Franklin lifted her hand to his beautiful mouth and kissed the back of it. Their eyes clashed, her body trembled at the contact with his lips, and she was unable to snatch her hand away. Millie loudly cleared her throat and the spell was broken. Mr. Franklin sighed and released her hand while Athena set about making up the herbs he would take with him.

An hour later, Byron had been persuaded to leave Meg, protesting loudly with a series of increasingly frantic whinnies that made Athena smile. Mr. Franklin saddled his horse and swung up into that saddle with an agility that defied his earlier near-dead condition. Really, the man had the constitution of an ox.

He waved to Athena and the girls as they stood at the door, and then cantered away.

'He is *such* a handsome man,' Lyssa said dreamily.

'I wonder where he's going,' Selene added as he disappeared from view, echoing Athena's private thoughts.

5

Eli was back at Winsdale Park in less than fifteen minutes. The short distance separating his palatial home from Athena's humble cottage might as well have been a million miles, given the difference in their living conditions. Eli was so accustomed to his estate that he took it for granted and never really thought about it, beyond being aware it was his responsibility to keep it running smoothly and profitably for the next generation of Sheltons.

As he approached the main house, trotting briskly up the long gravel driveway, gardeners straightened up from their labours to bow as he passed. He looked up at the rambling building, feeling both privileged and burdened by his obligations. He understood, as well as the next duke, that his role was vital. Someone had to be in charge or there would be anarchy. That he had been born to lead had been drummed into him since he was in short coats, and he prided himself on discharging his duties with a firm but fair hand. He looked after his tenants, took a keen interest in their farming methods, and concerned himself with local affairs.

There was one local affair he would very much like to concern himself with right now. Intimately. She lived in appalling conditions in one of *his* cottages, and Eli needed to understand how that situation had been allowed to arise. If he didn't receive a satisfactory answer, heads would roll.

The moment he rode into his stable yard, his head groom came running to take Byron's reins. Eli dismounted, barely acknowledging the man or his ill-disguised curiosity at Eli's bandaged head. He strode into the house by a side door, where his butler, Archer, awaited him. As always, he had anticipated Eli's arrival, or more likely observed him riding up the drive.

'Your grace,' he said, inclining his head. 'You're injured.'

'Very observant, Archer,' Eli replied, not breaking stride.

'Should I send for a physician, your grace?'

'Absolutely not.'

Eli wanted to tell Archer not to inform his mother — of his arrival, or of his injury — but knew it would be a waste of breath. Just like Archer, his mother would already be aware he was home. His mother always seemed to know.

'Have this sent up to my rooms,' Eli said,

handing Archer Athena's jar of herbs. 'And take care not to drop it.'

Archer looked rather offended that Eli considered him capable of dropping anything. He didn't have time to deal with his butler's wounded pride. Instead, he headed into the back corridor, where the estate office was situated.

'Bairstowe.' He impatiently threw open the door and strode into the room. 'Where the devil are you?'

'Your grace!' His steward cast aside his quill and jumped to his feet. 'Is something amiss?'

'What were you thinking, allowing tenants to take the old woodman's cottage in Whispers' Hollow?'

'Your grace, you gave me orders to find suitable tenants for all your vacant properties.' Bairstowe paled beneath the force of Eli's blistering glare. 'You were quite specific on the point.'

So he had been. 'Perdition, Bairstowe, I meant the habitable cottages. I didn't think I needed to spell that out to you.'

'I was fully aware of that, your grace. But the lady who took Whispers' Hollow was quite insistent it was the *only* location that would suit her requirements. I tried to explain it was unfit, but she was exceedingly

73

'. . . er, persuasive, that's not to say persistent.'

Eli rolled his eyes, well able to believe it. Just *how* persuasive had she been? Jealousy roiled through Eli's gut at the very thought of another man — any man — laying so much as one finger on his goddess.

'She particularly wanted a secluded location, and said Whispers' Hollow would suit her perfectly.' Bairstowe quailed beneath Eli's repressing glare. 'I only charged her a peppercorn rent, your grace.'

'A lady, Bairstowe? Where the devil is her husband?'

'I asked Mrs. Defoe the same question. She told me she was expecting him to return to these shores at any time, which is why she wished to be near to Portsmouth.'

'I would hardly call Whispers' Hollow close to Portsmouth. It's a good twenty miles away.'

'I made the same observation to Mrs. Defoe but, again, she insisted upon privacy. That, apparently, was more important to her than expediency.'

'Can't get much more private than Whispers' Hollow, I suppose. How long ago did she take occupation?' *How long has she been there without my knowledge?*

'A little over a month, your grace, if memory serves.'

'A month, you say.' She had been living in squalor all that time. Thank God, it was summer at least. Although the days were drawing in, and there was now a chill in the early morning air. 'Did she say how long she required it for?'

'No, your grace, but I assumed it would be for a short period. No one could live there in winter.'

'No one should be living there at all! Get a team of men over there first thing tomorrow.' Eli paced the length of the office, his booted tread ringing out on the boarded floor. 'I want the roof re-thatched, the inner staircase and upper floor made secure, the windows repaired, and two rooms made upstairs.' One for his goddess and one for the twins. 'Arrange for comfortable beds to be provided for those rooms, and make sure all the mouldy walls are repaired while you're at it. Oh, and tell Mrs. Defoe these repairs are being made on my orders, and there will be no increase in the rent.'

Bairstowe stared at Eli, open-mouthed. He wouldn't dare to ask how Eli had become so intimately acquainted with the cottage, or how he knew Mrs. Defoe's name, but it was obvious he was burning with curiosity.

'I'll make the arrangements at once, your grace.'

75

'See that you do.' Eli reached for the door. 'Oh, and Bairstowe, never put tenants in any unfit property ever again, if you value your position.'

He strode from the room without waiting for Bairstowe to respond, regretting how harshly he had treated a man who'd served him faithfully for as long as he could remember. It was thoughts of the way Athena had been forced to live, albeit by her own insistence, that had so angered him.

And her situation became ever more intriguing. She'd beguiled Bairstowe, or one of his underlings, into letting her have Whispers' Hollow, precisely because it was so isolated, or because she was sure to get it cheaply? She and her sisters were skilled in the art of lace-making, and yet weren't employed by any of the famous houses. Or were they? Is that what they were running away from?

Athena was married to a cove, damn his eyes, who appeared content to leave her and her sisters to their own devices. What sort of man did that make him? Hopefully, a dead one. Eli couldn't imagine anyone abandoning a precious flower like Athena for any lesser reason. She was reluctant to speak of her husband and wore no ring, but that meant little. Perhaps she was fleeing a brutal husband. The very thought filled Eli with a towering rage. The urge to ride back to Whispers' Hollow and assure her she was now safe, became more pressing by the second.

All in all, his Athena was an enigma. He could make her cottage habitable, ensuring her prolonged tenancy. He could, and hopefully already had, secured a market for her lace, providing her with an income. But it wasn't enough. He wanted to do more for her. So much more. He wanted to dress her in the finest style, enjoy her laughter and glowing eyes, worship her body, and protect her from the harsh realities of the world.

Eli looked around his fabulous home as he made his way to his rooms. There was activity everywhere as maids and footmen — all of whom bowed or curtsied and then flattened themselves against the wainscoting as he passed — cleaned, polished and brushed every inanimate object to within an inch of its life in preparation for the house party.

A house party that would see him selecting the woman with whom he would pass the rest of his life. Eli expelled a hollow laugh. Did his mother but know it, he had already found her. She was currently living in a hovel in his woods, and there wasn't any way in the world he could even include her in the festivities.

Was there?

He paused to glance out the nearest window, caught by the sight of a dozen men harvesting the corn in the nearest field, and rubbed his chin in thoughtful contemplation. For the first time since returning home, he felt the urge to smile.

Perhaps there was one more way in which he could assist Athena, and see a little more of her in the bargain. Of course, it would mean she would discover his true identity, but it was only ever going to be a matter of time before that happened anyway.

He entered his rooms and found Salter awaiting him, Athena's jar of herbs clutched in his hands.

'I need a bath, Salter?' He pulled his soiled shirt over his head, and unfastened his breeches.

'Already organised, your grace.'

'Good man. How did it go in the village?'

'Miss Dawson was delighted to be of service to your grace.'

Eli rolled his eyes. 'I don't doubt it.'

'She took all of Mrs. Defoe's merchandise, I understand, and thinks she will have no difficulty selling it. Apparently it's exquisite.'

She will certainly sell it if she puts out word that I endorse it. Eli refrained from indulging in another eye-roll. Quite apart from the fact the gesture tested his injury, and not in a good way, had he not deliberately thrown his name behind Athena's merchandise for that precise reason? He had never done anything of that nature before, and it was bound to create interest, and speculation. It would also guarantee Athena's success. There wasn't much point in being a duke if he couldn't use his position to his advantage, occasionally.

Eli eased himself into his steaming bath and sighed with pleasure as the heat seeped into his aching body. He had scrapes down one side where he'd fallen from Byron that he hadn't noticed before. The water made them sting. If only a certain copper-haired siren was here, with her soft, healing touch, he wouldn't feel the pain. His cock twitched and then hardened at the prospect. If Salter noticed it poking above the water, he had the good sense to remain silent on the point.

'May I enquire what this jar contains, your grace?' Salter asked deferentially. 'Mr. Archer said I was to take the greatest care of it.'

'And so you must, Salter. It's a herbal concoction that will heal my head wound. You must apply another poultice this evening before I retire, and then two more each day for the next six days.'

'Pardon my saying so, your grace, but would it not be better to summon a physician?'

'The same charlatan who has done so much to aid Lord Shelton's condition?' Eli twisted his lips in bitterness when he considered his brother's continuing decline. 'No thank you, Salter. We will do this my way.'

'As your grace wishes.'

'Salter held out a towel. Eli rose from his bath and wrapped it around himself.

'Get me something to eat, Salter. It's a while before dinner and I'm sharp set.'

Athena had offered to feed him again before he left the cottage. Much as he would have enjoyed the excuse to linger, and to make sure she ate something herself, he couldn't bring himself to steal more food from their hungry mouths.

No sooner had Eli expressed a need for food in his own establishment than a sumptuous array of cold cuts, bread and pasties was laid out in his sitting room. He ate quickly, barely noticing what he put in his mouth, satisfying at least one of his hungers.

The other would be far harder to gratify.

Fifteen minutes after he finished eating, Eli was dressed in pristine evening clothes. He was unrecognisable as the person who had chopped logs in the grounds of a tumbledown cottage a few hours earlier, apart from the bandage around his head, of course. He glanced at his hands. Blisters were forming where he'd wielded that axe with so much force. He was glad of them. They were a tangible reminder of just how much he had learned about himself that day. If he was master of his own destiny, he wouldn't hesitate to put that new-found knowledge to good use.

But Eli was not, and never would be, free to please himself.

With a heavy sigh, he straightened his already perfectly tied neckcloth, and headed for the drawing room, where he knew his mother would be lying in wait.

★ ★ ★

'Good heavens, whatever happened to you?'

Beatrice, who aspired to title herself Dowager Duchess of Winsdale, Eli's adored and respected mother, looked up from her embroidery and frowned at her son. She was the most level-headed lady of Eli's acquaintance. She possessed a quick wit, wasn't given to fits of the vapours, fortunately, and eyed Eli with a combination of amusement rather than alarm.

'A slight disagreement between myself and my horse, mother. No lasting damage done. No need to concern yourself.'

'Fortunately, I'm not in the least concerned about your head.' His perspicacious mother fixed him with a gimlet gaze. 'But I *am* curious to know if your accident is the only reason for your delay?'

'What other reason could there possibly be?'

'That is what I would give much to know. When you were a small boy, I always knew you'd been up to no good if you answered a question with one of your own.' His mother's lips twitched. 'That was most of the time, bye the bye.'

'I'm cursed with an enquiring mind,' Eli said, recalling telling a certain green-eyed siren the very same thing just a few hours previously.

'You haven't abandoned that habit, and I can see right through you,' his mother continued. 'I was on the point of sending out a much bigger search party.'

Eli frowned. 'I'm very glad you did not. I'm quite capable of taking care of myself.'

His mother's lips twitched. 'So I see. I also know you've been sowing your wild oats, which probably accounts for your tumble from your horse, if that's what really happened to you. I won't ask you anything else.'

His little sister, Susan, grinned up at him.

'You look like a pirate with that bandage wrapped around your head.'

'You will frighten off all your would-be wives,' added Charlotte, his older sister, now Lady Baintree.

'I very much doubt it,' Eli replied, swishing the tails of his coat aside and seating himself beside his mother. 'How is Harry?'

'Not so good.' His mother shook her head, looking anxious and distressed. 'I shall have to send for the physician. There's no help for that. I dare say he will bleed your brother again, but what good that's likely to do for an infection of the lung, I haven't the slightest notion. Still, he's the expert, so I suppose we must bow to his superior knowledge.'

Eli also frowned. 'I'll go and see how he is before dinner, if he doesn't come down.'

'I doubt if he will,' Charlotte said. 'All this upheaval, getting ready for the party, exhausts him, even though he isn't required to do anything. He likes peace and quiet.'

'Go and see him by all means, Eli,' his mother said. 'Your society always cheers him.'

'You can tell him what you've really been up to,' Susan added with a mischievous smile. 'I'm sure that will make him laugh.'

'What makes you suppose I've been up to anything, minx?'

'You never fall off a horse, Eli,' Susan

replied. 'Not unless you're intoxicated, or . . . well, I don't know, distracted in some way.'

Distracted? Eli's lips twitched. Yes, he'd certainly been that.

'Just three days to go, Eli.' Eli turned his attention to his mother, grateful for the interruption to his wayward thoughts. 'Are you ready to look at the names of the ladies I've invited for your inspection?'

'Heavens, no!' Eli scowled. 'The less I know about them, the better.'

'You're such a romantic,' Susan scolded.

'Having young ladies paraded before one like a string of race horses in training hardly inspires romantic notions.'

'You might be surprised,' Charlotte said, knowingly. 'My friend Lady Cynthia is quite convinced she understands your character and will make a perfect duchess. Furthermore, she's determined to make you fall in love with her.'

'So is every lady on Mama's list,' Susan added, grinning. 'Poor Eli.'

'I don't expect you to make up your mind immediately, Eli,' his mother said. 'Take the entire week to get to know the ladies in question better, see how they behave in company. Not that I would expect them to let you down in that respect. They've all been trained from the cradle.'

Eli tried very hard to appear interested, knowing how much trouble his mother had gone to on his behalf and well aware it was his duty to go through with this damned cattle market and secure the future of the Shelton dynasty. 'I dare say.'

'I thought we might have a grand ball on the penultimate evening. A masquerade,' his mother said. 'People tend to act true to their real characters when their features are hidden behind masks.'

'Oh, Mama!' Susan jumped up and clapped her hands. 'What a lovely idea. What do you think, Eli?'

Eli laughed at Susan's enthusiasm. 'You're just hoping for an opportunity to trap my friend Johnson with your feminine wiles.'

Susan laughed and blushed simultaneously. 'Why, Eli, the thought never crossed my mind.'

Eli groaned. 'Of course it didn't!'

He leaned forward and twitched Susan's nose. He was inordinately fond of his little sister and exceedingly protective of her interests, too. Susan, at least, could follow her heart's desire, and Eli knew her interest had been fixed on Lord Johnson for more than a season now. Hopefully, his friend was similarly minded, and this party would see the two of them engaged by the end of it. Johnson had certainly mentioned something during their carousing, drink having made him a little less reticent than normal. Eli couldn't remember what he'd said in reply — it was all a little hazy — but he hoped he'd given him suitable encouragement. Nothing would give Eli greater pleasure than to see Susan happily settled. Well, one thing would, but that was forbidden to him.

'Have a masquerade by all means,' Eli said to his mother casually. 'But personally, I shall be more interested to see how my would-be duchesses behave towards the tenants at the harvest dance.'

'Would you now?'

The duchess sent Eli another of her probing glances. Since this was the first sign of interest he had shown in the proceedings, Eli couldn't entirely blame her. It was a Shelton tradition that a party was held to celebrate the harvest, the gentry rubbing shoulders with the tenants on the sculpted lawns of Winsdale Park. It wasn't uncommon to see an earl or marquess treading a measure with a milkmaid or farmer's daughter. It just so happened that this year's event fell three days into his mother's house party. The way his mother's protégés conducted themselves with the tenant farmers and villagers would tell him a lot about their characters and, perhaps, help him to make a choice. More importantly, it would give him an opportunity to help Athena *and* see something of her.

'I assume you plan to use the large barn in the west paddock as the hub of activities, as usual?' he said casually.

'Yes, what of it?' His mother looked at him askance. 'Are you sure that bash on the head hasn't addled your wits, Eli? You've never shown any interest in the arrangements in the past.'

'Perhaps we should decorate the inside of the barn,' he said casually.

'I beg your pardon!' Three female voices spoke in unison.

'It always rains,' Eli replied, 'and that barn is a deadly dull place, especially when full of damp bodies.' He sent his mother a droll glance. 'Whatever will my would-be brides think?'

'I'm very glad you're so conscious of their feelings, my dear.'

'Knowing you are championing their respective causes, Mother, I wouldn't dare to neglect their feelings.'

'Harrumph!'

'Well, I think it's a splendid idea,' Susan said stoutly, and Eli could have hugged her for her timely intervention. 'We could decorate the place with corn dollies, and

'. . . well, harvest-type things from the fields and woods. I'm not sure what, precisely, but I expect inspiration will strike. It would look lovely. Can I take charge of that, Mama?'

'If you wish, darling,' the duchess replied, still sending Eli thoughtful glances. 'I'm not sure I can spare many servants to help you, though. We're stretched rather thin.'

Eli tried not to laugh. Winsdale Park was inundated with helping hands. His wily mother was obviously trying to find gainful employment for Susan, who would probably enjoy making the decorations. Except Eli recalled seeing an exceptionally fine decoration on a drab window sill in a tumbledown cottage, and had no intention of allowing her to tackle the project alone.

'Excuse me, Mother,' he said standing, having achieved his objective. 'I shall go and visit Harry before dinner.'

Eli made a detour to the estate office. Bairstowe looked anxious when Eli walked in, making him rather ashamed of the way he'd behaved earlier. Bairstowe had been bamboozled by a siren determined to have her way at all costs. He doubted very much if any man could resist Athena for long when she had her mind set on a particular course. Eli counted himself amongst their number. She intrigued him on many levels, and he was more determined than ever to discover what, or whom, she was hiding away from. Besides, had Bairstowe stood firm and obeyed Eli's orders then Eli and Athena would never have met. Worse, Eli might actually have bled to death on a bed of dried leaves in Whispers' Hollow.

'Bairstowe,' he said in a cordial tone that saw his estate manager immediately relax. 'When you send your team to Whispers' Hollow tomorrow, there's something I need you to do for me.'

'How can I be of service to your grace?'

Eli told him. He then went off to visit Harry, vowing to have a quiet word with Susan about his plans when the opportunity arose.

6

The thing Athena loved the most about Whispers' Hollow was the ethereal stillness in the woods at daybreak. The tranquillity, the oneness she felt with nature as the first fingers of daylight filtered through the leaves was worth the sacrifice of leaving her warm bed an hour before it was strictly necessary to do so. Peace and quiet, the opportunity to assemble her thoughts, was a luxury unavailable to her during her busy days.

Besides, the mushrooms would be gone if she left it any later.

Athena smiled at the typically practical turn her mind had taken. So much had happened since she had last come to Whispers' Hollow just the previous day. Was it really only one day? It seemed more like a year. And yet, she had found a market for their products and had a fat purse to prove it, had saved a man's life *and* had at least a week's worth of firewood chopped.

She pulled her shawl closer about her. The wind was picking up and she smelt rain in the air. Autumn was almost upon them. Her boots crunched over the leaves that had already fallen. She would have to look for somewhere else to live very soon, but at least she could afford something a little better. It was a shame they couldn't remain where they were. She really liked Whispers' Hollow. She felt safer in remote locations, where people were less likely to drop by unexpectedly and ask awkward questions about her past. She and Millie knew precisely how to respond to such inquisitions, but the twins were still so young, and their mouths sometimes ran away with them.

She bent to pick up a stick and threw it for Boris. The stupid mutt's woof disturbed slumbering birds. They took off from their leafy perches with a loud clatter of wings as Boris loped off in pursuit of the stick, ears flapping back against his head. She laughed at his antics when, stick discarded, he stopped to sniff the air, woofed again, and ran off in a different direction.

'Rabbits,' she said aloud, knowing Boris would never catch one.

Athena crouched to pick mushrooms, her thoughts returning to the previous day. She had discovered Mr. Franklin in this very spot, slowly bleeding to death. All signs of his presence had been eradicated, and she might almost have imagined it all. He really was the most fascinating man she had ever encountered — and mysterious, too. She was in a better position than most to know when a person was cutting a sham, which is why she hadn't asked any awkward questions of him. His activities were none of her business, just as her affairs had nothing to do with him. Even so, she couldn't help being curious. That horse, its quality saddle and bridle, Mr. Franklin's fine boots — all those things suggested he was a gentleman — and yet the rest of his clothing, his lack of a coat or attendants, told a very different story. She shook her head, wishing she had asked where he was going. She would have liked an excuse to see him again, but only to check on the progress of his injury, of course.

'Don't be ridiculous!' she muttered aloud.

Athena had too many responsibilities to indulge in fanciful dreams, and that was an end to the matter. Mushrooms collected, she called to Boris, and they made their way back to the cottage. The girls were at their breakfast and greeted Athena with their usual high spirits. Athena sat with them, eating just a little of the porridge Millie placed in front of her as they discussed their plans for the day.

'Miss Dawson needs more lace from us, girls,' Athena said between mouthfuls. 'I suggest we give her smaller items, such as purses, fans, and perhaps some lace ribbons.

They are quicker to produce, and we can make them unusual enough to catch the eye. If fine ladies are here for the duke's house party, they will have most of the things they require with them, and so we will need to tempt them with fripperies.'

'We could make a few lace cuffs as well,' Selene said. 'So that ladies can have their maids change the look of their gowns.'

'And fichus,' Lyssa added.

'Handkerchiefs, too.' Millie ladled more porridge in the girls' bowls. 'They always go down well.'

'That's true.' Athena shook her head at Millie when her ladle hovered over her own bowl. 'No thank you, Millie. I have sufficient here.'

Millie tutted. 'You've hardly eaten a scrap, lamb.'

'I ate a feast last night. Your mutton stew was a real treat.'

'Why is the duke having a house party at this time of year?' Lyssa asked.

Selene nodded. 'Yes, why? House parties are usually held in high summer, aren't they?'

'I heard it said in the haberdasher's shop yesterday his mother is insisting he find a wife. He's now thirty, you see — '

'That old,' gasped Selene, open-mouthed.

'It's positively ancient,' Lyssa agreed.

'Quite so.' Athena struggled not to smile. 'The duke has a duty to produce an heir to secure the future of the duchy. So, his mother has invited several young ladies and their mothers to stay for a week, and the duke has to choose one as his duchess.'

'Sounds brutal,' Millie said, sniffing.

'For the duke or his prospective brides?' Athena asked, her lips twitching.

'For the girls, of course. I don't care about a rich duke, who is probably very disagreeable and curmudgeonly. He'll just marry one of 'em, and then do as he pleases.' Millie sniffed. 'That's how gentlemen of quality behave.'

'What do you mean?' Selene asked, leaning forward expectantly.

Lyssa widened her eyes. 'Yes, what precisely would the duke do to please himself?'

'Never you mind about that.' Millie collected up their empty bowls. 'If you're finished, you'd best get to work, both of you.'

'Why do you always send us off — '

'Just when the conversation is getting interesting?'

Athena laughed at her sisters' aggrieved expressions as they left the kitchen and took themselves off into the other room to start a long day's lacemaking. At least Athena would be able to spend the entire day with them, without the distraction of ailing gentlemen or the responsibility for marketing their products plaguing her mind. She would tell them stories to keep them entertained. Athena had read a lot of classic literature, when she was at leisure to do so, and enjoyed passing on précis of those stories to the twins. She told herself it was education, of sorts, guiltily aware that, thanks to her, Selene and Lyssa were being denied the pleasure of learning.

'Hey up.' Millie peered suspiciously through the open doorway when the sound of hooves reached their ears. Boris removed himself from beneath the table, where he had been catching any scraps that happened to fall his way. His hackles were raised and a low growl rumbled in his throat.

'Go back in the other room now!' Athena told the twins, who had reappeared to see who their visitors were. 'Stay there until I tell you otherwise.'

Once they were gone, she and Millie exchanged an anxious glance. This was the moment Athena had been dreading. There was more than one horse coming, by the sounds of things, and they could hear the rumble of wheels on the uneven track, too. They had almost been caught on a couple of previous occasions, just managing to gather up their sparse possessions and flee in the nick of time. But on this occasion they wouldn't be able to run. If it had been just one man, then perhaps . . . but what could two women and two young girls do against what sounded like a small army?

'He must be really desperate to have us back,' Athena said bitterly, her stomach knotted with a combination of anger and fear. 'I should have known our good fortune of yesterday wouldn't last.'

'How did they find us?' Millie asked, scowling.

'The lace, I suppose. We're trying hard not to make it too obvious . . . but well, I suppose it's still different enough to lead back to us.'

'Even so.' Millie frowned. 'You only put it up for sale yesterday. It seems awful quick.'

'Yes, I know.'

'And you didn't tell Miss Dawson where we live.'

'No, but if my uncle discovered we were in the district, it wouldn't be too hard to find us. We've been careful, but still, we have been noticed.'

The two women hugged one another and stood arm-in-arm in the doorway as the small procession pulled up outside the cottage.

'That's Mr. Bairstowe,' Athena said slowly, the air leaving her lungs in an extravagant whoosh. 'The duke's estate manager. He's the man who agreed to let me have this cottage for a short time.' She stifled a smile as she recalled how she had badgered the poor man until she wore down his resistance. 'Eventually.'

'Well, we haven't been found then, but presumably it means the duke wants the cottage back.'

'I suppose so, but he will have to give us notice, won't he?'

'At least we can afford somewhere else now.'

'Yes, but I like it here.'

'Good morning, Mrs. Defoe.' Mr. Bairstowe doffed his hat. 'I trust I find you well.'

'Thank you, yes, but what is the meaning of this?' Athena waved a hand towards the cart and the men spilling from it.

'Duke's orders. We're to do repairs to the cottage before winter sets in. The thatcher will be here directly.' Athena and Millie gaped at one another, speechless for once. 'These men will repair the staircase and make the upper floor habitable. There will likely be disruption for a week or so, but at least you will be snug and secure for the winter.'

'We can stay?' Athena asked, barely able to believe her good fortune.

'Absolutely.'

'Wh-why are you doing this?'

'Duke's orders, ma'am,' he said for a

second time. 'He was displeased when he heard this cottage had been let in such poor condition and gave orders for something to be done about it.'

'Oh, I hope that didn't get you into trouble,' Athena said, her conscience pricking her.

'Not in the least.'

'We can't afford to pay much more by way of rent,' Millie said, wagging a finger at Mr. Bairstowe.

'The rent will not change.'

'It will not?' Athena echoed. She appeared to have lost the ability to say anything remotely intelligent, or to voice the myriad questions tumbling through her brain.

'Perhaps you will walk through the cottage with me, Mrs. Defoe, and we can discuss what is to be done,' Mr. Bairstowe suggested politely.

'Oh yes, of course.'

The tour didn't take long. Mr. Bairstowe gave instructions to two men and a lad, who appeared to have responsibility for restoring the stairs. Someone else set about the rotted windows with a chisel. Athena and Mr. Bairstowe were in the main room, where the girls stared at them with avid interest.

'These are my sisters, Mr. Bairstowe,' she said, not giving him their names.

'They seem very industrious.'

'Quite so.'

Mr. Bairstowe paused, apparently waiting for an explanation that Athena wasn't about to offer.

'This room doesn't seem to have suffered too much,' he said, glancing about him. 'We will arrange for the chimney to be swept, and for the window to be . . . I say, who made this?' Mr. Bairstowe picked up the ornament Athena had fashioned recently from dried leaves and forest fruits in an effort to cheer the room up and make it appear more homely.

'I did.' She flexed a brow, wondering why it could possibly be of interest a busy man like Mr. Bairstowe. 'I picked the berries in the woods around here. I hope I didn't take anything I ought not to have done.'

'You are very artistic, Mrs. Defoe.'

'It's kind of you to say so.'

'But it also puts me in mind of something. The duchess is having a house party next week, and the harvest party for the estate workers falls right in the middle of it.'

'Then presumably it will be postponed.'

'Oh no, the date is firmly fixed every year. The villagers are a superstitious lot, and wouldn't take kindly to it being changed. They would see it as a warning that next

99

year's harvest would fail, you see.'

'Oh.' Athena really didn't see what business this was of hers. The girls had abandoned all pretence of work and were listening avidly.

'The duchess sees no reason not to go ahead with the party, as usual. It is the one occasion every year when the villagers get to mix with the gentry on equal terms.' He shrugged. 'Well, almost.'

'Er, quite.' Athena sent a curious glance towards Millie, who stood in the open doorway, listening also. The older woman lifted her shoulders, equally puzzled.

'Lady Susan, his grace's sister, has taken it upon herself to decorate the inside of the barn that's used as the hub of the festivities. She has quite taken it into her head that something special ought to be done this year, owing to the fact there will be so many distinguished guests at Winsdale Park. But she . . . er, well, no disrespect intended, but she isn't blessed with your talent and originality of ideas.'

'Is that a long-winded way of saying she needs help?' Millie asked, sending Mr. Bairstowe an impatient look.

'She did happen to ask me if I knew of anyone who might be creatively inclined. It seems like a happy coincidence I should come here and see an example of precisely the type of

weren't usually up with the lark. 'It's still v
early.'

'Lady Susan is an early riser, as are all c
the duke's family.'

'What is he like? The duke, I mean, if you
don't mind my asking.'

Mr. Bairstowe looked surprised by the
question. 'You don't know?'

'How would I?' She laughed and shook her
head. 'In case you've forgotten, I live in a
tumbledown cottage in the woods, making
lace for a living. Our paths are hardly likely to
cross in the normal way of things.'

'Ah, I see.'

Mr. Bairstowe nodded, a faint smile
playing about his lips. Athena had absolutely
no idea what had become so blindingly
apparent to him. Since they had just turned
through a pair of magnificent gates, the pillars
topped by beautiful marble statues of rearing
horses, and the curricle was bowling along a
pristine gravel driveway, Athena's attention
was diverted, and she didn't ask him to
explain. There appeared to be a small army of
gardeners attending to grounds that didn't
appear to have a blade of grass out of place
Athena wondered what more there was f
them to do. There was a huge lake, spark'
off in the distance. Athena had a ch'
fascination for lakes and wondered   E

creativity she has in mind, Mrs. Defoe.'

Why was the man looking at her so
intently? Was this suggestion as innocent as it
sounded? Athena didn't see how the duke's
estate manager could be in league with her
uncle, but had long since learned not to take
anything at face value.

'Thank you, Mr. Bairstowe, but I'm needed
here.'

'I'm afraid it's going to be rather noisy and
crowded for the next week or two. Working
might be difficult.'

'Yes, but even so.'

'I hesitate to mention anything as vulgar as
money, Mrs. Defoe, but rest assured if you
were kind enough to help Lady Susan in her
hour of need, you would be amply rewarded
for your efforts.'

'The duke is already rewarding us by repairing the cottage and not charging more rent.
Besides, I'm sure he has no end of servants
who are more than capable of helping Lady
Susan.'

'They are more used to taking orders than
making suggestions.'

'You should do it, Athena,' Selene said. 'It
might be fun.'

'You would get to see Winsdale Park,' Lyssa
added, eyes wide with excitement.

'I'm sure you would all be invited to the

party,' Mr. Bairstowe said, smiling at the twins.

Athena had wondered how long their girls would hold their tongues, surprised it had taken them so long to speak. She glanced at their faces, animated at the prospect of a party, and her heart melted. They had so little pleasure in their lives.

'Very well, if you think Lady Susan might be interested in my suggestions, Mr. Bairstowe, then I will be happy to offer my advice. However, I have little experience of tackling such matters on a large scale. I merely dabble to amuse myself, so I might not be much help.'

'And I'm equally sure you will save the day.' Mr. Bairstowe inclined his head, treating her with far greater respect than she thought appropriate for a mere tenant, which was puzzling. Lady Susan must be really quite desperate.

'Perhaps I could find the time to come across to Winsdale Park this afternoon.'

'If it's no inconvenience, I shall be returning there directly, just as soon as I've set the men to work. I would be happy to take you myself.' He indicated a smart curricle, pulled up behind the cart outside the cottage.

'How will I get back?'

'Lady Susan will make arrangements, I'm sure.'

Athena wasn't sure of any such thin Grand ladies could be very high-handed.

'Go, lamb,' Millie said quietly. 'I'll keep weather eye on things here.'

Millie was the most suspicious creature o God's earth. If she thought there would b profit in Athena going, then who was she to argue? Besides, she admitted to a sneaking curiosity to see Winsdale Park for herself.

'Very well, Mr. Bairstowe. If you would give me a minute to wash my face and hands and tidy my hair, I shall be ready to come with you.'

'Change into your best gown,' Millie said, pushing Athena into her sleeping alcove, along with the gown in question. She pulled the curtain across and stood sentry outside while Athena, shrugging at Millie's assertive ways, dutifully changed her attire.

A short time later, Mr. Bairstowe handed Athena into his curricle and drove away at a brisk trot. Athena's head swam with the speed at which this had all happened. Less than two hours ago, she had been picking mushrooms and planning her day's lacemaking. Now she was wearing her best dress for the second day in a row, on her way to meet a duke's sister, no less.

'Will Lady Susan be about yet, Mr. airstowe?' she asked, aware that grand ladies

would have an opportunity to walk around this one while she was here.

They turned a corner and the house came into view. Athena gasped. With the sun bathing the honey-coloured façade with its morning rays, it looked magnificent. And enormous. Wide stone steps lead up from two directions at the front, converging on the terrace, from which Athena imagined there must be a fine view of the lake. She glanced up at the myriad windows, wondering what secrets lay behind them. Everyone had secrets — even people as rich as the duke obviously was.

Especially him.

The thought sprang unbidden into her mind, and she couldn't seem to shake it. Unlike Millie, she felt a moment's sympathy for the poor man, being expected to marry a woman he didn't love and hardly knew, simply because he was required to produce an heir. Suddenly her own existence didn't seem so very bad. At least when her pursuers gave up on her — as they would eventually have to — she would have the freedom to do as she pleased. Not for all the lace in Nottingham would she exchange her life for the duke's.

Mr. Bairstowe turned the curricle to one side of the house, presumably in the direction of the stables. It took a very long time to get there. They passed various gardens on the way. One was dedicated to roses. Although the blooms were past their best at this time of year, the perfume was delightful, even from a distance. She sat a little straighter when she saw an extensive herb garden. What she would give to explore that particular patch.

The curricle came to a halt, and a groom appeared to assist Athena from it. She thanked him, straightened her bonnet, although it probably didn't require any straightening, and looked to Mr. Bairstowe for direction. Nerves ate away at her insides and, not for the first time, she wondered what she was doing here. But still, her scalp wasn't prickling as it normally would if danger loomed, so she forced herself to relax.

'Please come this way, Mrs. Defoe.'

They entered the house through a side door. Mr. Bairstowe handed Athena over to a rather fierce-looking butler. 'Mrs. Defoe is here to see Lady Susan regarding the decorations in the barn, Mr. Archer,' he said.

'Please come this way, madam.' He walked ahead of her, down a long corridor, the walls of which were lined with elegant paintings, and opened the door to a small, prettily-decorated sitting room. 'Make yourself comfortable. I will inform Lady Susan of your arrival.'

'Thank you.'

Athena looked about the room as soon as Mr. Archer left her. The walls were painted sunshine yellow, the furniture was covered with a bright, floral fabric, and pictures depicting country scenes graced the walls. This clearly wasn't one of the formal rooms, but somewhere a family member would come to relax. There was an array of miniatures on a side table. Athena studied them, wondering if any of them were of the mysterious duke.

None the wiser, she gave up on the pictures and wandered to the window, feeling a strange premonition. Athena was unable to decide what it signified, or why she was so unsettled. She knew how to behave in good society and wasn't *that* intimidated by her surroundings. She had never actually met a duke before, it was true, but she was sure their paths wouldn't cross today. Even if they did, she would be beneath his notice. As for Lady Susan, it seemed she needed Athena's help. If she was too high-handed at that, Athena would simply leave her to her own devices.

No, she told herself, she had absolutely no reason to feel uncomfortable, but she *was* wasting precious time she could be putting to much better use. Although, if the duke really didn't mean to increase her rent, she would be saved the time and inconvenience of looking for a new abode. Under the circumstances, the very least she could do to repay the mysterious duke's kindness, was to help his sister in her hour of need.

She glanced out at a pretty garden that was completely unstructured, at direct variance to the strict maintenance of the formal gardens they had driven past on the way in. Athena thought this one far prettier. There were wild flowers mixed with azaleas, peonies, and honeysuckle. The perfume must be divine when they were all in full bloom, and she would give much to walk through it when it was.

★ ★ ★

Having risen with the dawn, Eli had been unable to settle to any occupation since. Anyone invited to help at Winsdale Park, especially when the request came directly from a member of the family, would ordinarily trip over their own feet in their haste to oblige. Athena, with her fear of whatever it was she was running from, was altogether another matter, and he had no idea how she would react to his — no, his sister's — summons. Bairstowe had damned well have been at his most persuasive, because Eli refused to take *no* for an answer. If he had to go to the cottage himself, reveal his true identity in less than ideal circumstances, and forcibly drag her back here, then that was what he would do.

Put simply, Athena Defoe intrigued him, and thoughts of her lovely face occupied his mind to the exclusion of almost everything else. He had planned to get through this damned party of his mother's in a permanent state of near intoxication. Now intoxication of a very different variety held him in its thrall. He could hope for nothing more than her friendship. For he was a duke and would never be free to follow his heart. But he could and would resolve her problems, whatever they were. She had saved his life, and he would return the favour by ensuring she could live hers, free of fear.

Fortunately, collecting her himself had proven not to be necessary, because Eli had the satisfaction of seeing Bairstowe's curricle bowling up the driveway, an immediately recognisable goddess seated beside him. She glanced up at the building, holding her bonnet with one hand as she tipped her head backwards. Eli was convinced her gaze was focused exclusively on the windows to his suite of rooms. She must have discovered who he really was and could feel the heat of his gaze burning into her profile.

'Idiot,' he muttered as the curricle moved away, and he could no longer see her.

Eli buried himself in his study, trying to concentrate on estate business. He dictated letters to his secretary, Jessop, a young man of good family and straitened circumstances, who was proving to be both intelligent and resourceful.

'There are a few requests for your consideration, your grace,' Jessop said, when Eli finished his dictation.

'When are there not?' Eli rolled his eyes. 'All right, let's hear them.'

It was the usual mixture of disputes, problems, and excuses that required resolution. Eli dealt with them quickly and, he hoped, with a fair hand. Jessop took extensive notes, and Eli knew his instructions would be carried out to the letter.

'What do you know about handmade lace, Jessop?' Eli asked, leaning back in his chair and pinching the bridge of his nose.

'Nottingham,' Jessop replied immediately. 'That's the place to go for it.'

'But it's in decline, is it not?'

'That it is, your grace. A man called Heathcoat invented a bobbin net machine that produces complex lace designs far quicker than they can be made by hand. It is my understanding that handmade lace, *if* it's

110

made by skilled craftsmen, can still fetch a high price, but the machinery has put a lot of people out of work.'

Eli raised a brow. Jessop's supply of ready information on the most obscure subjects never failed to impress. Mind you, Eli championing the handmade lace now for sale in Miss Dawson's establishment would be known throughout the house by now, probably raising more than one speculative eyebrow. He doubted whether there was a single scullery maid or humble under-gardener who didn't know of the interest he had taken in it. Jessop might have had reason to anticipate Eli's question, but Eli still admired his ingenuity.

'Send someone to Nottingham to make discreet enquiries, Jessop, with the emphasis on discreet. Choose a person with experience whom you trust but who can't be linked directly to me.'

'What should he look for, your grace?'

'I want to know if anyone is missing from a family or business renowned for producing handmade lace. Specifically, a woman of about four-and-twenty with younger twin sisters.'

'I shall make the arrangements at once, your grace.'

'See that you do.' Eli flapped a hand in dismissal, and Jessop stood up to leave. 'Oh, and Jessop. This is between you, me, and the person you send. Absolute discretion is called for. If anyone else hears of it, you will pay with your position.' Eli fixed the young man with a firm gaze. 'Understood?'

Jessop stood in the doorway, looking serious yet resolute. 'I understand absolutely, your grace.'

★ ★ ★

The door opened behind her, abruptly pulling Athena out of her tangled reflections. She turned to see a very pretty young woman of no more than nineteen, standing in the doorway. Dressed in a beautiful morning gown of pale pink muslin and with a profusion of dark curls, she smiled at Athena, immediately putting her at her ease.

'Mrs. Defoe. How kind of you to come. I've heard so much about you.'

You have?

The lady stepped forward, hand outstretched. Athena took it, and then remembered to curtsey.

'Lady Susan,' she said.

'Please sit down. Archer, some tea if you please.'

'At once, my lady.'

Athena glanced up and saw the butler in the doorway, regarding her with open curiosity. What did everyone find so intriguing about her? Her clothes were plain and dowdy, especially compared to Lady Susan's. Perhaps that's what it was. This stately butler obviously didn't approve of the tenants conducting business with the family. The thought amused Athena, driving away her residue doubts about being here.

Lady Susan was regarding her quizzically, head tilted to one side, a lively smile lighting up her features.

'I think I begin to understand,' she said, almost to herself.

'I beg your pardon?'

'Oh, nothing.' Lady Susan shook her head. 'I am so very glad you could come. I impulsively volunteered to liven up the barn for the dance, but I am really not qualified to do it alone. I thought it would be so simple, you see.' She wrinkled her brow, still smiling. Her good humour was infectious, and Athena found herself smiling, too. 'But it's not nearly so easy as it looks. I hope you have some inspired ideas that will save the day, Mrs. Defoe.'

'I'll certainly try. I often use berries and fruits from the forest to liven up my cottage. This is the same thing, except on a much larger scale, I suppose. I shall need to see the barn, of course, before I can offer any advice.'

'Naturally. Ah, here's tea. Thank you, Archer.'

Lady Susan poured tea into exquisite bone china cups and handed one to Athena, who thanked her, revelling in the luxury of drinking from such fine china. It had been a long time, and she had forgotten how good china could change the entire taste of the beverage it contained.

'I'm sure you must have an extensive orchard here, Lady Susan,' Athena said, when her companion paused in her chatter for long enough to allow Athena to get a word in. 'We could core apples and string them along the sides of the barn, and . . . '

'And make Chinese lanterns from pumpkins, too.' Lady Susan clapped her hands. 'You see, I knew you would be able to help me.'

'Well, it might not work, but — '

'Of course it will. Come, have you finished your tea?'

Athena hastily put her cup aside, although she would have enjoyed taking a second.

'Good, we will go and inspect the barn right away.'

Lady Susan was a whirlwind, reminding Athena of the twins at their liveliest. Having decided to visit the barn, she was up from her chair and out of the room in seconds. Athena almost had to run to keep up with her.

'Here we are,' she said breathlessly when they had negotiated yet another gravel path that led from the other side of the house to a large, recently harvested meadow. The barn was cavernous. Decorating it would be both a challenge and a thrill. It could definitely do with it. 'We have trestle tables in here for ale and lemonade. The landlord from *the Ram's Bottom* in the village supplies all of that. Then we have more tables over here for food for people to sit. Provided it doesn't rain, the family and our guests eat on the terrace, and there are tables laid out on the lawns for everyone else. The dancing takes place around the barn. In that corner over there we have musicians, also supplied by the villagers, and it's very jolly. It's impossible not to dance when you hear the fiddler strike up a jig.'

Athena tried to imagine it all, her mind already alive with possibilities. 'Hmm, you have certainly set yourself a challenge, Lady Susan.'

'But, surely it's possible?' Her face fell. 'I've quite made up my mind to do something memorable, you see.'

'And so you shall.' Athena resisted the urge to reassure Lady Susan by giving her a swift hug, as she would have done with the twins if they were discouraged about something. Athena bit her lip to prevent herself from

115

laughing. Hugging a duke's sister was hardly good form, she was absolutely sure about that. Even so, she liked the young woman immensely, despite the disparity in their situations, and would do all she could to help her. If money and labour was no object, then anything was possible. 'Now then, if we were to string — '

'Susan, are you there?'

'Oh, that's Eli.' Lady Susan sent Athena the most extraordinary smile. 'In here,' she called out.

The vague sense of unease Athena had felt since arriving at Winsdale Park intensified. It appeared she was about to meet the mysterious duke, and for some reason she was reluctant to turn in his direction, even when she sensed a large presence looming in the doorway.

'Mrs. Defoe has been kind enough to come to my rescue, Eli,' Lady Susan said.

'I'm sure we're all much obliged to her.'

No longer able to avoid doing so, Athena turned to look at the duke. He was impeccably attired in a green superfine coat and waistcoat in pale green and cream stripes. He wore an air of authority as elegantly as his coat sat on his broad shoulders. The only thing marring his appearance was the white bandage circling his head that thick black hair spilling across it couldn't conceal. Athena gasped, her legs wobbled, and she quickly leaned against the wall for support. She had survived no end of set-backs since leaving Nottingham without ever once losing her senses, but this was one shock too many, and she seriously doubted if she had enough strength to remain standing unaided.

'You!' she gasped.

7

'Mrs. Defoe.' Eli offered her an engaging smile. 'Welcome to Winsdale Park.'

Athena continued to stare at him, looking totally stunned. She swallowed several times, deathly pale and so bewildered, Eli felt wretched for having deceived her. She made no response to his greeting as a kaleidoscope of conflicting emotions passed across her lovely features, none of them especially encouraging. She was not only shocked, but angry with him.

Very angry.

Eli wondered if she knew just how endearing she looked when in a high dudgeon. She was simply magnificent in her justifiable rage and clearly not the slightest bit intimidated by Eli. Silence sucked the atmosphere dry as she continued to fix him with a penetrating gaze of focused fury. Susan, equally bewildered by the chilly silence, cleared her throat and sent Eli a speaking look. It broke the spell, and Athena finally acknowledged his presence.

'Your grace.' She imbued the words with sweet sarcasm as she dipped an elegant curtsey.

'I am very glad you were able to come to

my sister's aid.' He waved a hand around the cavernous barn, treating her as though she had just spoken with the utmost civility. 'She was quite at her wit's end over all this.'

'I was?' Susan looked surprised to hear it.

'I am no longer sure I can be of any help,' Athena said, a determined jut to her chin.

'Susan, I believe Mother needs you.'

'No she doesn't, Eli. She is discussing menus with Mrs. Coulton.' Susan sent him an impish smile and leaned her chin in her cupped hand, making her intention to remain with them patently clear. Eli supposed he couldn't blame her. Susan, the little minx, would be eaten up with curiosity about his connection to Athena. 'I should only be in the way.'

'You're in the way now,' Eli replied, through gritted teeth.

'Me?' She elevated her brows in innocent surprise. 'You must excuse me, but Mrs. Defoe and I are in consultation about decorating this barn. If anyone is in the way, it's you.' She settled herself on a stool and sent him a sweet smile. 'But don't mind me. If you have matters to discuss with Mrs. Defoe, I shall find something to occupy me.'

'Mrs. Defoe.' Eli held out an arm. 'Do me the goodness of taking a turn around the lake with me.'

His goddess sent him a lofty glance from

beneath her fringe of thick, curly lashes. 'Do I have any choice in the matter?'

'Absolutely you do,' Susan replied before Eli could. 'No one ever dares to say *no* to Eli. He will bark at them, and intimidate them if they attempt it, you see. But you are my guest, not his, and it's high time someone put him in his place.'

'Susan, are you absolutely sure there isn't something you ought to be attending to?'

'Thank you for your concern, Eli, but I believe my morning is completely my own.'

'Mrs. Defoe.' Eli again proffered his arm, an edge to his voice. 'Please oblige me.'

She inverted her chin, expelled a disgruntled sigh, and moved elegantly across the space that separated them. Eli felt victorious when she placed her small hand on his sleeve, even if she did so with obvious reluctance.

'Pray excuse me, Lady Susan,' she said. 'I will not be gone for long.'

'Take all the time you need, Mrs. Defoe,' Susan replied with a mischievous smile. 'I shall busy myself ordering the cutting of the blackthorn and elderberry branches you suggested.'

'Make sure they know to cut them as long as possible. These decorations need to be on a large scale in order to show to their best advantage.'

'Yes, I understand.'

Eli led Athena away in the direction of the lake. She looked straight ahead, but he could sense the fury in her fixed expression and rigid stance. What else could he have expected? He was unsure how to proceed or what to say to win her around, and so thought it best to wait for her to break the brittle silence that sprang up between them. It was several minutes before she did so — several of the longest minutes of Eli's life.

'I dare say you enjoyed a good laugh at my expense,' she said through tightly compressed lips.

'Quite the contrary, I do assure you. I've never felt more obliged to anyone.' He sent her a candid smile. 'You saved my life, and asked for nothing in return. I don't think you understand how remarkable that is.'

'Why did you not tell me who you were?' She stopped walking and glared at him, a rich burn turning her eyes the colour of molasses, her cheeks flushed delightfully pink with indignation. 'Or did you prefer to entertain yourself by making me look foolish?'

'What would you have done if you had known?'

'Sent word here at once.'

'Precisely.' He started walking again, compelling her to remain with him by placing his free hand over the one still resting on his other arm. 'And I couldn't have that.'

'You would rather sleep in a . . . just a minute.' She snatched her hand from beneath his and covered her mouth with it. 'The repairs to the cottage, selling our lace so easily, this request for help from your sister . . . that was all your doing?'

'Yes, I wanted to repay you in some small way.'

'So Miss Dawson wasn't impressed by our lace.'

She looked endearingly discouraged, and it took every last vestige of Eli's self-control not to pull her into his arms and kiss away the hurt.

'Oh, I believe she was,' he said in a languid tone. 'She ought to be. Even I can see that it is exquisite, and I'm told she has every expectation of it selling well.'

'It should. It's far cheaper than it ought to be.'

'Why is that?'

She shook her head, and it was obvious she didn't plan to say anything more.

'This may come as a surprise to you, your grace, but I was perfectly happy to help you, just as I would have helped anyone I found on the ground bleeding to death. You didn't have to interfere in my life in some obscure attempt to repay me.'

'Believe me, the ladies at my mother's house party will be in alt over your lace, so you have done me another favour. Besides, I'm persuaded you would have sold it without my help. As to the cottage, I had no idea it had been let, until yesterday.' He curled his upper lip. 'I wouldn't allow a dog to live in such conditions.'

'I suppose it must be difficult for a man in your position to keep track of all his interests.'

'You have no idea.'

Although Eli fully intended to keep very close track of the interest currently walking beside him. The heady herbal perfume he associated with her assailed his nostrils, sending his mind on a sensuous detour of aspiration and regret. He knew what he wanted from this beautiful, fiery, wilful lady, but also knew she would never agree to it. He grabbed her hand and returned it to his sleeve. He was encouraged when she didn't attempt to remove it again.

'Even so, you must charge me a fair rent,' she said, appearing slightly mollified.

'And as to inviting you here to help my sister, she was quite determined to decorate the barn, and I knew it would be beyond her. I saw your decoration at the cottage yesterday, and knew you would be just the person to help her.'

'Why is it so important to her?'

Eli laughed, glad to be on safer ground. 'Susan, as you will already know if you've been in her company for above half an hour, is delightfully high-spirited. She has received several offers from eligible parties, but I have rejected them all on her behalf because she has her interest fixed on my friend, Lord Johnson.'

'And he doesn't return her regard.' Athena wrinkled her brow. 'I find that very hard to believe.'

'Johnson is in a similar position to myself in that he's unsure if he's ready for matrimony.'

'In your case, I understood it was more by way of a . . . shall we say, contractual arrangement between suitable parties.'

Eli harrumphed. 'Well put, Athena.'

'But if Lord Johnson has feelings for Lady Susan and is free to do as he pleases, then what — '

'He needs a little encouragement, nothing more. He doesn't know Susan that well, and might mistake her lively manner for flightiness. The reverse is actually true. Johnson is a very keen farmer, and — '

'Ah, now I understand.' Athena nodded and smiled. 'If she can claim to have decorated the barn imaginatively to reflect the importance of the harvest, it might be enough to win his favour.'

'She hasn't admitted as much, but I believe that is her ulterior motive.'

Athena tilted her chin. 'Then we must ensure she succeeds.'

'So you will help her?'

'For her sake, not yours.' Athena frowned at him. 'Don't imagine I'm that easily persuaded as a general rule.'

Eli shuddered and was rewarded when her lips twitched into a reluctant smile. 'Believe me, I do not.'

'I dislike being manipulated as though I'm incapable of thinking for myself.' She wagged a finger at him. 'Especially by dukes who ought to know better.'

'I feel suitably chastised.'

'As you should. But you still haven't explained why you didn't tell me who you were.'

Eli stopped walking and waved a hand towards the house. 'I don't expect you to believe this, or for my problems to excite your sympathy,' he said. 'I know just how fortunate I am to have all of this, but it's also a heavy responsibility.'

He expected a lecture about not knowing when he was well off. Instead, she nodded. 'Strange as it might seem, I can understand that.'

'You can?' Eli allowed his surprise to show.

'Most people who heard me speak that way would accuse me of being spoiled and petulant. They would probably also offer to exchange places with me in a heartbeat.'

'I am not most people, your grace.'

No, you're not. But who are you, my beautiful, mysterious lady?

'Do you know, I can't remember a time when anyone spoke to me with anything other than deference, or downright obsequiousness. Everyone wants something from me, and it can become damned wearing, excuse the language.'

He paused beside the lake. Athena snatched her gaze from his face and looked out over the calm water, its surface gently rippled by a breeze, a few aquatic birds paddling lazily about. 'It's lovely,' she said. 'So peaceful. I love lakes.'

No, you're lovely. 'I thought you might enjoy it.'

'I'm still very vexed with you, your grace, and won't be fobbed off with pretty vistas. You have yet to offer me a satisfactory explanation for your peculiar behaviour.'

'You treated me like a normal man, sweet Athena.' He lowered his voice as he drowned in the depths of her fathomless eyes, falling ever more rapidly beneath her spell.

'Anyone would have done the same,' she

replied, sounding distracted.

'I disagree, and believe me, I am in the best position to know.' Eli steered her towards a bench on the lake's bank, waited until she had seated herself and arranged her skirts to her satisfaction, and then took the seat beside her. 'Your put my interests ahead of your own, even though it cost you time and money to do so, and expected nothing from me in return.' He drilled her with a look. 'Have you any idea just how unusual that is?'

'I dare say it is, but it still doesn't explain things.'

'I've never slept anywhere except the softest of beds — '

'Except when you go carousing with your friends,' she said, clearly fighting a smile.

Eli was less circumspect, threw back his head and laughed. 'Except then. I have never cleaned my own boots, prepared my own bath — '

'Chopped logs?'

'Precisely.' He fixed her with a dazzling smile. 'It was a liberating experience.'

'You will have blisters.'

He lifted up his hands and showed her his palms. 'You're right about that.'

'Ouch! I can mix you some herbs that will help with those. Speaking of which, how is your head?'

'Doing remarkably well. My valet is astounded at how quickly it's healing. He thinks I should be able to dispense with the bandage in another day or two.'

'That will be for the best. The fresh air will aid your recovery.' She offered him the ghost of a smile. 'Besides, we can't have your prospective brides put off by an ugly bandage.'

He scowled. 'Nothing will put them off, believe me.'

'No, I don't suppose it will.' She sounded slightly sorry for him, which surprised Eli, especially since he hadn't spoken with the intention of engendering her sympathy. 'Were you awake when I found you in the woods?'

He wanted desperately to lie, because he knew the truth would anger her, but couldn't bring himself to be anything other than honest with her. 'Yes,' he said softly. 'I woke almost immediately.'

She bristled with indignation. 'And yet you allowed us to struggle . . . to almost break our backs . . . Why did you do that?' She glared at him, her eyes flashing fire, her beautiful lips taut with anger.

Eli sent her a puerile grin. He simply couldn't help himself. 'I was about to regain my senses when I heard you say you would push me onto Byron by my backside. Well, I — '

'Of all the outrageous, disrespectful . . . Do you have any idea how heavy you are? We could have strained ourselves.'

'Oh, I wouldn't have permitted that to happen. And I did give you some help when you weren't aware of it.' He tried for a remorseful expression, but suspected he failed miserably. He was a duke, unaccustomed to showing remorse. It would take practise to perfect that expression. 'Athena, I was being treated like a normal person. Besides, I was enjoying myself far too much to go back to being myself.'

'You do realise that your enjoyment could have resulted in permanent damage to your thick head.'

'You see. You've just proven my point. No one outside of my immediate family has the courage to accuse me of being thick-headed.'

She arched a delicate brow. 'Even when you are?'

His lips twitched. 'Even then.'

'You really are impossibly arrogant,' she said, a deeply capricious expression replacing her earlier condemnation. 'But, I suppose, in your circumstances I might have behaved in a similar fashion.'

'So I'm forgiven.'

'I shall have to think about that.'

'While you're thinking, may I ask another

huge favour of you?'

She looked surprised. 'Yes, I suppose so. What is it?'

'I have a brother, Harry — Lord Shelton. He has a weak chest, finds it difficult to draw enough breath into his lungs, and often can't leave his chamber for days at a time. He's particularly bad at the moment, and my mother is on the point of sending for the physician, who will bleed him.'

'For an infection of the lung!'

'Precisely my reaction. I wondered, given you saved my life — '

'To say nothing of your beauty.'

'Are you teasing me, Mrs. Defoe?'

'I believe you deserved to be teased, *Mr. Franklin*. I doubt many people dare to attempt that, either.'

'You're right. However, you now own me, you see — '

She widened her eyes. 'I beg your pardon.'

'You saved my life and so, according to ancient folklore, I am now your responsibility. This area is full of suspicious people. It wouldn't do to upset them by ignoring superstitions that have been handed down through the generations.'

She sent him a quelling look. 'Are you laughing at me?'

'No, sweet Athena. I'm desperately trying

130

to persuade you to help me.'

She looked away from him. 'I have already said I will. I absolutely don't own you, your grace, nor do I have any wish to, but I will see what I can do for your brother.' She stood up. 'Shall we go?'

Relief swept through Eli as he stood and offered her his arm again. 'By all means.'

8

'This is the quickest way.' The duke led her back to the house by a different path. 'By the way, you never did tell me where Mr. Defoe is, or why he has abandoned you and your sisters in such an unlikely location.'

'That is no concern of yours, your grace.'

'*Touché!*' A wicked smile flirted with his lips. 'Still, you can't take me to task for being curious. If you were mine,' he added, lowering his voice to a seductive purr, 'I would not leave you unattended for five minutes.'

'If I was yours, we wouldn't see anything of one another.'

He blinked. 'Whatever do you mean by that?'

'Do not dukes and duchesses lead separate lives?'

'That,' he replied, with a smile, 'would depend entirely upon the duke's choice of a duchess.'

'I definitely should have left you to bleed to death,' she muttered, averting her face so he couldn't see her blush.

The duke chuckled but had the good sense to fall silent.

Although the grounds were beautiful, Athena still felt too dazed to fully appreciate them. Was it shock that still afflicted her, or could her light-headedness be attributed to the close proximity of a devastatingly attractive duke who seemed determined to make her think well of him? Perhaps he had only just realised how close he had come to death and felt obliged to her. That was a natural enough reaction, she supposed, but not one she would have expected from an aristocrat accustomed to having an army of servants dancing to the beat of his particular drum.

There again, he seemed genuinely fond of his sick brother. A shadow had passed across his countenance when he spoke of his illness, and it was apparent just how frustrated he had become with traditional medicine. Hardly surprising if the physician's only answer was to bleed the poor man, Athena thought in exasperation.

She was touched by the duke's faith in her ability to help Lord Shelton. Faith or desperation? Either way, she would do her very best for him, even if it did make her more visible than she would like. Athena had made an art form out of being a wraith. She also had a gift for healing and owed it to those in need to lend them her aid, provided no one attempted

133

to interfere or brand her as a witch. That had happened before, when her methods triumphed over the conventional, because people could be so narrow-minded.

The duke didn't say anything more to break the silence that had sprung up between them as they walked towards the house. He cast frequent glances in her direction, his expression now brooding and unreadable. She found it difficult to equate this commanding, elegant sophisticate to the shirtless rogue who had lain in Millie's humble cot and then taken considerable pleasure in chopping logs outside their tumbledown cottage. How Millie would laugh when she learned the truth about their visitor. She had said from the start he wasn't what he appeared to be and, not for the first time, her judgement had proven to be sound.

An air of expectancy hovered between herself and the duke, interfering with her tangled reflections. He was aware of it, too. She could tell by the manner in which he frequently glanced at her face, casting her long considering looks as though he didn't quite know what to make of the charged atmosphere, either. His beauty, his sheer animal magnetism, stole her breath away, filling her body with forbidden desires. The situation didn't please her one jot.

Why, oh why, had he come into her life? She needed no such complications, even if she was secretly grateful for his intervention in her affairs. She did not share his view that she would have sold all of her lace, or for such a good price, had it not been for his seal of approval. She believed him when he said he didn't know Whispers' Hollow had been let, and that he wouldn't allow anyone to inhabit it in its current state. So for that, too, she had reason to be grateful.

But as for the rest — for being here at Winsdale Park to aid Lady Susan and Lord Shelton — was that really necessary? She persuaded herself that with regard to Lord Shelton it very likely was, and Lady Susan had been a convenient ruse to get her here. Presumably, Athena would be treating Lord Sheldon without the duchess's knowledge. She was sure his mother was unaware of the part she had played in saving the duke's life. If she was content to allow some butcher to bleed her son, further reducing his strength and causing him unnecessary distress, then she would hardly approve of Athena's methods. That must be why they were entering the house by a side door.

Numerous gentlemen had been keen to claim Athena's hand over the years, several of whom had been brought to her attention by her avaricious relations for reasons of their own. None had excited her passions, and she had rejected them all. Athena saw no reason to surrender her independence and place herself and her activities beneath the control of a man, unless she felt a deep-seated love and respect for him. None of her suitors had aroused those feelings. Glancing at the duke's noble profile, and recalling her extreme reaction to him the previous day, she finally understood the exquisite nature of carnal desire. Unfortunately, the gentleman who had awakened that emotion within her was quite simply out of her league.

The duke was about to select a wife from amongst the most eligible, best-born ladies in England. The pathos in his tone when he explained it was his duty had dented Athena's soft heart. Yes, he had money, power and all the privileges associated with his elevated rank but, unlike Athena, he wasn't free to follow his own heart.

Recalling what was expected of him snapped Athena out of her momentary regret. What possible interest could the duke have in her, and why would she encourage such an interest, even if it did exist? She was a runaway lace-maker, definitely not duchess material. She had managed very well for the first four-and-twenty years of her life without a tyrannical male dictating her every move and had no wish to alter that state of affairs.

'I wish I knew what you were thinking.' The duke looked down at her through eyes that gleamed with unsettling intelligence, recalling Athena's attention to him. 'You look so very distant and remote.'

'I can't imagine why my thoughts would be of the slightest interest to your grace.'

'Will you please stop *your gracing* me,' he said, his tone edged with annoyance.

'Then how would you have me address you?'

'My name is Eli.'

She laughed. 'You are a duke of the realm. I can't possibly use your name.'

'That's precisely the point I was trying to make earlier. If we were still at Whispers' Hollow, and you thought I was Mr. Franklin, would you have objected to using my name then if I asked you to?'

'I see what you mean.' Athena mangled her lower lip between her teeth as she thought the matter through. 'It would have been unconventional, but then so were the circumstances, so I suppose I wouldn't have demurred.'

'Then take pity on a humble duke who is about to marry a stranger when he would much rather not. Allow me to hear my name spill from your lovely lips, at least when there's no one around to overhear us.'

Lovely lips? 'Let's be clear on one thing. There is, your grace, absolutely nothing humble about you.'

He narrowed his eyes at her. 'What did you just call me?'

'Oh, very well, there is nothing humble about you, *Eli*.' His mood appeared to have taken a capricious turn, and she felt herself being swept along by it. 'There, does that satisfy you?'

'Not nearly, sweet Athena,' he replied softly, eyes burning dark and intense into her profile. 'But it's a start.'

'Tell me more about Lord Shelton's condition,' she said quickly, searching for a change of subject. One that wouldn't make her insides surge with intense longing when he fixed her with a look that heated the air between them, depriving her of the ability to think straight.

'His weak chest has plagued him since his school days,' the duke replied, frowning, all flirtation absent from his expression. Good. That was her intention, was it not? 'The best doctors have attended him, but nothing they do gives him any lasting reprieve.'

'Do you know what methods they have tried?'

'Besides recommending sea air, or bleeding him, nothing that's been effective.'

'Well, just so long as you don't expect me to work miracles.'

'Where did you gain your knowledge of herbs?'

'From my mother, who learned from her mother before her. Both were accused of being witches.'

'Just as you have bewitched me.'

He spoke so quietly, she thought at first she must have misheard him. Then she saw the scorchingly intense longing in his eyes as he rested his gaze on her face for far longer than was necessary. Desire pooled deliciously deep within Athena's core, and a small gasp of surprise slipped past her lips. She disciplined herself to ignore her arousal, aware just how dangerous it would be to engage in a flirtation with this experienced *roué*. She straightened her spine and tore her gaze from his.

'I think damage to your head was more extensive than you realise,' she said with asperity. 'Perhaps Lord Shelton's physician should bleed you instead of him.'

He laughed, the intimate mood was broken, and they covered the remaining short distance to the house in silence.

'Here we are,' he said, opening a side door that lead into a vast entrance vestibule with a chequered floor and a stunning candelabra overhead.

The butler appeared out of nowhere, as butlers were want to do.

'Your grace?'

'Archer.'

The butler looked askance at Athena, clearly anxious to know how she could possibly have business with the master of the house when she was supposed to be helping Lady Susan. The duke showed no indication to satisfy his curiosity. The relaxed, teasing Eli was gone, and in his place was the imperial duke, used to doing as he wished without recourse to anyone. The alternation was quite remarkable, reminding Athena of the chasm that separated them, if any reminder were necessary.

'Is Lord Shelton in his rooms, Archer?'

'Yes, your grace, I believe he is.'

'Come,' he said softly, taking Athena's elbow and leading her to a grand sweeping staircase, wide enough for four people to ascend it side by side.

There was a magnificent gallery at the top of the stairs, lined with portraits, presumably Eli's ancestors. Athena would have liked to pause and examine them, but Eli's fast pace didn't slow. She imagined he wanted her out of sight as soon as possible, which made her wonder why he hadn't brought her up the back stairs. The answer to that question soon became obvious. Maids and footmen paused in their duties to defer to Eli, and then flattened themselves against the walls so as not to hinder his progress. So used to them scattering before him was he that he didn't seem to notice them. The duke escorting an unknown — albeit very lowly dressed lady — through the body of the house would not excite undue comment because they would assume she had a legitimate reason for being there. Bringing her in through the servants' entrance would engender endless gossip and speculation.

'Here we are.'

Eli paused before a door in what appeared to be the main wing of the house and entered without knocking.

'Eli, is that you?'

Athena walked through the door Eli held open for her, and then stood back as he called out to his brother, feeling like the intruder she was. The first thing that struck her was the oppressive heat. She was in a large sitting room, with a roaring fire blazing up the chimney, all the windows firmly closed. There was a cloying smell in the room she associated with ill-health. There was an open door at one end of the room, which presumably led to Lord Shelton's bedroom.

How could Eli be sure his brother was in a

141

fit state to receive a stranger, she wondered. The idea he might not be didn't appear to have occurred to the duke. He strode into the room, his irritated expression far from convincing. Even Athena, who didn't know him well, could detect the concern he was trying to conceal.

'Are you still lazing about in that damned chair, Harry?' he asked, shaking his head in a poor display of disapproval. 'Anyone would think there was no work to be done around these parts.'

'You know me, Eli. I never miss an opportunity to shirk.'

Athena stood at Eli's shoulder, examining the gentleman who had just spoken. Even these few words caused a dry cough to rattle through his body. He appeared to be almost as tall as Eli, with a similar shock of thick black hair and piercing, intelligent eyes. His body, what she could see of it, was far thinner than the duke's and, in spite of the overwarm room, his face was deathly pale. A thick blanket was tucked over his legs, and covered half his chest. He must have been sweltering.

'I've brought a lady to meet you.' Eli reached for Athena's arm and brought her farther forward. 'This is Mrs. Defoe. Mrs. Defoe, may I present my brother, Lord Shelton.'

Athena curtsied and then took Lord Shelton's outstretched hand. His eyes lit up with interest as he examined her, and a speaking look passed between the brothers.

'It's a pleasure to meet you, Mrs. Defoe. Please excuse me if I don't get up. This cough, you understand.'

'I understand completely, Lord Shelton. Don't give it another thought.'

'That's why Mrs. Defoe is here, Harry. She has extensive knowledge of herbs, and I thought she might be able to help you.'

'I'm sure she can help me no end.' Lord Shelton's eyes continued to sparkle, but his words stalled as he again coughed. Athena tried not to frown, but knew things were very bad for this engaging young man. 'Not sure about the herbs, though.'

'Nonsense. The damned quack mother keeps sending for does you no good.'

'That's true enough.' Lord Shelton sent Athena such a gleaming smile, so like his brother's, that she couldn't help responding. 'Will you take a seat, Mrs. Defoe? Parker, some refreshments for my visitors.'

A man Athena hadn't previously noticed extracted himself from behind Lord Shelton's chair and rang the bell.

'Mrs. Defoe treated this,' Eli said, pointing at his bandaged head.

'Did she indeed? I won't ask how she happened to be on hand to do so, but it's all over the house that your wound is healing at breakneck speed. Even I got to hear of it, stuck away in here.' Lord Shelton sent his brother a teasing grin. 'How come you fell from Byron, anyway, Eli? The brute doesn't usually get the better of you.'

Eli snorted. 'You obviously haven't been drinking with Franklin or Johnson recently, or you wouldn't ask such a damned fool question.'

'Franklin?' Athena canted her head and elevated one brow at the duke. 'I had not thought you quite so lacking in imagination as all that.'

'I wasn't myself.'

'No, I don't suppose you were.'

She was openly laughing at him, something which she suspected not many people dared to do. Well, she had no reason to curry favour. Besides, had he not just told her he enjoyed being treated like a normal person? Lord Shelton looked bemused by the exchange, but Athena didn't think it was her place to enlighten him.

'I haven't been drinking with anyone recently,' he said, sounding rather aggrieved. 'However, those two have skulls even thicker than yours, Eli. If you tried to keep pace with them, I suppose you can be excused for losing your balance.'

'Thank you,' Eli said, his lips twitching. 'However, thanks to Mrs. Defoe's skill and quick thinking, no lasting damage was done. I'm a convert to her herbal cures.'

'So am I,' Lord Shelton replied, with another engaging smile for Athena. 'And I haven't even tried them yet.'

'I'm lending Mrs. Defoe to you *only* so that she can treat your malady,' the duke said in a castigating tone.

'Just a moment, your grace.' Athena fixed him to a lofty glance. 'I'm hardly yours to loan. You make me sound like an item of merchandise.'

Lord Shelton's man visibly stiffened at Athena's tone of address. Lord Shelton, on the other hand, guffawed, which made him cough.

'Good for you, Mrs. Defoe,' he said, when he recovered himself. 'Do not, on any account, allow him to bully you.'

'Oh, I can assure you, Lord Shelton. I do not.'

'She speaks the truth,' Eli said with a rueful smile, and Lord Shelton found that amusing, too.

A maid appeared with a tea tray, her eyes widening when she observed Athena. Lord

Shelton's man poured, and passed around the cups. Then he withdrew a respectful distance, presumably listening intently to their conversation, details of which would be all over the servants' hall within the hour.

'His grace tells me you've been plagued with weak lungs for some years, Lord Shelton,' Athena said with quiet sympathy. 'Has nothing the doctors recommended helped you?'

'Not really. Sea air is all right, if the weather's fine. But, of course, most of the time it isn't, not in this country, and the damp seems to make it worse.'

'It has been recommended that Harry goes to live in warmer climes,' Eli said. 'But none of us are keen on that idea. Not even Harry himself.'

'It might be a temporary cure, Lord Shelton, but in my opinion it's necessary to treat the underlying cause of your ailment.'

'Which is?'

'Inflammation of the lung.' She frowned. 'Do you feel the cold, Lord Shelton?'

'No, I'm insufferably warm, but the doctor insists that I remain trussed up like a turkey. Draughts, apparently, could be my undoing.' Athena shook her head. 'You disagree with that assessment, Mrs. Defoe?'

'There's such a thing as being too warm.

146

Forgive me, but the air in this room is stale. Provided you are suitably attired, I think you would benefit from opening the windows for a while during daylight hours, and airing the room.'

Parker cleared his throat. Athena glanced at him and could see he violently disagreed. He opened his mouth, presumably caught sight of Eli's warning frown, and as quickly shut it again.

'Mrs. Defoe,' Lord Shelton said with feeling. 'You can have no idea how ardently I yearn for fresh air.'

'The windows, Parker,' Eli barked. 'Open them. Get rid of the damned blanket that's near suffocating Lord Shelton, and get some fresh air into this room.'

'As your grace wishes.'

Parker walked towards the windows, his spine rigid with disapproval. Out of Eli's sphere of vision, he turned to bestow a suspicious glare upon Athena. She had met this type of prejudice towards her methods more times than she could count, and ignored him.

'I feel better already,' Lord Shelton said when the blanket was removed and a soft breeze filtered through the open windows.

'I am very glad to hear it.' Athena smiled at him. 'Presumably you have a well-stocked stillroom here at Winsdale Park.'

'Is our stillroom well-stocked, Parker?' the duke asked.

'Indeed, your grace. It's my understanding that it contains herbs from all over the world.'

Athena's fingers were already itching to sort through them. 'Well then, with your permission, Lord Shelton, I shall make free use of it. If the herbs I require are there, I can make an inhalation which I'm fairly sure will bring you immediate relief.'

'If you can do that, Mrs. Defoe, then I shall do whatever is necessary to steal you away from Eli. He definitely doesn't deserve you.'

Athena laughed. 'Then if someone could show me the way.'

The bell was rung and the same maid escorted Athena through a maze of corridors, until they reached a cool stillroom in the bowls of the house.

'Here we are, madam,' the maid said. 'Can I help you at all?'

'No, but watch carefully what I do. If it works, it will need to be repeated. Don't leave me. I shall never find my way back to Lord Shelton's room on my own.'

The walls of the stillroom were lined with shelves loaded with glass bottles, all neatly labelled. It would have been an apothecary's delight. Even Athena was unsure where some of them had originated. She disciplined herself not to get side-tracked and, to her delight, found all the ingredients necessary to aid Lord Shelton's recovery, principally thyme, coltsfoot, rosemary, and comfrey. Lavender and jasmine joined the mix as she placed an exact measure of each into a bowl and passed it to the maid.

'What is your name?' she asked.

'Bertha, ma'am. I am head parlour maid here.'

'You seem very young for such a responsible position.'

Bertha's round face broke out into a wide smile. 'I worked my way up from scullery maid,' she said with pride.

'And do you enjoy your work?'

'Oh yes. The family are ever so good to us.'

She wouldn't have expected Bertha to denigrate her employers in front of a stranger, but her glowing testament said much about the way the Shelton family treated their servants. Having met three of the four siblings and found them all charming, Athena easily believed it. But the duchess? She who insisted upon her younger son being bled and forced the heir to marry a woman he hardly knew. Athena shuddered, deciding to reserve judgement about that lady's character, hoping their paths would never cross.

'This needs to be taken to the kitchen,

Bertha,' Athena said. 'Add half a bowl of water and crush the mixture over a hot flame. Stir it well, until it becomes thick in consistency, then bring it straight to Lord Shelton's room before it cools.'

Bertha nodded. 'Very good, madam. I shall take you back first, then attend to this myself?'

'Thank you.'

Now she wasn't in the duke's company, Athena was conscious of maids and footmen staring at her with open curiosity. She was well aware her best gown was woefully inadequate, and no one in this establishment would mistake her for a lady. She held her head high and ignored the interest her presence created as she was conducted back to his lordship's room.

Unlike Eli, she didn't feel she could simply walk in unannounced. She tapped on the door, which was opened for her by Parker. Eli stood when he saw her, sending her a warm smile. So, too, did Lord Shelton, although he didn't stand.

'Your stillroom is truly remarkable,' she said with enthusiasm. 'An inhalation is being boiled up for you in the kitchen, Lord Shelton, and should be here directly.'

'Do you really think it will work?' he asked, cautious optimism in his tone.

Athena offered him a reassuring smile. 'I have every expectation of it doing so, but I must stress it won't be a cure. You will never be rid of this affliction. I might be able to ease the symptoms, enabling you to be more active than you are at present, but the weakness will always be there. As you have already discovered for yourself, damp weather, over-exertion, and all manner of other circumstances could cause a recurrence.'

'A respite is more than I dared hope for an hour ago.' He flashed another mischievous smile. 'I am quite determined to dance at my brother's betrothal and wish him and his bride joy, you see.'

Eli shot him a sour look, and said nothing, which made Lord Shelton laugh.

'I'm sure you will be able to dance within the week,' Athena assured him.

'Dancing is one thing. It would be too much to hope for some help with my duties from my baby brother, I suppose,' Eli complained.

'Oh, absolutely.' Lord Shelton shared a complicit smile with Athena. 'Work is quite out of the question, I'm sure. Is it not, Mrs. Defoe? Minor situations can cause a recurrence, and work is certainly not minor.'

Eli rolled his eyes. 'How would you know?'

Athena could sense the anxiety beneath Eli's teasing tone, and truly hoped she lived up to their expectations. She was about to find out since Bertha had returned with the boiled herbs. Athena tested the consistency and declared herself satisfied with the result.

'Well done, Bertha, this is exactly right.' The maid beamed. 'Now, Mr. Parker, be so kind as to move a small table directly in front of his lordship.'

Once the table was in place, Athena placed the steaming bowl on it and the aroma of jasmine, mingled with lavender, filled the room. Lord Shelton looked anxious.

'What am I to do, Mrs. Defoe? Drink it?'

Athena laughed. 'No, Lord Shelton. I wouldn't wish that upon you.'

'Then you are in indeed an angel.' He grimaced. 'If you could only see what some of the quacks have expected me to ingest.'

'This is not nearly so intrusive. Now, if you would kindly lean your face as close to the bowl as you can manage without burning yourself?' He did so, and Athena placed the towel she had asked Bertha to bring with her over his bowed head. He completely disappeared from view, and there was little space for the steam to escape. 'Breathe as deeply and evenly as you can, Lord Shelton.'

Athena was conscious of Eli and Mr. Parker looking on anxiously.

'Don't look so concerned, your grace. The

worst that can happen is it will make no difference at all.'

'I can smell jasmine and lavender. What else is in there?'

'You have coltsfoot in your stillroom,' she said reverently. 'It's very rare, so we were fortunate in that respect. It has been used by the ancient Egyptians to treat such maladies for millennia.'

'If I may ask a question, ma'am?' Mr. Parker said, scepticism mingling with the deference in his tone.

'By all means.'

'If this comfrey is such a magical cure, why have none of the doctors who have attended his lordship suggested its use before now?'

'Because they are narrow-minded fools,' Eli answered for her, expressing himself more forcibly than she would have done, but essentially saying the same thing.

'Quite,' Athena agreed, meeting the duke's gaze and holding it for a second too long.

'How long must he keep doing this?' Eli asked.

'Until the mixture cools.' She sent him a questioning look. 'Have you noticed anything unusual since Lord Shelton started inhaling?'

'No, what?'

'He hasn't coughed at all.'

Eli's gaze flitted between his brother and

Athena. 'Well I'll be damned!'

'Very likely,' Athena replied with a wry smile. 'Right, that ought to be enough.' She removed the towel from Lord Shelton's head and he looked up at her, red in the face, but smiling. 'How do you feel?'

'Do you know, I think it did some good.' His smile was broad and infectious. 'Who would have thought it?'

'I would have,' Eli said, grinning also.

'Your breathing is certainly less laboured, Lord Shelton,' Athena said. 'But don't get carried away. These things take time. I have given Bertha precise instructions on how the infusion should be made up. If the quantities are wrong it will be less effective. His lordship should inhale twice a day for four days, Mr. Parker.'

'Can't I take it as often as I feel the need?' Lord Shelton asked.

'No, long term some of the herbs will do more harm than good.'

'So what after four days.'

'I will see you again, if you would like me to, and we will discuss it.'

'He would like you to,' Eli replied for his brother.

'Thank you, Mrs. Defoe.' Lord Shelton rose to his feet, without appearing to feel the effort, grabbed Athena's hand and kissed the back of it. 'I'm greatly in your debt.'

'It was my pleasure. But now, if you gentlemen will excuse me, I am supposed to be in the barn, helping Lady Susan to decorate it.'

9

'Harry, what are you doing down here?' The duchess stared at her young son, with a mixture of surprise and concern. 'You ought to be resting.'

'I have done nothing but rest since I can't recall when,' Harry replied, leaning down to kiss his mother's brow. 'I feel a great deal better, and I'm sick of the sight of the four walls in my rooms.'

'You certainly look a great deal better. I can't imagine what caused this transformation. I was on the point of sending for the physician again, even though you were opposed to the idea.'

'As you can see, there is no need.'

'You do look much more like yourself,' Susan said, kissing his cheek. 'You actually have some colour in your face.'

Charlotte kissed him, too. 'Welcome back to the land of the living, Harry,' she said.

Eli leaned against the mantelpiece, watching his brother, delighted by the changes in him, in spite of the problems they were about to cause for him. His mother would discover how those changes had been wrought, if she didn't already know, but that was a small price to pay in the light of Harry's improved condition. Athena's knowledge of herbs and their properties was nothing short of miraculous, and Eli was almost tempted to believe she *was* a witch. He had certainly fallen totally and completely under her spell.

After treating Harry, she had returned to the barn and spent the rest of the day with Susan. Where she took luncheon, and with whom, Eli didn't know, but his sister would have ensured she was fed. Eli had pressing matters to attend to with Bairstowe, and forced himself to concentrate on them when he would have much preferred to spend his last few hours of freedom with Athena. He knew she had been driven back to Whispers' Hollow by one of his grooms and tried not to resent the blaggard's good fortune in having her to himself for the duration of the short journey. Ye gods, but he was in a bad way!

'Come and sit by the fireside, Harry,' Eli's mother said. 'Don't tire yourself by standing about.'

'I have had more than enough of fires,' Harry replied with great good humour. 'I am now a firm advocate of fresh air.'

Charlotte sat beside her brother. 'Tell us how you come to look so much better,' she invited. 'Who wrought such miracles?'

'I have Mrs. Defoe to thank,' Harry replied. 'She made a herbal inhalation that cleared my lungs almost immediately.' He shook his head. 'I can still scarce believe it. All the cures that have been tried, and it was that simple.'

'Mrs. Defoe?'

The duchess looked bewildered. Could it be, for once, the latest gossip had failed to reach her ears, Eli wondered, or was she being deliberately obtuse for reasons best known only to her?

'Mrs. Defoe is one of our tenants, Mama,' Susan said. 'She is kindly helping me to decorate the barn. She is *such* a talented lady, and so very beautiful. I am quite in awe of her abilities.'

'That's as may be, Susan, but I fail to understand how poor Harry's condition came to her notice.'

'I asked her to look at Harry, Mother,' Eli replied languidly.

'You!' The duchess fixed Eli with a considering look. 'I fail to appreciate how you could know anything about her.'

'It was she who treated my head wound. I fell from my horse near her cottage, she found me, and probably saved my life,' Eli replied, the master of understatement.

'She actually saved your life!' The duchess looked truly shocked, and appalled. 'You told me your injuries were not serious.'

'They are not, but would have been, had not Mrs. Defoe been on hand.' Eli would much rather not relate all this to his mother, and spellbound sisters. 'I happened to see her in the barn with Susan this morning, and it occurred to me she might be able to help Harry, too.'

'And she did, as you can see.' Harry shared a smile between them. Eli rejoiced to see him attired in full evening clothes for the first time in weeks, looking far more like his old self. 'She warns me not to expect miracles, but as far as I'm concerned, that is what she has wrought.'

'I must meet this paragon, and thank her personally. It seems I am indebted to her for both of my sons' wellbeing.'

'She will be here again tomorrow, Mama,' Susan said, sending Eli frequent sideways glances and mischievous smiles. 'Shall I bring her to meet you?'

'Yes, my dear, I think perhaps you should. Bring her to luncheon. I very much look forward to making her acquaintance.'

'When will your husband join us, Charlotte?' Eli asked, keen to change the subject.

'Oh, he is still in Brighton with his royal highness. Goodness knows when he will be free. Being equerry to the prince is far more time consuming than we had supposed would be the case. His royal highness doesn't seem able to manage without him, and poor Charles is quite exhausted.' Charlotte sounded both exasperated and proud. 'Goodness knows when he will be able to get away.'

'In that case, why do you not go to Brighton and join him?' Susan asked.

'And miss the fun of seeing Eli choose a bride?' Charlotte grinned, shaking her head. 'Not likely. I have been looking forward to this day for years. I can give you chapter and verse on all of Mama's choices, if you think it would help you make up your mind, Eli.'

'Thank you, Charlotte,' Eli replied drolly. 'Your selflessness never fails to impress.'

Archer announced dinner and the family moved into the dining room together. It was rare for them all to be at home and without company. Eli looked forward to a quiet family dinner, even if he would be required to tolerate his sisters' teasing, to say nothing of his mother's inquisitive glances. He was acutely aware that his interest in Athena Defoe had not gone unnoticed by her.

Both of Eli's sisters seemed to be in especially capricious moods during the meal — excitement at the thought of the forthcoming festivities, or perhaps they shared Eli's pleasure at the improvement in Harry's health.

'That's a lovely ribbon in your hair, Susan,' Charlotte remarked. 'Quite unusual.'

'Isn't it beautiful?' Yes, Eli thought, it is, and I've seen it before. 'Mrs. Defoe gave it to me.'

'You take gifts from our tenants now, Susan?' the duchess asked, arching a brow. 'Should it not be the other way around? Especially since Mrs. Defoe has already done so much for your brothers.'

Harry shot Eli a wry smile, implying he would very much like to know precisely what Mrs. Defoe had done for Eli. *Not nearly as much as I would like her to, little brother.*

'Oh yes, I agree, but you see, Mrs. Defoe and her sisters make lace. I happened to admire this ribbon in her hair today, and she insisted I take it.'

'She made it herself, presumably,' Charlotte said. 'She must be very talented. I shouldn't know where to start.'

'You have never had to make your own living,' Harry pointed out, grinning.

'True, but even so.'

'Lace?' The duchess canted her head. 'Did I not hear something about Miss Dawson having a large consignment of handmade lace in her premises which she is assured of selling because you have endorsed it, Eli?'

'The lady saved my life, mother,' Eli replied

indolently. 'It was the very least I could do for her in return.'

'I disagree. You have the power to bestow just about any gift of your choosing upon her, as you should, if she really did save you. I'm still not persuaded your accident was so very serious.'

'You think Mrs. Defoe has exaggerated in order to win favour with Eli?' Harry asked frowning. 'Having met the lady, I find that very hard to believe.'

'You, too?' The duchess sent Harry a mildly censorious glance.

'Unlikely as it seems, Mrs. Defoe wouldn't accept a reward for what she did . . . for either of us.' Eli glanced at Harry as he spoke. 'And so I had to think of more inventive ways to thank her.'

'The lace and repairs to her dwelling,' Susan said. 'She told me about that, and I think it was very thoughtful of you, Eli. She might be poor, but she has her pride, after all.'

'Where is her husband?' the duchess asked.

'Abroad somewhere, I believe,' Eli replied.

'Well, I must definitely meet her tomorrow and thank her,' the duchess said, a firm set to her jaw.

'And I fully intend to be well enough to stand up with her at the harvest festival.'

Harry added, sending Eli a challenging smile. 'Eli will be too busy dancing attendance upon his prospective brides to spare her a second thought.'

'Will she come, do you suppose?' Charlotte asked. 'Have you invited her, Eli?'

Hell no, how could I have overlooked something so obvious? 'All of her family will come,' he replied off-handedly. 'She is one of our tenants and all the tenants attend.'

'And she is also responsible for making the barn look so wonderful,' Susan said. 'Without her I would have made a complete mull of it. She deserves the lion's share of the praise.'

★ ★ ★

Athena felt great satisfaction with the progress she and Lady Susan had made with the barn. She experienced even more satisfaction from what she had been able to do for Lord Shelton. Every time she thought of that stuffy, over hot room he had been told to shut himself away in, she wanted to scream with frustration. Was that really the best advice their considerable wealth could buy?

She climbed into the curricle that was to take her home at the end of the day, feeling wary now the full implications of her actions had come home to her. Making a public

163

exhibition of herself was the surest way for her pursuers to catch up with her. Not that Winsdale Park was public, precisely, but word of what she had done for Lord Shelton would get out. So, too, would the part she had played to save the duke in his hour of need. She would be looked upon as anything from a miracle-worker to a witch and, once again, would become the subject to endless gossip and speculation.

What was the point in burying herself away if she then did everything she could to draw attention to herself? Athena sighed. She really liked it here, felt settled, and did not wish to move yet again. The duke's patronage of their lace ensured them a steady income for the foreseeable future. It wasn't just the duchess's house party that would bring customers for it, but the ladies in the other grand houses in the area would also take an interest. The rich dwellings in the locality had attracted Athena to it for that very reason.

As to the duke with his devastating smiles, seductive eyes, outrageous flattery and mercurial charm . . . well, she simply wouldn't think about him and the most peculiar effect he had upon her. His prospective brides would be at Winsdale Park in two days' time, and Athena would ensure she went nowhere near the place once they were in residence. Instead, she would remain quietly with her sisters in their newly renovated cottage and work her fingers to the bone to ensure their survival.

They had been making lace for the past six months, ever since escaping from Nottingham, stockpiling it until they found the right market. A market far enough away from Nottingham to sell it without fear of their unique handiwork — albeit disguised — being recognised. She hadn't anticipated selling it all at once, but certainly didn't feel the need to complain because they had. Their stocks were virtually depleted, and they must work night and day to replenish them while the going was good.

It was the perfect antidote to the strange cravings wracking Athena's body. She knew from experience if she worked herself to the point of exhaustion, she wouldn't have the energy to think about anything else.

'Excuse me, ma'am.' The groom who would drive her home joined her on the seat of the curricle and handed her a wrapped parcel. 'This is for you.'

'For me?'

A note accompanied the package. Athena opened it with shaking hands as the curricle moved off. The handwriting was sprawling and confident — a man's writing.

Mrs Defoe, it said. *To replace the one you*

*sacrificed for the greater good of my head.
Winsdale.*

Yea gods, the package was from Eli! And Athena would bet her last farthing it contained a petticoat. How the devil had he managed to get hold of one? Presumably, he had mistresses dotted all over the county and bought them intimate apparel all the time. Her face heated as she considered that very real possibility. She couldn't accept such a gift from a stranger, could she? But what was the alternative? To try and return it to him? That would create more difficulties than it would resolve. Unless she handed it back to the groom, unopened, asking him to return it from whence it came. Perversely she couldn't quite bring herself to do that.

Athena threw back her head and blew air through her lips, quite out of charity with the duke. The man was completely impossible — a law unto himself. He seemed to think he could do precisely as he pleased, without caring about the damaged reputations he scattered in his wake. Really, it was too much, and she would give him a firm talking to the next time she was in his company. She fingered the parcel, severely tempted to open it. The wild side of her character longed to know what he had chosen for her — if he had chosen it himself, of course. It was far more likely some minion had done the choosing in his stead, she mused, which helped to rein in her fanciful imagination.

Her reflections were brought to an end when the curricle came to a halt in the clearing outside the cottage. All was activity there. The thatcher had obviously arrived and half the rotted thatch had already been removed. A posse of men were in and out of the cottage, carrying tools, timber and any number of other items Athena couldn't begin to identify. She very much doubted if the twins had achieved much work today in the middle of all that upheaval. Indeed, the two of them danced into sight at that moment. Selene was in deep conversation with a young man, causing Athena to frown. Why wasn't Millie keeping a closer watch on them?

The answer became obvious when she observed Millie standing in the door to the cottage, keeping a weather eye on the workmen as they came and went. She couldn't possibly be everywhere at once, and the twins were very lively when in company, mainly because they spent so much time in isolation. That was all her fault. She had dragged them away from everything familiar to them, and the guilt that thought engendered helped Athena to absolve them of any wrong-doing.

Boris noticed the curricle and came

bounding over, tail spiralling.

'Hello, darling.' She leaned down from her perch and scratched his ears. 'Have you been a good boy?'

Woof!

The twins saw Athena and came running over.

'You've been gone for ever,' Selene said.

'You should see how much work has been done to the cottage already,' Lyssa added with enthusiasm. 'You won't know the place.'

'I can see differences even from here,' Athena replied, taking the groom's hand and jumping down from the curricle.

Millie noticed her and came across. 'What's in the parcel?' she asked.

Athena shook her head. 'Show me what has been done.'

It was indeed remarkable, if chaotic, reminding Athena of the duke's ability to get things done. A short time later, the workers left. Selene lingered at the door, waving off her apprentice, her eyes shining. Athena shared a glance with Millie, who merely shrugged.

'Tell us all about your day,' Millie said as they sat down to their meal.

Athena briefly told them how she had helped Lord Shelton, and about Lady Susan and the decorations for the barn.

'But here is the most astonishing thing.' Athena knew they would find out soon enough, but they ought to hear it from her. 'Prepare yourself for a huge shock.'

'What is it?' the twins asked together, their eyes round and wary. Dear Lord, did they always assume any news she had would be bad? Had she really trained them to expect only the worst these last months? Once again, she was consumed with feelings of guilt.

'Well, Mr. Franklin, the gentleman who fell from his horse isn't Mr. Franklin at all.' Athena paused. 'He is actually the Duke of Winsdale.'

'No!'

The girls clasped hands to their mouths. Even Millie looked shocked. Then she laughed.

'So, a duke slept in my bed. Well, there's a thing. I knew there was more to him than met the eye. That air of authority. He wears it like a mantle and probably doesn't even know it.'

'Quite.'

'So, I take it the lace, the repairs here, are his way of repaying you?'

'Yes.'

'Why didn't he tell us who he was when he regained his senses?' Lyssa asked.

Why indeed? 'He said no one ever treats him like a normal person, and he enjoyed the novelty too much to bring it to an end.'

Athena thought it better not to mention he had actually been conscious when she and Millie hoisted him so unceremoniously onto Byron's back. Duke or no duke, Millie would probably take him to task for his forwardness if she knew of it.

'Well, if he thinks I would have kowtowed to him, even had I known, then he would have been disappointed,' Millie said, hands on ample hips.

'Imagine us knowing a duke,' Lyssa said reverently.

The girls and Millie marvelled for some time about having had a duke beneath their humble roof and asked endless questions about Winsdale Park.

'Is it very grand?' Selene asked.

'Oh yes. It's quite magnificent.'

'You saved a duke's life,' Lyssa said wondrously.

'It's hardly surprising he wants to do something for us in return,' Selene added.

'Off you go now, girls,' Millie said, clapping her hands. 'The chores won't do themselves.'

When the girls went off, Athena was able to express her fears to the only person who might be able to supply answers.

'Tell me,' Millie said. 'Something is bothering you.'

'I'm nervous,' Athena admitted.

'Of being found here?'

'Yes. Sometimes my gift for healing feels more like a curse. But, Millie, if you could have seen that poor young man . . . all the money in the world, and yet nothing was being done to help him. I simply had to do what I could.'

'Of course you did.' Millie sent her a shrewd look. 'What is it, lamb? What are you not telling me?'

'Oh nothing. I'm just being fanciful. I must be more tired than I realised.'

'It's the duke.' Millie's compassionate gaze rested on Athena's face. 'You like him?'

Athena had never been able to keep a secret from Millie. 'Yes,' she said with a heavy sigh. 'God help me, but I do. It's ridiculous, all the opportunities I've had, and it's a duke who breaks through my reserve. Not that it matters. I'll get over it soon enough.' She shook her head. 'I've never felt like this before. When I think of all the men who have wanted to . . . and I have not. Now I choose to fall for a man so far above me, he might as well be the king of England.'

Millie, instead of laughing or lecturing, patted Athena's hand. 'He's a charming rogue, and I could sense the attraction between you, even when you thought he was a plain Mister. But have a care. He knows how close he came to death, and that you are responsible for saving him. The fact that you wouldn't accept a reward is probably unusual enough to give him pause. You said yourself people always want something from him, and he's come to expect that.' Millie's eyes softened. 'You're beautiful, Athena, far too beautiful for your own good. If you were not, we wouldn't be in the mess we're in now. Anyway, it's only natural he should think well of you, but he's to be married to another before long and there's an end to it.'

Millie's calm common sense was Athena's undoing. The floodgates opened and tears rolled freely down her cheeks.

'Oh, Millie, what am I to do?'

Millie pulled Athena into her arms, probably alarmed because Athena prided herself on *never* crying. She needed to be strong for the others, and not once during all the setbacks they had lived through had she resorted to tears. Now a dashing rogue with compelling charm and a not entirely civilized air about him had reduced her to a watering pot. Millie soothed her back as she sobbed on her shoulder, simply letting her cry. Boris pushed his damp nose beneath her hand in an instinctive gesture of solidarity, causing her to cry harder still.

She cried for everything they had worked

for and been forced to leave behind, for the straitened circumstances the twins now found themselves in. Most of all, she cried for the emptiness she felt inside and for what could never be.

10

Athena woke at her usual early hour and slipped out of bed without disturbing the twins. She intended to visit the woods again, but this time she wouldn't be searching for mushrooms or injured dukes. Instead, she had noticed a patch of common elder flourishing in a clearing that would give a fresh, outdoors appearance to the walls of the barn. She doubted whether elder was permitted to show itself in the sculpted grounds of Winsdale Park, and so Athena would just have to take it there herself.

With Boris for company, Athena cut as much elder as she could manage to carry and staggered back to the cottage with it spilling over her arms. Having given vent to her emotions the previous evening, she felt much more in command of herself, and could even chide herself for her silly, unrealistic infatuation. She would face the duke with equanimity, should their paths happen to cross and was perfectly prepared to wish him joy in his forthcoming marriage to whichever lady engaged his affections. And after that, she would think of him no more.

She absolutely would not!

Thus resolved, Athena turned her mind to the tasks she must undertake that day. She would be driving herself to Winsdale Park, after visiting Miss Dawson's establishment with the rest of the merchandise they had so far produced for her. In spite of the upheavals at Whispers' Bottom, the twins had applied themselves the previous day quite industriously. Athena vowed to spend the afternoon working alongside them. Helping the local gentry to prepare for a party was all well and good, but Athena had a living to make.

'Breakfast,' Millie said firmly, placing a bowl of porridge in front of Athena. 'And don't try telling me you're not hungry. You barely ate a bite at supper last night.'

Athena knew better than to argue with Millie when she was in such an intransigent mood. She dutifully ate her breakfast, listening to the twins' bright chatter as she did so. Selene mentioned Ned more than once. Apparently, he was the young man with whom she had been in such animated conversation when Athena arrived home yesterday.

'His father is the village blacksmith,' Selene said, her face pink with pride.

'Don't worry,' Millie said, presumably in response to Athena's appalled expression. 'The young man wouldn't dare take liberties, or he'll find himself on the wrong end of his father's branding iron.'

No, he certainly would not take liberties — not with Millie acting as the twins' chaperone. It was the thought of them reaching the age to need a chaperone at all that worried Athena. They were only fourteen — surely too young for their thoughts to be turning in *that* direction?

'Right, girls, I must be away. I shall only stay at Winsdale Park for a short time. Will you start on that new pattern for the fans which we discussed last night?'

'Yes,' Selene replied.

'I wish we could come with you to Winsdale Park,' Lyssa said wistfully.

'It must be very grand.'

'Were they kind to you?'

'What is the duke's brother like?'

'Did you make him better?'

Athena threw her hands up as the questions came too thick and fast for her to keep track of them all.

'We will spend the afternoon together,' Athena replied, laughing. 'And I will tell you all about it then.'

A short time later Athena drove off with the bed of the cart full of elder, her precious lace carefully packaged and placed beneath the seat to keep it safe. She blushed when she recalled the superb lawn petticoat that sat beneath her gown, rubbing against her skin like an elicit promise. Eli had given her not one, but two, beautiful undergarments, the likes of which she had never thought to own. Millie didn't approve and was all for sending them back. Athena knew she ought to, but simply couldn't bring herself to part with them. When had she last treated herself to anything? Any spare money had gone towards the twins clothing these past six months. Athena's gown might be shabby when set against the spectacular backdrop of Winsdale Park, but at least she had the comfort of the soft lawn nestled beneath it. It gave her a perverse sort of confidence and, should the situation arise, the strength to resist the duke's unquestionable charms.

When she halted the cart outside Miss Dawson's establishment, the proprietor herself came out to greet her, her face wreathed in smiles.

'Mrs. Defoe. How nice to see you again. Your lace is causing quite a stir already, and the duke's guests haven't even arrived yet. Mrs. Peterson is quite put out because she cannot compete and is losing customers as a consequence.' Miss Dawson nodded with evident glee towards her rival's establishment across the street. 'Do you have more things for me?'

'I've brought you everything we have, Miss Dawson, and we're working as fast as we can to produce more.' *Except I am not.*

'Do bring them inside. Here, let me help you.'

Several early customers browsing inside the shop glanced at Athena with open interest. Damnation, that was just the sort of attention she especially didn't wish to attract. She smiled absently at the ladies, but didn't allow herself to be pulled into conversation with them. Promising Miss Dawson more of their lace as soon as they could produce it, she climbed back into the cart and drove towards Winsdale Park, her heart fluttering with nerves. She felt a perverse sort of pleasure, driving her ancient cart and nondescript pony up the pristine driveway. The cart, she and the pony were so out of place in such surroundings it made her smile.

To their credit, the duke's grooms didn't sneer when she arrived at the stable yard. Instead, one lad came to hold Meg's head and another offered her a hand down.

'Is this for the barn?' he asked, indicating the foliage in the bed of the cart.

'Yes, if you would be so kind.'

'I believe Lady Susan is already there.'

'Then I shall go in search of her.' A whinny sounded from deep inside the yard, causing

178

Athena to smile. 'Oh dear, I fear his grace's stallion doesn't have very good taste. He's rather taken with my poor pony, you see.'

Athena wished the same could be said of his grace, and he might be attracted to her for reasons other than gratitude. Reminding herself she had vowed to think of him in that light no more, she followed the two grooms carrying the elder and applied her mind to the decoration of the barn.

'Oh, Mrs. Defoe, there you are.' Lady Susan sent her a dazzling smile. 'What do we have here?'

Athena explained her plans for the walls. 'I thought we could use rose hips, hawthorn in berry and sloes, if you have any here, and twine them around honeysuckle. If we then add fruits and nuts to the mix, perhaps some wild hops, too, and it will be very festive.'

'Oh, that is such an inspired suggestion!' Lady Susan turned to the grooms. 'Please see if you can find any of those things for us. Consult with the gardeners.'

'At once, your ladyship.'

'I was thinking, we could fashion extravagant sheaves of corn and bind them with autumnal coloured fabric fashioned into rosettes. Do you have anything suitable?'

'I'm sure something could be found in the attics. I will send word and have my maid conduct a search.'

How easy it must be, Athena thought, to have an army of people just waiting to do one's bidding.

'How is Lord Shelton?' Athena asked, as she worked beside Lady Susan, threading nuts and apples onto long pieces of string.

'Oh, I meant to say. He came down to dinner last night, looking just like he used to. We could scarce believe the difference in him. And today, he has ridden out with Eli to inspect the coppicing taking place in the northern spinney. He would go, even though Mama thought it might be too much for him.'

'You must trust him to know how he feels.'

'Yes, you're right, of course. He's been indoors for far too long, and the weather is still so mild, at least during daylight hours. Anyway, we are most terribly grateful to you. You have saved not one, but both of my brothers.'

'Hardly that. Lord Shelton will never be cured, but hopefully we've found a way to control his malady.'

'You are so clever, Mrs. Defoe. I wish I possessed one tenth of your skills.'

'Mine, such as they are, are mostly born of necessity.'

'Meaning I have never had to do anything to help myself if I had rather not?' Lady Susan's smile took the sting out of her words.

'Well yes, I suppose, if you put it like that.'

'Be that as it may, you are a very good example to me, Mrs. Defoe, and I shall certainly apply myself to these decorations.'

Athena laughed. 'If you will take the other end of that honeysuckle, Lady Susan, we might try and twine it around these strung apples to see how it looks.'

As they worked, Athena was conscious of every footstep made by the people who came and went, running errands for Lady Susan. At one point, she heard a deep, rich voice, so like the duke's, her heart quickened. Was he here? Had he come to find her? No, it wasn't him. Athena persuaded herself it was just as well, but couldn't dispel the sinking feeling that gripped her when she considered his inconsistency. Yesterday, he would have her believe she had bewitched him. Today he appeared to have recovered from that temporary aberration with a speed that belied true conviction. He was cruel and unkind, and Athena was quite out of charity with him.

'There.' Lady Susan stood back to admire their handiwork. 'That really does look very wild and pretty. After luncheon I shall have some of the gardeners fix it to the walls, and then we will get a better idea of the overall effect.'

'I believe Lord Johnson will be impressed

with your inventiveness.'

'Oh.' Lady Susan blushed. 'How did you know — '

'The duke mentioned something,' Athena said hastily. She had spoken out of turn, and hoped she hadn't overstepped the mark or given offence.

'Eli told you that?' She raised a brow, suddenly the haughty daughter of the house, a side of her character Athena had not yet seen. 'How extraordinary.'

'You must excuse him, Lady Susan. When we conversed yesterday morning, I was unsure if I could spare the time to help you, knowing what a large task it would be. He told me how very much it would mean to you personally, which is what persuaded me.'

'Ah, that explains it.' She sighed. 'The problem is, though, even if Lord Johnson does admire the decorations, I can hardly pretend they are a result of *my* inventiveness. All of the ideas were yours.'

'He doesn't need to know that.'

'You're too generous, but how can I lie?'

'We shall be economical with the truth, nothing more.'

'Well, I suppose that's not so very terrible.' Lady Susan laughed, her good humour restored, and Athena knew her blunder had been excused.

The morning passed quickly after that. Some order was emerging out of the chaos, and Athena decided it was time to leave.

'Oh no, you can't go yet. Mama wishes to meet you. We are to have luncheon together.'

The duchess! 'Why would she wish to meet me? I am hardly — '

'You saved both of her sons, you goose. Of course she wishes to know you and to thank you.'

Athena glanced down at her crumpled gown and despaired — at that and at this family's assumption she had nothing better to do than to dance attendance upon them. 'I am really not sure I can spare the time.'

'Please, for me.'

Athena had formed a great attachment to Lady Susan during the hours they had spent together in the barn. She treated Athena quite as an equal, chatting to her extensively about her feelings for Lord Johnson, now she was aware Athena knew of her attachment. Athena suspected she had no one else to confide in and was glad to lend a sympathetic ear. She even offered a little advice, suggesting Lady Susan might make her feelings less apparent and allow Lord Johnson to pursue her.

'Flirt with other gentlemen, you mean?' Lady Susan wrinkled her brow. 'Do you imagine that will work?'

Athena laughed. 'If the gentleman has feelings for you then I am sure it will incite his jealousy.'

'But what if he does not and merely thinks me inconstant?'

'Is it not better to know?'

Lady Susan bit her lip. 'Yes, you're right. I would rather know what's in his heart.'

It was strange to see such a privileged, assured young lady looking . . . well, unsure of herself. She reminded Athena of the twins when they encountered setbacks. Athena did everything within her power to reassure them and was equally determined to set Lady Susan's mind at rest.

'Very well,' she said in response to the luncheon invitation. 'Since *you* insist.'

'I'm sure you will like Mama. She isn't nearly as terrifying as people imagine.'

Lady Susan linked her arm through Athena's as they left the barn.

'We can wash our hands in here,' Lady Susan said when they reached the house.

The room Athena was ushered into on the first floor was clearly Lady Susan's bedchamber. It was large and airy, decorated in light colours, and enjoyed a lovely view over the park. A maid Athena had already seen once or twice, coming and going from the barn, had a ewer of steaming water waiting for them, and Athena was also able to tidy her hair. She looked like the lowliest of poor relations, but of course she couldn't even lay claim to that position.

'Come,' Lady Susan said. 'If you are ready, Mama will be expecting us.'

Lady Susan led the way into a small sitting room with yet another, different view over the gardens. There was a round table in front of the window laid up for four. Who was the fourth? Athena's heart stammered. Please, not the duke!

'Mama, I've brought Mrs. Defoe to meet you.'

A tall lady with immaculate hair pulled into a neat pleat, looked up at Athena, assessing her through eyes as gray and candid as her son's.

'Your grace.' Athena curtsied.

'Mrs. Defoe.' The duchess offered up her hand and Athena shook it. 'I believe I am indebted to you.'

'You owe me nothing, your grace. Anyone would have done the same.'

'That's a matter for debate, and we will not fall out over it. Suffice it to say, I am exceedingly obliged to you.'

'The pleasure was all mine.'

The duchess was formidable. The self-assured matriarch determined her son should marry, and marry well. The duchess sent Athena frequent glances, openly assessing her, suspicion occasionally flitting across her features. Athena was in no mood to be intimidated and fell back on the manners that had been drummed into her as a child, when her life had been so very different, to see her through this initial inquisition.

'Ah, and here is my sister, Lady Baintree,' Lady Susan said.

Again, Athena curtsied to a woman a year or two older than Lady Susan and not quite so handsome. She too had easy manners, but wasn't quite so carefree as the engaging Lady Susan. Marriage was not always the panacea guileless young ladies supposed it to be, Athena thought, reminding herself that was one of the reasons she was determined to avoid matrimony. Such autonomy as she currently enjoyed over her own affairs would be taken from her in a trice, and that would never sit comfortably with Athena. She would prefer to live in the hovel they currently occupied than give up her independence.

'Your lace is quite exquisite, Mrs. Defoe,' Lady Baintree said as soon as they were seated. 'My sister showed me the ribbon you gave her. I am quite in envy.'

'Then I shall bring you one as well, Lady Baintree,' Athena replied. 'I could not have a dispute between sisters on my conscience.'

Lady Baintree laughed. 'That would be so very kind. But you must allow me to pay you for it.'

'I wouldn't think of it.'

'The barn is going to be transformed, thanks to Mrs. Defoe's vision,' Lady Susan said, smiling. 'You really will not know it, Mama.'

'I understand you have sisters who help you to make the lace, Mrs. Defoe,' the duchess said.

'Yes, your grace. They are twins. Fourteen years old.'

'Where did you learn your trade?'

These were the sorts of questions Athena dreaded, and usually managed to avoid answering. But how did one gainsay a duchess? 'In Nottingham.'

'And who taught you?'

'I was taught at a time when machinery was just coming into fashion, replacing the dying art of hand lacing.' Athena thought she had avoided a direct answer rather well, without giving offence.

'Machine lace will never match up to the hand-produced,' Lady Susan said stoutly.

'Your husband is abroad, I'm given to understand,' the duchess said after a short, awkward pause.

'Yes.'

'Oh, where is he?' Lady Susan asked. 'You must miss him terribly.'

'I cannot say precisely where he is at this moment.' Well, that was true enough.

'Mine is in Brighton with the Prince Regent,' Lady Baintree said, a shadow passing across her eyes. 'And I have no idea when I shall see him, either.'

'Whispers' Hollow seems rather a remote location for lace production,' the duchess remarked, a suspicious edge to her voice.

'We prefer to be isolated,' Athena replied, no longer caring if her abrupt responses gave offence.

'Your answers are very short and precise,' the duchess said, making it sound as if that was very remarkable.

'I would not wish to bore, your grace.'

'On the contrary, Mrs. Defoe. You are quite the most remarkable person I have met in many a long year.'

'You see,' Lady Susan said, beaming. 'I told you as much, Mama.'

The food was delicious — poached salmon, tiny potatoes, crisp vegetables — it literally melted in Athena's mouth. The sweet courses especially appealed, and Athena couldn't help thinking how much the twins would have enjoyed them.

'You and your sisters will attend the harvest

188

party, of course,' the duchess said.

'Attend?' Athena's entire body jerked. Mr. Bairstowe had issued an invitation, of course, but Athena hadn't taken it seriously. 'I hadn't thought of it.'

'Oh, but you must!' Lady Susan cried. 'You must be here to see the barn admired. I insist.'

'We agreed the credit for that was to be yours, Lady Susan.'

'Oh stuff and nonsense. No one who knows me will believe I did it alone. We shall take the credit together.'

'I really don't think I . . . ' Athena glanced down at her gown. Her *only* decent gown. Besides that, she really didn't want to draw attention to herself. 'We shall have to see.'

Athena noticed an incredulous look pass between the ladies, making her wonder what she had done wrong now.

'The duke told me you were a headstrong young woman,' the duchess said, not unkindly. 'It's a refreshing change.'

The talk became more general after that, and as soon as she politely could, Athena took her leave, promising to return the following morning to help Lady Susan with the final touches to the barn's decorations.

11

'You look beat, little brother.' Eli felt both concern and guilt as he and Harry rode through the Park at a walk. Against Eli's better judgement, he had agreed when Harry insisted upon a flat out gallop across the lower meadow. Harry had been so enthusiastic Eli had been unable to refuse him. It was like old times, but probably hadn't done Harry much good. 'That was too much for you.'

'Nonsense. I've never felt better, thanks to your Mrs. Defoe.'

'I am glad she was able to help.'

'The proof of her genius sits beside you.'

'And beside you,' Eli replied with a wry smile.

'She's talented, beautiful, and very mysterious. Why the devil does she want to hide herself away at Whispers' Hollow, and what does her husband think he's about, leaving her there unprotected?'

'I have absolutely no idea.'

'But, unless I miss my guess, you intend to find out.' Harry flashed an irrepressible grin. 'I know you, Eli. She has fascinated you, and you won't rest until you discover her secrets.'

'Perhaps she doesn't have any. And even if she does, what right do I have to interfere in her affairs?'

'That is undeniably true, what with you about to embark upon matrimony. I, on the other hand, am free to do as I please.'

'Leave her alone! She's mine.'

Harry roared with laughter. 'I thought so,' he said smugly.

Eli regretted allowing Harry to goad him into making an inappropriate response. Athena wasn't his and never could be. More was the pity. Even so, when it came to her, he was as a moth to flame, totally compelled, even though he knew it was a dangerous and pointless attraction. As Harry had so kindly just reminded him, he was about to be married, even if he didn't yet know the identity of his bride.

They returned to the stables and Byron whinnied. Meg was obviously here some-where, Eli thought, grinning.

'You and me both,' he muttered, patting Byron's neck.

Once they had dismounted, Eli slapped Harry's shoulder and told him to go and rest. 'Don't overdo it and ruin all of Athena's good work.'

'Athena, ah? What a very pretty name.'

Harry waved to Eli as they parted in the back corridor. 'Until later.'

Eli went to his study and had food brought to him there. He was acutely aware of Athena's presence in the building. She would be taking luncheon with his mother and sisters, enduring their endless questions about her circumstances — questions he knew she wouldn't adequately answer. His Athena was a master at dissembling. The desire to join them was strong, but Eli resisted. He had already shown more interest than was wise in Athena. He never joined his mother for luncheon and if he did so today, it would only fuel her speculation.

Instead he tried to work on the papers Jessop had left him to look over — a contract for the purchase of additional land adjoining one of his other estates — all the while keeping a weather eye on the driveway. He would see Athena leave, and when she did, he would go after her. He urgently needed to speak with her.

Half-an-hour later his vigil was rewarded, and he saw her ancient cart making its way down the drive at a slow plod. Eli was up and out of the room in two bounds. He saddled Byron himself and was on his back a very short time later. He knew better than to follow Athena down the drive. He would be seen from the house. Questions would be asked. Instead, he cut through the woods to the west of the stables. A track brought him out about halfway to Whispers' Hollow. He halted Byron and waited.

It was a full ten minutes before he heard the rumble of the cart approaching. Not wishing to scare her, he joined the track and rode towards her so she would see him in good time. Her adorable head jerked up when she heard Byron whinny, and a small gasp of surprise slipped past her lips. Just for a moment, she could have sworn those lips turned upwards, but she straightened them again before he could be entirely sure, leaving him no nearer to knowing if she was pleased or annoyed to see him again.

'Out for an afternoon ride, your grace?'

'No, Athena, I was waiting for you.'

'Good heavens. Why?'

'Are you absolutely sure that contraption is safe?' he asked, eyeing the cart with scepticism.

'We can't all afford the best of everything, your grace.'

Eli sighed. 'If you don't stop *your gracing* me, I shall put you over my knee, right here and now, and spank obedience into you.'

She sent him a look of frozen surprise. Her face coloured and this time the corners of her lips definitely lifted. 'You wouldn't dare.'

He imbued his responding grin with wicked intent, conscious of his blood heating and his cock stirring. 'My advice to you, my dear, is not to put yourself in a position where you might find out. I never could resist a challenge.'

'I don't intend to put myself anywhere near you. Please move aside so I can pass.'

'Besides,' Eli added, remaining right where he was, blocking her path, 'I have already offered to purchase you a safer form of transport.'

'But I don't want you to.'

'Worried what your husband would have to say?'

'Precisely. He's a very jealous man.'

'Which makes him an even bigger fool for leaving you alone and unprotected.'

'We are not all free to do as we would like, *Eli*.'

His heart plummeted. 'I of all people can attest to that fact,' he said, suddenly feeling the full weight of the burden that rested on his shoulders.

'I am not alone,' she said, her face heating as he continued to look at her. 'I have Boris and Millie. Two fiercer protectors it would be difficult to find.'

'And yet still you hide yourself away.' Eli

sent her a probing glance. 'What are you hiding from, sweet Athena?'

'What makes you think I'm hiding from anything?'

He moved aside, she encouraged the pony forward, and Eli rode alongside her. 'By not denying it, you have just confirmed my suspicions.'

'You are too clever for me, your grace.'

'Athena, by all that's holy, if you don't — '

'Stop it, just stop it!' Her eyes blazed with an emotion he couldn't put a name to, and she looked close to tears. 'Go and find someone else to take your frustrations out on. I don't have time to play games with you.'

Eli sighed, long and deep. 'Why are you so intent upon defying me?'

'Ignorance is the curse of God: knowledge is the wing wherewith we fly to heaven.'

Eli looked at her askance. The more he got to know her, the more of an enigma she became. She would have the world believe she was a mere lace-maker, and yet her manners were pristine, her voice educated, she and her sisters were named after Greek goddesses, and now she was quoting Shakespeare at him.

'King Henry, if memory serves.'

'Yes.' She shook her head, as though just realising what she had said, or rather quoted, and what it must tell him about her. 'As to defying you, why are you so determined to hound me?'

'*Touché*,' he said softly.

'I have already made it clear you owe me nothing. I was glad to be able to help you, and Lord Shelton, and that's an end to the matter.'

'Did you enjoy my mother's society?' he asked in an abrupt change of subject.

'She is *interesting*.'

'Interesting?' Eli roared with laughter. 'That is a very unique, or perhaps delicate, way of describing her.'

'She wasn't at all what I expected, since you ask.'

'Oh, and what had you expected. An autocratic duchess who rules with a rod of iron?'

'Well yes, something like that, I suppose.'

'You think I would allow anyone to dictate to me? Especially my mother.'

'She is dictating your choice of bride.' Athena blushed again when she spoke, as though she hadn't meant to say the words aloud. 'Not that it's any of my business.'

'I am only going along with her plans because I'm not in a position to choose my heart's desire,' he replied, fixing her with a pointed look.

'Then I feel very sorry for you.'

'Thank you.'

She burst out laughing, presumably because they were suddenly being very stiff and formal, something that hadn't happened in any of their exchanges up until now. Her musical laughter was a delight to hear, and Eli found himself laughing, too. At that moment he would have parted with all his wealth, all his privileges, in exchange for the freedom to court this vibrant, lovely young woman. She had secrets she refused to share with him, which made her seem mysterious, and incited his protective instincts. His intuition told him she was in danger, and Eli would move heaven and earth to keep her safe, if only she would allow it. Even if she did not. Did she not realise the extent of his influence? Whatever it was she was running away from, he could make it go away. At least he could do that much for her. Eli was filled with a firm determination to make her tell him what it was.

'Are you planning to return to Whispers' Hollow with me?' she asked.

'It would probably be for the best,' he said, striving for a mock-serious tone. 'I'm not satisfied that death-trap of yours will make it. Besides, I doubt whether I could get Byron to go the other way, even if I wanted to. Just look at him.'

Athena laughed. Eli's stallion was prancing

sideways, tail held high, tossing his head whenever Eli released his firm hold on the reins, and occasionally pawing the ground. Meg continued to ignore him.

'He's just showing off,' Athena said. 'The male of the species tends to do that when a lady takes his fancy, I find.'

'I'm sure you would know,' he replied in a smoky, provocative tone.

'Petticoats,' she hissed at him. 'Who gave you the right to gift me petticoats?'

'It was the least I could do. You *did* sacrifice yours for my sake.'

'Yes, but even so, it was an unseemly gesture.'

'You didn't like them?' Eli raised a speculative brow. 'I thought you would be pleased.'

They reached the cottage before she could respond, but Eli sensed she was struggling not to smile. What woman didn't enjoy receiving gifts of intimate apparel? At least in that respect, Athena appeared no different to the rest of the female race, and he was glad to have brought a little pleasure into her life.

Everything was activity within the vicinity of the cottage. The twins saw them, came running over, then appeared to recall who Eli was and stopped dead in their tracks. He had known everything would be different, of course, and would give much to have the carefree twins of yesterday back again.

'Hello,' he said to them, jumping down from Byron and then extending a hand to Athena to help her down. 'What have you been doing?'

'Are you really a duke?' Selene asked.

Yes, he thought she was Selene. Both girls wore silver crucifixes, and he had noticed yesterday that Selene's had a tiny ruby in its centre. Lyssa's was decorated with a sapphire. That was how he had told them apart.

'Why didn't you tell us?' Lyssa added in a note of feint injury.

Both girls belatedly remembered their manners and curtsied. Eli made them giggle when he offered them a courtly bow in return. Millie joined them, and at least she showed no inclination to be obsequious.

'Come for another nap in my comfy bed?' she asked.

'I actually came to see how things are going?'

Eli strode off, waving the men off when they would have stopped to bow. Everything seemed to be in order, the work coming along nicely. He spent a moment or two speaking with the men repairing the staircase, satisfying himself that they were doing a thorough job. Couldn't risk his goddess turning an ankle on an uneven board.

With nothing further to delay him, Eli returned to Athena and Millie. They were unharnessing Meg, watched with intent interest by the smitten Byron.

'Are you looking forward to the harvest dance, girls?' he asked.

'Dance?' They looked at one another.

'Are we invited?' Lyssa asked, hope flaring in her eyes.

'Mr. Bairstowe said something, but we weren't sure.'

'Well of course you are invited. All the tenants go. It is the highlight of the year, and you wouldn't want to miss it.'

'Can we, Athena?' they asked in unison.

Athena sent Eli a damning glance. It was evident she hadn't taken Bairstowe's invitation seriously, or had told the twins it wasn't serious. It was equally evident they were very eager to attend. It was just as well Eli had come here with the specific purpose of setting her straight, even if Athena didn't appreciate his intervention. She shared a look with Millie, who shrugged, and then returned her attention to the twins' eager faces.

'Of course we shall attend,' she said with a weary sigh.

★ ★ ★

Two days later, Eli's mother's guests started arriving throughout the afternoon. So far Eli had managed to avoid them all by burying himself in his study, short-tempered and out of sorts with anyone who happened to cross his path. Most people appeared sensibly to avoid him. Another two days before the harvest dance, when at least he would see Athena again. He had denied himself that pleasure on the day after his visit to the cottage, when he knew her to be with Susan. Seeing her would only ignite the deep desire he felt for her, the palpable, pulsating ache that flamed his blood whenever he caught a whiff of her unique scent, heard the rustle of her skirts, or the sound of her melodic voice.

Now she was no longer on the estate, he would have suffered death by a thousand cuts just to spend a few minutes in her engaging and lively company. But Eli stayed away from Whispers' Hollow because nothing could be achieved by his going there. Curses flowed from his lips at his inability to do as he pleased.

He had pointed out to Susan she would likely have nothing to wear. Susan had risen to the occasion and insisted she accept the gift of one of her old gowns. Athena was a little taller than Susan, but no doubt she could use some of her lace to rectify any shortfall in the hemline. It pleased him to think his goddess would have something fresh and pretty to wear, along with her new petticoats, even if he wouldn't be free to admire the resulting image.

Eli suddenly realised he hadn't yet received a response from Jessop regarding the enquiries he had asked him to make in Nottingham.

'What the devil is the hold up?' he asked aloud, tugging the bell so hard that the cord creaked.

Jessop responded immediately and stood respectfully in front of Eli's desk. 'Your grace rang.'

'What news from Nottingham?'

'Nothing as yet, your grace. I have sent one of our best men to make enquiries and anticipate hearing from him at any time.'

Hmm, nothing obvious then, otherwise Jessop's man would have heard of it right away and sent word by express. Even so, the delay angered Eli. Just about everything angered him at the moment. But it wasn't Jessop's fault, and it would be unfair to take his unsettled mood out on his secretary.

'All right, Jessop. Let me know the moment you hear anything.'

The dressing gong sounded, and Eli could hide away no longer. He made his way to his chambers, saying nothing to Salter as he helped Eli to dress. He tied his own neckcloth in a flamboyant waterfall, straightened his embroidered waistcoat, and turned towards the door. Tonight he would be without his bandage for the first time. His wound was healing well, but there was still a large and colourful bruise on the side of his face, partially covered by his hair.

'Good luck, your grace,' Salter said, a tinge of sympathy in his tone.

'Thank you, Salter,' Eli replied, grimacing. 'I shall most certainly need it.'

The drawing room was full of beautifully attired people, speaking in low, elegant voices, laughter occasionally ringing out as battle lines were drawn between the ambitious mothers and their offspring. Eli managed a brief smile when he noticed his friend Johnson and Susan in close conversation. His baby sister had wasted no time in staking her claim.

Eli's presence was noticed. Conversation gradually subsided as all heads turned in his direction. So it begins, he thought, striding into the room, greeting acquaintances as he went. There was no one present whom he did not know, and he could tell immediately from the calculating glances in their mothers' eyes which ladies were on his own mother's list of desirable partis.

'Your grace.'

Lady Denton stepped into his path and

dropped into a graceful curtsey, winning the race to be the first ambitious mother to do so. Her daughter Caroline followed suit, and Eli greeted them with every appearance of civility. Caroline Denton was a pretty blonde, large of bone, wide in the hips. Child-bearing hips his mother would approve of, he thought absently. He tried to imagine making children with Lady Caroline and singularly failed.

'Lady Denton, Lady Caroline. Welcome to Winsdale Park. I hope you've been made comfortable.'

'Perfectly so, I thank you, your grace.'

'It is a very pretty estate, what I've seen of it,' Lady Caroline said. 'I would enjoy a more extensive tour.'

Damned impudence! 'I dare say a tour is on my mother's list of entertainments.'

Eli moved on, thinking at least Lady Caroline spoke without simpering and didn't gush. He was grateful for small mercies. Next to accost him was Lady Evans and her daughter the honourable Emily. *Oh no, mother. Surely not?* Emily couldn't be described as pretty, not even by her most ardent admirer. She had small eyes, a long jaw, and there was something not quite right about her nose. Eli knew nothing to her detriment, but if he had to marry a stranger, at least let her be pleasing to the eye.

'It looks as though your party will be blessed with fine weather, your grace,' Lady Evans remarked.

'Oh no, Mama,' Emily contradicted. 'It's harvest time, and it always rains on the harvest, does it not, your grace?'

Eli retained his composure only by dint of the stringent training he had gone through since the cradle. Did Emily but know it, she had just ruined any minute chance she might otherwise have had of becoming his duchess by reminding Eli of the harvest. Harvest made him think of the dance, the dance made him think of Athena, and the urge to flee this circus and join her in the relative peace of Whispers' Hollow had never been greater.

Lady Louisa Broughton was exquisite to look at, but couldn't string a single intelligible sentence together. Worse, she giggled each time Eli addressed a word to her. *Give me strength!*

Charlotte's friend Lady Cynthia Parsons had possibilities. Pleasant, intelligent, and seemingly as disinterested in the proceedings as he was, she was the lady to whom he proffered his arm when dinner was announced. Eli sensed annoyance in the other ambitious mothers as Eli and Lady Cynthia made their way to table. His dinner partner accepted his company with composure and answered any questions he addressed to her with intelligence and, mercifully, lack of giggling. There was nothing spontaneous about her, though, nothing to hold his interest for long. She and Lady Caroline were very much the best of a mediocre but oh-so-suitable bunch.

Eli smothered a sigh. It was going to be a very long, very trying, week.

12

Athena sat with her sisters, fingers moving deftly back and forth across the lace she was making, while she re-told the girls the story of King Lear.

'It hardly seems fair of the king to dispose of estate based on the level of flattery he received from his daughters,' Selene said, wrinkling her nose.

'Well, he *was* mad,' Lyssa pointed out. 'So I don't suppose we ought to judge him too harshly.'

'I don't think the king could have been an agreeable person.'

'I agree, Selene. It's very mean to set one sister against another.'

'Imagine if anyone tried to do that to the three of us.'

Athena listened to the seamless conversation flowing between her sisters, a nervous smile playing about her lips. Even their opinion of mad King Leah couldn't keep her thoughts away from the afternoon to come. It was the day of the harvest festival party, and she would see Eli surrounded by his bevy of would-be duchesses. How was she supposed to endure that agony without giving herself away? She glanced at the girls, so excited at the prospect of seeing the Park and chided herself for her selfishness. She would get through it. Somehow. The place would be crowded, no one would notice her, which was just the way she wanted it.

Millie was to come, too. There had been much argument about that. Millie declared she had no time to waste with parties, but Athena stood firm. Millie deserved a respite from their daily routine as much as the rest of them. Probably more. She cajoled and then resorted to bribery. The girls needed to be watched, and Athena couldn't be everywhere at once. It did the trick, and only Boris would remain behind at the cottage.

'It's time to get ready,' Athena said, putting her work aside.

Lyssa grinned. 'At last we get to see you wearing your lovely gown, Athena.'

Athena hadn't wanted to accept the beautiful muslin dress from Lady Susan, even though she insisted she no longer wore it because the colour was wrong for her. But Lady Susan's argument that the colour was exactly right for Athena was irrefutable. It was a bright burnished copper almost exactly the same shade as her hair. A little too short, she and the girls had made a pretty lace flounce in cream, worked through with gold thread, and stitched it to the hem. Similar lace now also adorned sleeves, finishing halfway down Athena's forearms. She had a shawl in exactly the same colours, which she draped across her arms, deciding she might as well use the opportunity to show off their handiwork and generate more business.

Athena didn't bother to put her hair up. It would only escape again — it always did. Instead, she tied it back with a ribbon to match her shawl, but tendrils broke free and framed her face. Sighing, she squashed a straw bonnet on top of her unruly locks. It was trimmed, not with the usual decorations but, of course, more lace.

'You look a picture,' Millie said, wiping a tear from her eye when she saw Athena dressed and ready. 'Your Mama would have been that proud.'

'Shush now, Millie, enough of that. If I must attend this party then I intend to enjoy myself. Don't mention anything to make me sad.'

'That I won't, lamb.'

'Are the girls ready?'

'Yes, we are.'

For once, they weren't dressed alike.

'We're tired of no one being able to tell us apart,' Selene said by way of explanation.

Athena didn't have the heart to point out that would still be the case. Lyssa wore a pretty cream gown, Selene's was pink, but unless they wore their names around their necks, that wouldn't help their cause much. As in Athena's case, it had been necessary to trim the hems of their gowns with lace since the girls had grown since making the garments for themselves over a year previously. Lyssa had followed Athena's example and simply tied her hair back. She hadn't bothered with a bonnet and her locks tumbled and rippled down her back like liquid gold. Selene's hair was piled tidily on top of her head and she, too, wore a straw bonnet trimmed with lace.

'Well, Boris,' Athena said, giving him the chop bone she had saved as compensation for being left alone. 'Guard the place for us. We shall see you later.'

Boris's tail flapped, and he looked momentarily forlorn to be left. Then he remembered the bone and was already crushing it into submission in his powerful jaws as they left the cottage.

The four of them clambered into the cart, to which Meg was already harnessed. As Athena drove the now familiar route to Winsdale Park, she was suddenly glad they had decided to come. The twins' excitement was infectious and, regardless of the risks involved, Athena found herself looking forward to the afternoon, even if she would have to endure the agony of seeing Eli in all his ducal splendour. Perhaps this visual reminder of the chasm that separated them would bring her to her senses. After today she would stop wasting time thinking about him, which would be a good thing.

Of course, it would.

The cart joined a long line of similar vehicles making slow progress up the long driveway to Winsdale Park. People called cheerfully to one another, and an atmosphere of great good humour prevailed. Everyone, it seemed, was in the mood for a party. The girls' eyes were round with excitement, and they seemed to be looking everywhere at once, asking endless questions. Athena answered them absently, concentrating on keeping Meg in line behind the cart in front of them.

When they finally reached the stable yard, the groom recognised Athena and treated her with great respect. She gave Meg and the cart over to him with a nod of thanks and jumped down to join her sisters and Millie.

'There is so much to see,' Lyssa said.

'Jugglers and fire-eaters,' Selene added, pointing to a spot in front of the terrace where trestle tables were set up for the tenants' luncheon.

'And games, by the looks of things.'

'Where is the barn you decorated, Athena?'

'Can we meet Lady Susan?'

'I should like something to eat.'

Athena laughed. 'When are you two not hungry? Come, we must find a place at the tables. We eat first, and then the fun begins.'

There were two rows of tables. Athena found a spot for them all at the far end of the back row, where they were least likely to attract attention. There must have been about eighty people jockeying for position around them, a lot of the men looking uncomfortable in their Sunday best, while the women seemed to enjoy shedding their everyday clothes in favour of something a little finer. Athena glanced up at the terrace. A long table was covered with a snowy white cloth and there was a dazzling array of crystal glasses. About thirty people were converged there, talking amongst themselves, looking out at the sea of people gathered on the lawns with varying degrees of uncertainty.

She saw him at once, and her breath caught in her throat. She was struck, as always, by his sheer vitality and animal magnetism. Even from a distance, he cut a commanding figure in a beautiful blue coat and creamy waistcoat, a thousand times removed from his appearance when they had first met under such unconventional circumstances. Athena counted four elegant young ladies buzzing around Eli like flies, which is when it finally struck her just how ridiculous she was actually being. She had told herself as much on an hourly basis since meeting the duke.

The time had come to accept it.

'Oh look,' Selene said, pointing. 'There's the duke. Doesn't he look regal?'

'Imagine him sleeping in Millie's bed,' Lyssa added, giggling.

That was precisely what Athena didn't wish to imagine.

As though sensing her presence, Eli broke away from the conversation he was conducting with one of the ladies and looked out over the lawns. His gaze roved slowly along the lines of people. It stopped when it reached her position.

And didn't move on.

★   ★   ★

Eli had been summoned to his mother's sitting room before the festivities got under way. He stood with his back to the fire, watching the crowd growing steadily bigger on the lawns below. He knew what his mother wanted to speak to him about, but resented the need to answer her. Wasn't it enough he had agreed to this charade? He would tell her of his decision when he had reached one. Until that time came, there was nothing to be said. Could it be she sensed the changes in him since he had met Athena and felt the need to remind him of his duty?

Duty? Eli hated the sound of the damned word.

'I think we might actually avoid being rained on this year,' he said, absently glancing up at the sky, trying to tell himself he wasn't watching for Athena's cart. It would be impossible to spot it amongst a collection of so many similar vehicles, but he looked anyway.

'I didn't call you here to discuss the weather,' his mother replied crisply.

'Yes, I am aware.'

'Then do me the goodness of giving me your attention, and tell me if you have yet reached a decision.'

'The Evans girl is out of the question.'

His mother's lips twitched. 'Yes, I thought she probably would be.'

'So, too, is Lady Louisa.' Eli sighed. 'All that stupidity *and* giggling. Whatever made you imagine she would suit?'

'She has the right pedigree.'

Eli's lips quirked. 'You make her sound like a dog.'

'Yes well, that leaves Lady Caroline and Lady Cynthia.'

'So it does.'

'Do try to show a little more enthusiasm, Eli.'

'Believe me, Mother, this *is* enthusiasm.'

'Oh, Eli, my dear, do you think I enjoy doing this to you? I have waited so long for you to make a decision without any coercion from me. I just want you to be happy, but — '

'I know. Don't distress yourself. My life is not my own. I have responsibilities.'

'Precisely. Your father didn't love me when we married, nor was I foolish enough to imagine he did, but we became fond of one another over the years, and reached an understanding that suited us both.'

Ah, so his mother was reminding him marriage wouldn't necessarily bring an end to his personal pleasures. But it would, because he had fallen deeply and passionately in love with a woman he could never marry, and it was slowly tearing him apart.

'I thought you understood what was expected of you, Eli.'

'How could I not?' he replied, a trace of bitterness underlying his words.

'What is it, my dear? Surely you're not balking because you think romance ought to play a part in your decision?' Her laugh was bitter. 'I thought you had more sense than that. When it comes to choosing a wife, there's no room for emotion for a man of your stature. You and your future bride must both understand the importance of maintaining the exclusive lineage of the duchy, and she can only properly do so if she comes from a similar background to your own.'

'I dare say.'

'Love complicates everything, Eli,' she added briskly. 'Besides, it doesn't last. Flick through the pages of any history book if you doubt my word. See what quivering wrecks powerful men have become in the name of love, and how comprehensively they have come to regret their foolishness.' She shook her head. 'No, my dear, take it from one who knows and think with your brain, not your emotions.'

'We ought to go down,' Eli said, wishing to curtail this excruciating conversation. 'It's time.'

'Very well, but I *will* have your decision by the end of the week?'

Eli firmed his jaw. 'I have already said you will.'

His quelling tone prohibited further discussion on the point and they descended the stairs in taut silence.

Their guests were assembled on the

terrace, the tenants on the lawn. The two parties would only inter-mingle after luncheon.

'Oh, your grace, such a crowd,' Lady Caroline said, fluttering her lashes at him. 'I had no idea so many people would be here.'

'It's the highlight of our year,' Eli replied drolly.

'I didn't mean to imply it isn't the greatest fun imaginable. It is so very generous of you to open your grounds to all these people.'

Eli wanted to point out the grounds would be a shambles, and there would be no harvest, were it not for these people. In the end, he decided to save his breath.

'Quite so,' he replied.

Lady Cynthia appeared on his opposite side. Her initial reticence had given way to a quiet determination, no doubt the result of her mother's lecturing, or his own sister's encouragement.

'No rain after all,' she said.

'It would seem not.'

She was here. Eli was convinced he could sense her presence. That was ridiculous, given the throng collected on the lawns beneath him, settling themselves at the tables amidst a loud cacophony of cheerful good humour. Lady Cynthia said something else to him. He gave every impression of being enthralled by her fascinating insight, but didn't have a clue what it was she had actually said. Instead, he scanned the crowd with his eyes until he found her, right at the back, at the far end, the twins to one side of her, Millie to the other. It was as though she was trying to fade into the background. Eli suppressed a snort. As if she ever could!

Dear God, her hair was loose, tumbling down her back like fluid copper. Even from this distance, she looked like an angel. Eli wanted to run down and plant his fist in the face of the man who had just dared to speak to his goddess. *She's mine, leave her alone, damn it!* Except she wasn't his, and never could be. He died a little inside as reality struck home. Eli ground his teeth and kept his gaze focused down on her, until she looked up and their eyes clashed. He inclined his head, and smiled, transfixed, unable to look away.

Archer appeared on the terrace and rang a small bell. His guests took their seats, but Eli, at the centre of the table, remained standing. Immediately a hush fell over the boisterous tenants and a sea of faces looked up at him.

'Another year has passed and the Winsdale estate continues to flourish,' he said, 'thanks in no small part to all of you.' A loud cheer. 'We have successfully gathered in another year's harvest and are here today to give thanks for that. We, the Shelton family, have never lost sight of your loyalty, nor will we ever forget how much we owe to you. So thank you all. This day is for you.' He raised his glass high. 'Enjoy yourselves, you have earned the right, but don't drink too much!'

There was loud laughter and more cheering. Then the cooper, by tradition the self-appointed spokesman for the villagers, stood up. Once again there was quiet.

'We appreciate your generosity, your grace,' he said with suitable gravitas, raising his glass in return. 'Three cheers for The Duke of Winsdale.'

Everyone stood up and cheered. The men threw caps in the air and a hundred voices echoed loud in the still afternoon air. It was impossible for Eli not to be moved by their loyalty, a timely reminder of all that was expected of him. He inclined his head in the cooper's direction and took his seat.

With the formalities over with, everyone tucked into the sumptuous food provided by the Park's kitchens. Eli insisted the tenants and gentry shared the same menu, even if crystal glassware and silver cutlery didn't extend beyond the terrace.

'They all adore you,' Lady Caroline said, in awe. 'Which is only right and proper since you have behaved munificently.'

'You sound as though you don't approve.'

'Oh no, on the contrary, your grace. I admire the way you keep them loyal.'

The feasting finally came to an end, the noise getting progressively louder as the ale flowed and both parties relaxed. When the final plates had been removed, Eli stood, indicating it was time to mingle with the tenants.

'Susan,' he said, grasping his sister's arm. 'It's time to admire your handiwork.'

'Oh yes, all right.'

All of the guests had heard of the decorated barn, but none had been permitted to view it in advance. Harry appeared at Eli's side, as did his friends Franklin and Johnson. Together the entire party descended the steps from the terrace, Eli in the lead. The tenants bowed as he passed, then went back to drinking and enjoying themselves. Eli didn't hear much of what was said to him because his goddess was no longer in her seat. Where the devil was she? Heaven help any rogue who placed so much as one inappropriate finger on her. The violent possessiveness that spiralled through him at the thought of any other man getting anywhere near her took him by surprise.

'Oh my!' Lady Caroline cried when she saw the barn. 'Did you really do all this yourself, Lady Susan?'

It was the first time Eli had seen the results, and he was more than impressed. Athena's guidance had seen the large space transformed into an indoor woodland, the fragrant perfume of honeysuckle and jasmine dominating. There were huge sheathes of corn held together with plaited robe and bold rosettes of fabric. A large display of harvest produce covered one wall — pumpkins, potatoes and carrots, together with fruit and green vegetables, blending into a fresco that typified the season. There were herbs, too, of course — lots of them. It was inspired.

Just like its creator.

'I had some help,' Susan said, grinning. 'Well, quite a lot of help, actually.'

'It's a triumph,' Lord Johnson said to her, taking her arm and leading her a little apart from the rest of them. Eli was amused to see Susan blush. What he knew and Susan did not was that Johnson had made up his mind. He'd spoken to Eli just that morning, and Eli had given him permission to address his sister. Well, at least someone in the family would soon have her heart's desire. 'Come, if I'm not mistaken, they are serving cider from that table yonder. We ought to try it. Allow me to collect you a cup, Lady Susan.'

'Mrs. Defoe!'

Susan's delighted cry had Eli's immediate attention. He turned slowly, and almost didn't recognise her, even though he had spent most of the meal gazing at her from afar. She looked . . . well, she looked like his goddess, only a thousand times more beautiful. A small, nervous smile flirted with her lips as she met his gaze and didn't look away. He broke away from his party, went up to her, and took her hand.

'You intoxicate me,' he said quietly, lifting her hand and brushing the back of it with his lips, his eyes burning into hers. 'I want to whisk you away from here and . . . well, I hadn't better tell you what I would like to do to you. Your husband would horsewhip me, and rightly so.'

'We are being watched by two very angry-looking ladies,' she replied, her lips moist and shiny and altogether too tempting as she parted them to speak.

'Did you make the lace on your gown yourself?' he asked, perfectly indifferent to his enraged audience.

'Yes. Your sister gave me this gown, but it was too short.'

'Did you have the right petticoats to go with it?' he asked, sending her another scorching glance.

'Oh, yes. I have an endless supply given to

222

me by gentlemen admirers.'

He narrowed his eyes and growled at her. 'That had better not be the case, Mrs. Defoe. I have already warned you what to expect if you displease me.'

'I'm not afraid of you, your grace.'

'Then you damned well should be.'

'Eli, stop monopolising Mrs. Defoe.'

Harry joined them, full of cheerfulness, and kissed her hand also.

'How are you, Lord Shelton?' she asked.

'The inhalations have worked wonders, as you can see, and I shall be forever in your debt,' he replied. 'But don't forget I need your advice on how to proceed with them.'

'Then I shall discuss it with you, perhaps after his grace has chosen his wife and your guests have all departed.'

Eli choked on an oath. Harry appeared to find the situation very amusing.

'Begging your pardon, your grace.' The village blacksmith hovered at Eli's elbow. 'We're ready to start the tug of war, if that's convenient.'

'Tug of war?' Athena asked, smiling.

'Oh, yes.' It was Harry who answered her. 'It's an annual tradition. The villagers against us lot.'

'And I suppose the duke is always allowed to win.'

'Not a bit of it,' Eli replied with a puerile grin. 'No quarter is asked for or given. It can get quite vicious.'

'In that case, I wouldn't recommend you take part, Lord Shelton,' Athena said. 'You are not nearly strong enough yet.'

'I would disagree, except if I'm a bystander, I can watch with you, which will more than compensate for my disappointment.'

Eli scowled. 'Have a care, little brother.'

'Shame Baintree isn't here,' Harry said. 'His bulk is always a big help for our side.'

Eli frowned again, for a different reason this time. He couldn't put his finger on why precisely, but he had always disliked and mistrusted Charlotte's husband, and had been opposed to their union. But Charlotte had been determined to have him, and their mother had supported her cause. The Earl of Baintree, a good looking and charismatic man, was perpetually short of blunt, had needed Charlotte for her dowry, and clearly didn't return his wife's adoration. Eli suspected the blinkers had finally fallen from Charlotte's eyes, and she now knew it. She was disappointed with her marriage, and Eli was sorry her illusions had been shattered.

Baintree was equerry to the prince regent. A womaniser at best, there was a dark side to his nature that Eli found repellent. Married men took mistresses as a matter of course. Even his mother had indicated to Eli earlier today it was a perfectly acceptable state of affairs. Dear God, was she implying that he should — Athena? No, she was worth more than that! Baintree wasn't discrete and didn't limit himself to one woman at a time. Presumably, the rumours had reached Charlotte, accounting for her low mood and disillusionment. There was nothing she could do about it, though and had taken the only course available to her, wisely ignoring the rumours.

'He said he was coming up from Brighton today,' Eli replied to Harry's question. 'He must have been held up.'

Eli summoned up the seven gentlemen who would tug for his side. He shed his coat and passed it to Harry to hold, before one of his tenacious admirers could lay claim to it.

'We shall be more comfortable over here, Mrs. Defoe,' he heard Harry say to his goddess as he took her elbow and led her away.

Eli glanced around the bustling grounds, the gentry mixing freely with the tenants and farmers. His mother would be keeping a careful watch over her selected candidates for his hand, Eli guessed, and observing how well they took to the event. The duchess herself was very good indeed at mingling. He glanced up and saw her deep in conversation with several of the ladies who had baked cakes for the occasion. His mother had, to the best of Eli's knowledge, never baked anything in her entire life, but that didn't prevent her from taking a lively interest in the village ladies' activities, and rightly so.

He noticed the twins, eating toffee and gingerbread from a nearby stall. It amused him to see them on the brink of adulthood, yet still drawn towards childish pleasures. Several lads hovered around them, causing Eli to frown. He didn't want anything to mar his goddess's pleasure today. Then he noticed the reassuring figure of Millie standing close enough to keep a weather eye on them, and relaxed.

'Are we ready, gentleman?' asked the cooper, acting as adjudicator for the tug of war.

Eli declared his side were, as did the blacksmith. The two men grinned as they shook hands, equals for the next few minutes.

'Take up the slack, gentleman,' the cooper yelled when all the men had taken a firm hold of the thick rope.

Both sides complied.

'On my signal. Three, two, one . . . heave!'

Both sides put their backs into it. The crowd cheered as fortunes waivered — first one side appearing to have the ascendency and then the other. Allegiances became apparent when those supporting the villagers stood to their side, yelling encouragement and advice. Eli's supporters were no less vociferous, if slightly less uninhibited. Athena and Harry stood diplomatically between the two groups, laughing at Eli's endeavours. The healing blisters on his hands were being opened up by the abrasive rope as he put all his weight into pulling. He barely felt the pain, filled instead with a childish desire to win and impress Athena.

The teams were evenly matched this year. Eli felt sweat trickling down his torso as he continued to lend his weight to his side of the rope. They were suddenly jerked forward as the opposition put in a concentrated effort, roared on by the crowd. Eli led a counter-attack and it was the villagers' turn to stumble clumsily forward. Ebb and flow, ebb and flow. Both sides were tiring.

'Now!' Eli yelled to his team.

All seven of them gave it all they had and tugged the villagers out of their half of the field, across the winning line. Eli's team all fell over when the villagers let go in defeat, much to the amusement of the crowd.

Laughing, Eli got up and shook the blacksmith's hand.

'Good fight, Tate,' he said, slapping the man's huge shoulder.

'We almost had 'yer, your grace.'

Eli brushed the grass from his backside, straightened his waistcoat and joined Harry in order to retrieve his coat.

'Well done,' Athena said. 'It was quite a tussle.'

'I did warn you. There is nothing the villagers would like more than to see me flat on my back.'

Harry cleared his throat and sent Eli an amused grin. 'And they have,' he added. 'More than once. Something, or someone, must have inspired Eli this year.'

'One of your prospective brides, perhaps?' she suggested with a playful smile that didn't reach her eyes.

'Hardly.'

'Are you such a bad landlord, your grace, that your tenants feel the need to knock you down?'

He fixed her with a languorous gaze. 'You tell me.'

Eli found himself detached from Athena by one of his persistent aspiring duchesses. The fiddler struck up a jig, couples flooded onto the grass to dance, and so Eli swept a delighted Louisa into their midst. She would be wise not to read too much into his choosing her as his first partner. She just happened to be convenient, and it was his duty to dance with each of the four of them. Eli planned to get it over with as quickly as possible.

He noticed Athena avoiding the dance, keeping to the shadows, watching her sisters as they both accepted eager partners. He saw her decline several invitations herself and could see she was nervous about something. He yearned to go to her, and force her to tell him what troubled her, but he could not.

At least not just yet. Duty first.

He danced with all four ladies, one after the other, and then went in search of Athena. It was twilight, and the party was nearing its end. He found her at the side of the barn, completely alone, leaning against the wall and staring off into the distance. Her hair, even tied back, hung almost all the way to her waist, a dozen different shades of autumnal colours reflected in its thick mass. Eli longed to run his fingers through it. She looked sad, vulnerable, almost afraid. She must have heard him approaching and glanced up, her expression apprehensive.

'What are you doing back here all alone?' he asked quietly.

'Taking a moment to myself, that's all.'

'Then you are being very unkind. You look so beautiful today, you have a duty to put yourself where I can admire you.'

'You were busy admiring your aspiring duchesses.' She sent him a teasing smile that did little to dispel the sadness in her eyes. 'Have you made your selection yet?'

'Dance with me, Athena.' He held out his hand. She looked at it for a long time before slipping hers into it. 'You have opened up your blisters.'

'I know. That was my intention.'

'Good heavens!' She raised a brow. 'Were you that desperate to win the tug?'

'No.' He caressed her with his eyes. 'The blisters make me think of how I came by them in the first place, which makes me think of you.'

'Oh!'

The fiddler was playing a country dance. Several sets had formed up. Eyebrows were raised when Eli joined one of them with Athena. He ignored everyone and relished the sight of Athena's slender body swaying, enjoying the sound of her laughter as she tripped lightly down the dance. She clearly enjoyed dancing and was no stranger to the art, another aspect of her past that intrigued him.

'You look happy,' he said to her when they next came together.

'I love to dance,' she replied, stating the obvious. 'It has been some time since I had the opportunity.'

'Where did you learn?'

She shrugged. 'Where does anyone learn?'

'Remain a mystery then,' he said, smiling into her shining eyes. They were green now. No, blue, with silver shards. A man could spend the rest of his days trying to identify their exact colour. He would never manage it because it seemed to change with her moods, but Eli would be prepared to die trying. 'But I shall find you out, never doubt it.'

'Why?' she asked. 'Why would you waste your energy? I am nothing to you.'

Oh, Athena. Can you not feel it?

The dance came to an end far too soon for Eli's liking.

'Allow me to fetch you a cup of orgeat.'

'The syrup of orange and almond type?' He nodded. 'Oh, yes please. I love orgeat, but haven't tasted it for a long time.'

He took Athena's arm to lead her in that direction when, glancing up, he noticed Baintree approaching.

'Ah, my sister's husband has finally arrived.' Eli tried to sound more enthusiastic than he felt. 'Charlotte will be pleased.'

Athena followed the direction of Eli's gaze, watching Baintree and his companion approach. Eli had no idea who the man with him was. Baintree always just assumed he could bring whomsoever he wished to the Park. But it wasn't his unknown companion that intrigued Eli, but Athena's reaction. A horrified gasp slipped past her lips, and she pulled her hand from Eli's grasp.

'Excuse me,' she said, her face ashen as she slipped between the crowds and disappeared from view.

'What the devil,' he muttered aloud, staring after her in disbelief.

13

Blood rushed through Athena's ears, her scalp tingled, her heart pounded against her ribcage, unadulterated terror streaked through her body — all her usual reactions when Blake was close at hand. Athena was no witch, but she did have a heightened sense of perception, and always knew when danger — specifically Blake — was anywhere near her. That gift had saved her from capture on more than one occasion during the past six months.

So why hadn't her senses warned her he was close by this time?

The answer was as simple as it was vexing. She had enjoyed dancing with Eli so much she had foolishly let her guard down. The touch of his hand, the laughter in his eye, the heady intoxication of the moment, the feel of his strong arm circling her waist — all of those factors had had a profound effect upon her, and she forgot to be cautious.

Dear God, she was paying dearly for that lapse now!

She leaned against the outside wall of the barn, breathing deeply, scared half out of her wits. How the devil had he found her here?

She thought they had moved far enough away to be beyond his reach. Apparently not. More to the point, had he seen her? Baintree had been heading for Eli, but had Blake noticed the duke's partner? Athena fled without waiting to find out.

The twins! Athena's hand flew to her mouth, and she pushed herself away from the wall with a great sense of urgency. She had to find them and Millie. If Blake hadn't seen her, he would surely see them. They were so alike they stood out even in a crowd. Thank God they weren't dressed the same today, but even so, he would notice them sooner or later. Was it safe to reveal herself yet? If she hadn't been seen, perhaps Blake wouldn't recognise the twins after all, she thought, wishing rather than expecting it to be so. It was her he wanted. The twins were just a means to an end. Besides, in their grown up gowns, they were unrecognisable from the young girls he knew. What to do?

She tensed when she heard footsteps approaching her solitary location. She couldn't be caught here. It would be safer to lose herself in the crowd. But her legs refused to move, and before she could force them to she became conscious of a large body looming over her. She recognised the aroma of sandalwood soap and imperious duke, and was suddenly afraid of him, too, but for very different reasons. She looked up and the concern in Eli's eyes was almost her undoing. He grabbed her shoulders to support her, which is when she realised she was trembling quite violently.

'What is it?' he asked. 'Who has frightened you?'

'It's nothing.' She shook her head against his chest, overwrought and exhausted.

'Nothing, you say. Then why are you shaking like a leaf? Tell me, Athena. Tell me what it is and what I can do to be of service to you?'

'Find Millie and the twins, if you want to help me. We must leave at once.'

'Selene is dancing with Ned. I saw her just a second ago. Lyssa is with Millie in the barn. They are all perfectly safe.'

She glanced up at him, her eyes moist with unshed tears. 'You checked on them before coming to find me? Why would you do that?'

'I assume whatever frightened you applies equally to them, and so it follows you would be worried about them.'

She sagged with relief, her knees almost giving out beneath her. One of his arms slipped to her waist, supporting her as it pulled her against him. She fell against his chest, comforted by its solidity. She couldn't afford to lean on him — on anyone — for long. Even so, she rested her head against his shoulder and drew on his considerable strength. She had borne her responsibilities alone for so long it was impossible not to feel the pull of someone stronger, someone she instinctively trusted. It was impossible not to be tempted to confide in him.

But she simply couldn't take that risk.

'Tell me,' Eli said softly, speaking into the top of her head. 'Let me help you.'

She shook her head against his shoulder. 'You can't help me. No one can. Besides, you have more than enough problems of your own.'

'For the love of God, Athena.' He grasped her shoulders again, pulled her away from the comfortable pillow formed by his shoulder, and glared passionately into her eyes. 'Do you realise how much influence I have? I might sometimes resent my position, but at least I can use it for the good of people deserving my help. What would be the point otherwise? There is nothing, absolutely nothing I can't achieve if I set my mind to it.' The urgency in his voice gave way to a soft, persuasive purr. 'Let me be of help to you, Athena. I can't bear to see you like this.'

'Eli, I want to, but I can't.' She screwed her eyes shut, unable to meet the entreaty in his expression, truly conflicted. 'It would do no good. Even you aren't above the law.'

She sensed his surprise. 'You are in trouble with the law?'

'In a manner of speaking.'

'Oh, this is ridiculous!'

He appeared to be losing patience with her and would soon leave her alone. She felt the loss right to her very core, but knew it would be better that way. He couldn't afford to involve himself in her affairs. If he did so, her uncle would have every right to publicly castigate him for his interference, and she wouldn't have his reputation being called into question on her account. She loved him with quite single-minded passion, and so the very least she could do was to protect him from himself.

'Just find the twins for me, and we shall leave at once.'

'All right, and then we can talk tomorrow.'

'No, Eli.' She forced herself to remain firm. 'There will be no more tomorrows for me in Whispers' Hollow. We shall just have to move again.'

'No, I won't let you go!' He pulled her against him so violently her body collided with the hard imprint of his, sucking the air from her lungs. She could feel his strength as his muscles bunched and tensed beneath his clothing, and once again she was tempted, sorely tempted, to confide in him. She closed her eyes for an expressive moment, thought of the twins, and the moment passed.

'Can't you feel it, Athena, the connection between us? The deep, abiding pull. There is an unfamiliar feeling tugging at my heart which ensures my every conscious thought is focused on you.'

She could sense the emotional investment behind words that were persuasively, passionately sincere, and died a little inside. Why, oh why, had she fallen for a wretched duke of all people?

'Only you, my precious love, and I can't bear to see you so frightened.'

She gasped because his words so closely mirrored her own feelings, when all the time she had imagined it was just her being foolish. She didn't want to admit to it, but was incapable of lying to him. 'Yes,' she whispered. 'I do feel it, but it does us no good. You are to be married, and I must move. Again.'

She felt tears seeping from beneath her lowered lashes. He tilted her chin with his forefinger until she was obliged to look directly into his eye. His smile was a tender caress, as tender as the finger that gently wiped an errant tear away.

'I don't want you to go,' he said softly.

'I must.'

'I won't let you.'

He lowered his head, reducing the already short distance that separated them. His breath peppered her face, and she knew he was going to kiss her. She absolutely couldn't allow that to happen. If she did, all would be lost, since she was incapable of resisting temptation. Of its own accord, her head lifted up anyway, meeting his half way. Without giving them permission to do so, her lips parted in anticipation, brazenly inviting him to cover them with his own. His arms closed around her body so tightly she couldn't breathe. She could feel the erratic beat of his heart and could hear the uneven tenor of his breathing.

His kiss, when it came, was practised and persuasive, although no persuasion was necessary. Athena was an enthusiastic participant in that kiss, keen to take as much of him as he was prepared to give, for she was serious in her intention to leave here, and she would never get another chance. Eli's tongue invaded her mouth in a series of bold, exploratory sweeps as their mouths fused and sensation rioted through her body. So this was how it felt to be kissed by a gentleman she admired. Athena wouldn't know, since she had never before desired a gentleman's advances. Although, she had much practise in fending them off. Eli groaned as he deepened the kiss, and it became unashamedly carnal. Her body was pressed tightly against the solid length of his own, and she could feel the state of his arousal. Dear God, how could she ever walk away from such unadulterated bliss?

She could because she had no choice. The only alternative was to involve him, and that she would never do.

He released her, and they were both breathing heavily.

'I've wanted to do that since I first met you,' he said quietly.

'Yes, I know.'

'Oh my sweet love, what shall we do about this?'

'There's nothing we can do,' she replied, looking everywhere except at him. If she met his gaze, which she knew would be searing and intense, she would lose her resolve. 'I have to go.'

'Your husband,' he replied urgently. 'Are you waiting here for him to return?'

She looked up sharply, wondering at the sudden change of subject. 'No, I don't anticipate seeing him again for years. If ever. Why do you ask?'

Eli expelled a long breath. 'Then I have a suggestion to make.' He pulled her back into his arms, but held her gently this time, daylight separating their bodies. 'If I could choose for myself, I wouldn't hesitate.'

She blinked up at him in surprise. 'What do you mean?'

'There's only one lady on the estate today whom I would choose for a wife, and I'm holding her in my arms.'

Athena gasped. 'You can't possibly mean that.'

'I thought we had already established our feelings for one another.' A wolfish smile replaced his melancholy expression. 'I would be happy to remind you if — '

'Eli, let's not talk of impossibilities. It does no good.'

'You're a lady, I know it.'

'Perhaps, but not nearly high-born enough to become a duchess.'

Eli laughed. 'Allow me to be the judge of that. Besides, I wouldn't care if you were a woodsman's daughter, but for my mother. She has such high standards, such expectations, and I must choose between breaking her heart, or breaking mine.'

'I understand.'

'You don't need to leave the area, sweet Athena. In fact, I won't let you. I have a house, a very nice house, on the other side of the village, in a remote location. It's yours.

For you and the twins, if you will accept it.'

She blinked up at him, wondering if he was proposing what she thought he was. 'What are you asking of me, Eli?' She needed to be sure.

'I want you for my wife, Athena, but it can't be.' His expression was tortured, and he hesitated before saying anything more. 'Will you be my mistress instead?'

'I-I can't — '

'Don't say that!' he cried passionately. 'I love you a thousand times more than I will ever love whomever I marry. She will be my wife in name only, whereas you are in my heart and soul.'

'Oh, Eli!' Athena's body was awash with emotion.

'I will cherish you and protect you at the expense of my own life. You will have servants. The twins will have an education. You will be safe, since no one who wishes you harm will ever get anywhere near you, and I will never again see such terrible fear in your lovely eyes. I will give you money, clothes, everything your heart desires, except the thing I most long to give you and cannot, which is my name.'

'Don't tempt me.' She bowed her head against his shoulder and shook it from side to side.

'We won't talk about it now,' he said. 'I

242

have to go back to the party. Tomorrow would be better. Meet me at dawn in the hollow, in the place where you saved my life. It seems only fitting. I will take you to see the house, and we can talk some more then.' She lifted her face from his shoulder, and he traced the line of her cheek with a gossamer touch that sent tremors down her spine. 'Stay here, darling. I will fetch the twins and Millie.'

'Yes, thank you. I will.'

Athena again relied upon the support of the barn wall, but this time it was Eli's actions, and ardent words, that had set her reeling. She had no time to assemble her thoughts and only just enough to straighten her clothing, before Eli returned with the twins and Millie. Athena exchanged a glance with her faithful servant and saw the fear in her eyes. She had seen Blake, too.

'Oh, is it time to leave already?' Selena asked, blithely unaware of the danger.

'We were having such fun,' Lyssa added.

'Everyone is leaving now,' Eli said, ushering them behind the barn to a path they could use to reach the stable yard without anyone in the house seeing them. 'Someone is bringing Meg out for you.'

Even with her mind frozen, Athena wondered at Eli's ability to make things happen so effortlessly. By the time they reached the yard, Meg was harnessed to the cart, her head being held by a groom. Eli himself helped each of them into it. If the grooms thought this unusual, they had the good sense to keep their thoughts to themselves.

Athena was the last to ascend, and Eli's hand lingered on hers.

'Will you be there?' he asked, so softly that his words couldn't be heard above the twins' excited chatter.

She looked down into his glowing gray eyes, knowing she should not keep her appointment with him. No good could possibly come of it.

'Yes,' she whispered, unable to help herself.

She saw satisfaction and relief flash through his eyes as the groom released Meg's head, Eli let go of her fingers after giving them a reassuring squeeze, and Athena drove away.

'Drive that thing carefully,' he said, a hint of humour entering his voice.

'You saw him,' she said quietly to Millie as soon as they had left Eli behind.

'Yes, but thank the lord he didn't appear to see you,' Millie whispered back. 'That, at least, will buy us some time. What the devil was he doing there? Do you think he came looking for us? Could he have heard already about the lace?'

'I don't know. He was with Lady Baintree's

husband. Perhaps it was just a coincidence,' Athena said optimistically.

'What shall we do?'

'Shush.' She joined the procession of vehicles leaving the estate, and nodded over her shoulder to the cheerfully chattering twins, unwilling to spoil their pleasure. It was a commodity in precious little supply in their lives these days. 'We will talk when they are asleep.'

That would give Athena a little time to consider the extraordinary events of the day, specifically Eli's proposal. She would have to tell Millie about it, even though she knew her servant would be violently opposed to such drastic measures. But Athena was so tired of running, so conscious of all the things the twins were entitled to, and which she could no longer supply them with. Would being a duke's mistress be such a very bad thing? Especially when that duke was Eli Shelton, and she was already so very much in love with him? If he was to be believed, and she *did* believe him, he was similarly enamoured of her. Oh, what a farrago!

★ ★ ★

The twins were exhausted and were soon in bed, leaving Athena and Millie in the kitchen with the freedom to talk.

245

'What's happened, lamb?' Millie asked with her usual perspicacity.

Millie deserved to know, and to have her say. She had been her own mother's closest friend and was more of a mother to Athena than a mere retainer. She was fiercely loyal and had encouraged Athena to leave Nottingham rather than fall prey to Blake's vile clutches.

'I was dancing with the duke when Blake appeared,' she said.

'Yes, I was watching you. It was lovely to see you smile and him, too.' Millie chuckled. 'Although, judging by the sour faces on a couple of his prospective brides' faces, they didn't share my joy.'

'I should have known there would be a price to pay for a few moments entertainment,' she said bitterly. 'But I didn't realise it would be quite such a heavy one.'

'What did you do when you saw Blake? One moment you were there, the next the duke was standing alone, staring after you. I tried to find you, but in the crush you were nowhere to be seen. I thought it better to make sure the twins were safe.' Millie flashed a sapient smile. 'The duke appeared to be taking care of you.'

'Do you think Blake noticed you or the twins?'

'No, they went into the barn, him and that Baintree fellow, then headed back to the terrace and disappeared into the house. They barely looked at us lesser mortals.'

'Thank goodness for that.' Athena fondled Boris's ears and stared into the dwindling fire. 'Presumably Lord Baintree will leave at the end of the party, and Blake will go with him. We just need to stay out of sight for three more days.'

'What if he identifies the lace, or hears about it?'

'Yes, there is that.' Athena bit her lip in frustration. 'We have been careful not to make the lace in the Cunningham way, but still, if he hears about handmade lace being sold by a stranger, he will become curious.'

'We will have to go from here before he finds us,' Millie said decisively.

'There might be another way.'

'Then I would be very glad to hear it. I have no desire to up sticks again.' Millie patted Athena's hand. 'Tell me, lass.'

And so she did. Not looking at Millie, she told her all about the duke's proposal, omitting all mention of the passionate kiss they had shared. She expected Millie to roundly berate the duke for his audacity — she had been stout in her defence of Athena when men of all rank had previously tried to exploit her. To her considerable surprise, she merely smiled.

'And you are tempted,' she suggested.

'Yes, God help me, but I am. You know how I feel about him, Millie, and I believe those feelings are reciprocated. Whether they will last is another matter, but the more time I can buy for myself and the twins, the better.'

'It would mean sacrificing your virtue, lamb. I know you don't intend ever to marry, but still, it's a big step.'

Not so very big when the man offering to seduce me is Eli. 'Yes, I'm aware of that. I would also be branded a *mistress*.' She managed a wan smile. 'My reputation, such as it is, would be destroyed. There's no help for that, but would it have a worse effect upon the twins' chances for happiness than their current situation?'

'They too would fall beneath the duke's protection.'

'Are you saying I should meet with him in the morning?' Athena couldn't hide her surprise. 'I thought you would be adamantly opposed to the idea.'

'See him,' Millie said, lumbering to her feet and stoking up the fire. 'See what his terms are first.'

Athena frowned. 'Terms?'

'Oh aye, these things are usually contractual agreements drawn up by lawyers.'

'Good heavens, how on earth do you know that?'

Millie chuckled. 'You don't get to be my age without learning a thing or two.'

Athena actually smiled at that. 'What aren't you telling me, Millie? Do you have dark secrets in your past?'

'Never you mind about that. If you're so set on doing this — '

'I am.' Athena scratched Boris's ears even more violently. 'I must. For all our sakes.'

'Especially your own. You've fallen for him hard, I know.'

'That helps, of course. I can't pretend I'm indifferent. Besides, if I was, I wouldn't do it, no matter how dire our situation.'

'I know that, lamb. Still, if you are determined, take my advice and insist upon a contract so that you know where you stand financially.'

'You don't make it sound very romantic, Millie.'

Millie laughed. 'You can have all the romance you want, once he's agreed to keep us all in style.'

Athena's glance clashed with Millie's, and her lips twitched. All the vicissitudes of the day warred inside her tired brain, the stresses and strains, pleasures and passions merged, and the two of them dissolved into fits of nervous laughter.

14

Eli returned to the party, brooding as he watched the long train of carts making their way down the driveway, wondering if Athena's was still amongst them. It was impossible to tell from this distance. Damnation, he hadn't handled things well just now! Time constraints and the crowds of people milling just feet away from them had made it impossible for him to insist she tell him what had frightened her so badly, why her husband had abandoned her, what or whom she and her sisters were hiding from.

Instead, he'd blurted out a request for her to become his mistress. Eli threw back his head, closed his eyes, and stifled a groan. What a fool! At first, he had been elated when she agreed to consider his proposition, but he could see now she would have agreed to anything simply to get away from him. He had probably frightened her off for good simply because he'd been thinking with the wrong part of his anatomy. Now he must face the unpalatable truth, which was that he might never see her again.

Impossible!

Eli's heart lurched, and he refused to accept that possibility. He'd only known her for a few days, but in that time she had managed to turn his well-organised existence on its head, and he couldn't imagine his life without her in it. She could never be what he wanted her to be, which was his wife, but they would find a way. Perhaps he was being selfish. Except he knew from the way she had responded to his kiss, his feelings were returned. She understood his dilemma, and they would reach an understanding. Somehow.

Eli became conscious of his mother sending him strange, considering looks, presumably because he had been absent for some time. Now he had rejoined his guests, but wasn't dancing attendance on any of his prospective brides.

The hell with that!

He strode into the drawing room and poured himself a substantial measure of brandy, downing it in two swallows. He refilled his glass and sipped more slowly this time, trying to figure out who had spooked Athena. She had been so carefree, her dazzling smile completely bewitching him, while they danced together. He had never seen her in such a light-hearted mood before. It was as if she had put aside all thoughts of the responsibilities that weighted so heavily on her slender shoulders and given

251

herself over to her own pleasures for once. Eli had wanted time to stand still.

Then something had happened to spoil it all.

But what? She had obviously caught sight of someone who scared her witless. Whoever it was, and it had to be a man, Eli would throttle him with his bare hands when he discovered his identity. A murderous rage consumed him as he thought about the cowardly, faceless blaggard who took pleasure from frightening a helpless woman. No one, but no one, scared his goddess and lived to tell the tale.

What connection that person had to her, and how it involved the law, Eli was at a loss to know. She was right in one respect. If the person was a relation who wielded legal powers over her, then he had right on his side, but that wouldn't deter Eli. He had power and influence enough to stop a dozen irate relations in their tracks. But first he would install Athena and the twins in Amulet House, where no one would be able to get to them. Even if she decided against becoming his mistress, he would still insist she take the house. He smiled to himself as it occurred to him that a house had never been more aptly named. It would suit his witchlike goddess perfectly.

Harry and Franklin joined Eli, bringing an end to his mental perambulations. He poured brandy for them both and forced himself to chat with them about nothing more taxing than their plans for the coming hunting season.

Then Baintree and Blake came in, too, and the relaxed atmosphere became strained. Eli had even less time for Blake than he did for Baintree, and was annoyed Charlotte's husband had just assumed he could bring him along. It wasn't the first time he had sprung an uninvited guest on them. Eli would need to talk to him about his habit of treating the Park as though *he* was its owner.

Blake was witty and charming, and the ladies were attracted to him. But Eli had never taken to him, and thought there was something sinister about the man. Blake's father was Lord Michael Blake, the younger brother of the Marquess of Trent. Blake himself was Lord Michael's second son and, apparently, a great favourite with his mother. The well-established family didn't lack for blunt, and Blake didn't appear to do anything with his time except gamble and cling to the Prince Regent's wild set, making him an ideal companion for Baintree in many respects.

Eli provided the new arrivals with brandy but was actually glad when the ladies found them and he no longer had to suffer Blake's annoyingly high-pitched voice relating endless raucous stories. Since they had all eaten so well at luncheon, his mother had arranged a light buffet supper, allowing the indoor servants to join what was left of the harvest party. There was no formality attaching to this meal, but Eli was still plagued by his four would-be brides the entire time. His training kicked in, and he entertained them with witty anecdotes, with no real idea of what was said or by whom.

All the while he was conscious of his mother's piercing gaze resting upon his profile. He might be able to fool the rest of the world, but she knew there was something on his mind that had nothing to do with his forthcoming nuptials. He could only hope she had the good sense not to cross-question him upon the matter.

He got through the evening, somehow, and retired to his chamber as soon as he politely could, but not to sleep. He needed to think this thing through. If Athena didn't meet him in the morning then he would go to the cottage and drag her out, forcibly if necessary. She *would* hear what he had to say to her, and that was an end to the matter. He also needed to think of another way to find out what bothered her so. Direct questioning clearly wouldn't work. She didn't trust him completely, which saddened but didn't surprise Eli. Someone had frightened or disappointed her so badly she was suspicious of everyone. But he would prove to her not everyone in the world was out to manipulate her. He would put himself out to earn her trust, because it was worth earning.

He was up before dawn, dressed in plain breeches and shirt, just as he had been on the morning when she rescued him. He wanted her to see him as an ordinary man, not an aristocrat. He saddled Byron himself, waving the surprised night-groom whose sleep he disturbed back to his cot in the tack room.

He cantered away from the Park and reached the hollow before he could expect to see Athena there. He dismounted, leaving Byron to graze, as he watched the dawn light filter through the leafy canopy, counting the moments until he could reasonably expect her to appear. Wondering if she would lose her nerve. He was deep in thought when he heard a twig snap behind him. He turned, and there she was, early morning mist shrouding her as she walked towards him wearing her old gown, hair floating loose around her shoulders. Relief flooded through Eli, and he sent her a heated smile, thinking she had never looked lovelier.

'You came.'

She stopped a short distance away from him. 'I said I would.'

They were awkward with one another, as though their passionate kiss had never taken place.

'Where is Boris?'

'I left him with the twins.'

Ah, of course, she was concerned for their safety. 'The men will be back to work on the cottage today. They will be quite safe.'

'I can't be away for long.'

'Then come.' He held out a hand and, after a moment's hesitation, she stepped forward and placed hers in it. The moment his fingers closed softly around her palm, he felt a strong surge of desire just from that simple contact. Her eyes widened, implying she felt it, too. 'Shall you mind riding behind me on Byron?'

'Not if Byron doesn't object.'

'Oh, he can be quite obliging.' He touched her face and lowered his voice. 'Just like his master.'

She swallowed and looked away from him, obviously nervous. 'Where are we going?'

'I want to show you Amulet House.'

'Amulet House?' There was a hint of amusement in her tone. 'What a peculiar name.'

'The house could have been named for

you, my sweet.' He so wanted to kiss her, but sensed the moment wasn't right. She didn't look as though she had slept well, and anxiety was making her both shy and skittish. 'Come.'

He whistled to Byron, who obediently trotted across. Eli swung himself easily into the saddle and then reached both hands down.

'Now it's my turn to help you onto Byron's back.'

She weighed nothing at all, and he lifted her from the ground with ease. She swung her leg agilely over Byron's quarters, and he then had the pleasure of feeling her belly pressed close against his own. She wrapped her arms around his waist and leaned her head against his shoulder.

'I could get used to this,' he told her, sending her a sensual smile over his shoulder as he pushed Byron forward.

Their journey skirted the village until they were approximately equal distance to it on its opposite side from Whispers' Hollow. Eli slowed Byron as they approached the house he hoped to persuade Athena to call home.

'We're here.'

He tried to see the house through her eyes. It was a square, solid building, standing in its own grounds of about an acre, no other buildings within sight. There was a spinney off to one side, common land on the other, and a small stream marked the end of the garden.

'This is it,' he said, riding around the house to a small stable at the back, acutely aware she hadn't said a word yet. He threw his right leg over Byron's withers and slid to the ground. Then he reached up to place his hands around Athena's waist and helped her down. An old groom emerged from the stables and took Byron's head.

'Morning, Walters,' Eli said.

'Your grace.'

Walters led Byron away, showing no interest in Eli or his guest. Walters was the soul of discretion, which was one of the reasons why he was such a good and trusted employee, rewarded well for his service.

'Who was that?' Athena asked.

'Walters looks after the grounds. His wife keeps the house tidy.'

Athena looked alarmed. 'Oh, is she inside now?'

'No, don't worry. I sent word I would be here early today and required the house to be empty. I thought you might be embarrassed, otherwise.'

'Thank you. I would have been.' She paused. 'I am. This is all so unexpected. I haven't had time to adjust to the idea.'

He touched her cheek. 'There's no need to worry, my love. I know this is strange for you. I don't want you to feel any pressure, but — '

She sent him a twisted smile. 'You can have no idea *how* strange. I never imagined it would come to this.'

'Do you find the idea so very repellent?'

At last, she met his gaze. 'You know I do not.'

'Then I'm glad.' He took her hand and led her towards the house. 'The Walters live in an apartment above the stable, which I imagine is where Mrs. Walters is now. There are rooms in the attics for more servants, as you will see in a moment. When you live here I shall hire more people to take care of you.'

'I haven't agreed to live here yet.'

'No, but I plan to persuade you. And, just so you know, my powers of persuasion are legendary.' He stood back, his arm wrapped lightly around her waist, and looked at the house with her. 'What do you think of it?'

★　★　★

As elegant as its owner and just as compelling, the house appeared to be the answer to Athena's prayers. She had laughed at Eli when he said it could have been named for her, but secretly she agreed. It had to be a

259

good omen, surely? She was still reeling from riding behind him on Byron, and the excuse it provided her with to snuggle up against his lovely broad back and breathe in the intoxicating scent of the man she loved. He was hatless and his dark hair had blown back in the breeze as they sped along, touching her face, just as Eli had indelibly touched her vulnerable heart.

'Who's land is this?'

'The house and spinney is the farthest most reach of the Winsdale estate. The common is . . . well, common land. The occasional rider comes by, and sometimes local famers graze their livestock on it, but mostly no one comes here.'

'Are you telling me that because you think it is what I wish to hear?'

'I'm merely telling you the truth.' His glance was faintly condemning. 'I would never lie to you, Athena.'

'No, sorry, of course you would not. You must forgive me. I'm nervous, and I tend to blurt out the first thing that comes into my head when I am nervous.'

'There is absolutely nothing to be nervous about.' He stood behind her, his arms circling her waist. 'I will take care of you. All of you.' His lips brushed the top of her head. 'Never doubt it.'

She tilted her head backwards and smiled up at him. 'Yes,' she replied softly. 'I know you will.'

'There's a lovely sunny patch on the south side of the house,' he said, pointing to it. 'I thought your herbs would grow well there.'

Athena thought the same thing. She could already imagine herself here, tending to them, with nothing more taxing on her mind than the rate of their growth or the twins latest escapade.

'Come, let me show you inside.'

Eli reached into his pocket, produced a key and opened the door. They were greeted by the smell of beeswax polish and a feeling of homeliness that told Athena this was a happy house. Athena exclaimed with delight when she stepped into a drawing room with large windows looking out over the gardens. She could just imagine a roaring fire dancing up the chimney on a cold winter's night, her and Eli cuddled up on a sofa in front of it as she rested her head in his lap and he stroked her hair. Except that wouldn't happen too often, she reminded herself. He would soon have a wife to think of, as well as his duties at Winsdale Park to keep him occupied. Jealousy cramped her insides. *Don't think of those things. Think only of yourself and the twins.*

There was a dining room and small study on the ground floor, as well as a wide entrance vestibule, all of which were spotlessly clean and elegantly, yet simply furnished.

'The kitchens are through there,' he said, waving a hand. 'Do you want to see them?'

'Perhaps later. Show me the rest first.'

'So eager, Mrs. Defoe,' he said with a mocking smile.

'You have a wife to select, and I have work to do,' she replied, turning away so he wouldn't see her blush.

'You have a happy knack for spoiling the mood,' he said, lightly swatting her behind as she ascended the stairs ahead of him.

'Just being practical, your grace.'

There were four bedrooms on the first floor, the largest sharing the same extensive view over the gardens and countryside beyond as she had just admired from the drawing room. She entered it with a hesitant step, knowing what would happen in it very soon, if she agreed to Eli's proposition. Surprised at just how desperately she actually wanted it to happen.

Eli led her to the window, and they sat together on the bench seat in its embrasure. He took one of her hands in both of his, turned it over, and planted a soft kiss in the centre of her palm.

'If you agree to become my mistress, I will have my lawyers draw up a binding agreement, just so you know where you stand. I will support you and the twins, bearing all of your expenses as well as providing them with a governess.'

Athena gasped. 'You would do that?'

'With gladness in my heart. They will be my responsibility, as you will be. I will supply you with a clothing allowance and pay all the household expenses.' He lowered his voice. 'I will also acknowledge and support any children resulting from our liaison.'

'Children?'

He sent her a quizzical smile. 'They would be a distinct possibility, because you need to be aware I won't be able to keep my hands off your delectable body.'

'Oh, I hadn't thought as far as children.'

'You will associate with no man other than me during the term of our agreement. Should that agreement come to an end for any reason, and provided you haven't broken the terms of it, I will supply you with somewhere to live and the means by which to live there unless or until you take up with another man.'

'You make it all sound so . . . well, formal.' Athena shuddered.

'That isn't how I feel about you, sweet Athena, but it would be best to establish where we both stand.'

She stared out of the window, too embarrassed to look at him. 'Yes, I expect you're
right.'

'I know what a big step this is for you, and
so the contract is for your peace of mind
more than mine.'

'If you say so.'

'What terms would you like to impose, my
sweet?'

Athena shook her head. 'I can't think of
anything at all.'

'Then you agree?' He looked disbelieving,
quite unlike the autocratic duke she had
come to know over recent days. A slow,
devastating smile broke across his face. 'You
won't run away from me?'

Part of Athena wanted to run. Being a
mistress — even Eli's — seemed tawdry
somehow, and she was still worried about the
effect it would have on the twins. But she was
also tired, so tired of running. Besides, there
didn't seem to be anywhere she could run to
without Blake finding her — not unless she
gave up lace-making, and then how would
she support herself? And she loved Eli with a
passion that stole her breath away.

Yes, she could definitely do this.

'No, Eli,' she said, reaching up to stroke the
curve of his face. 'I won't run away, and I

agree to be your mistress.'

'Oh my love!'

He stood up, pulled her into his arms and kissed her with brutal passion, crushing her lips as firmly as he crushed her body against his. His large hands splayed her back as he pulled her closer still, causing desire and a deep, alien longing to pool deliciously inside her. When he released her and she looked into his eyes, she gasped at the deep, burning passion reflected in them.

'I have one additional condition of my own,' he said. 'When the agreement is signed, you must tell me who you are running from and why. I can't properly protect you unless I know.'

'Yes, all right.' She had planned to tell him today and get it over with. She would, too, but there was something else she needed to do first.

'I had best get that agreement drawn up pretty damned quick,' he said, breathing hard. 'I want you and the twins safely installed here without delay.'

'We don't need an agreement in order to seal our . . . er, agreement,' she said, astonished by her own forwardness.

The plain fact of the matter was that she needed to do this now. Not only was she aroused, but she was also anxious, worried

265

she might not live up to his expectations, or lose her nerve all together. She could just tell him she was an unmarried virgin, of course. But her sixth sense told her he would call the whole thing off if she did and refuse to consummate their union. Having waited all these years, eschewing all attempts to drag her to the altar, Athena was now in a tearing hurry to find out what all the fuss was about. She trusted him, but still wouldn't tell him about Blake until *after* she had lain with him. She was convinced that was the correct order in which to do things even if, deep in her heart, Athena knew that having only part of Eli would never be enough for her.

'Athena, are you sure?'

'I trust you not to renege,' she said lightly.

'Oh, my darling!'

Eli swept her into his arms and carried her to the bed, his intensely passionate smile sending spirals of anticipation roiling through her. He laid her down and then sat beside her, running thick strands of her hair repeatedly through his fingers.

'That's something else I've wanted to do since first meeting you,' he said softly, dropping a line of delicate kisses across her brow. 'I wish I had more time this morning. I would like to lick and kiss every inch of you, and

266

spend the entire morning doing it. You are so beautiful, so deserving of my adoration, so perfect in every way that I sometimes think I must have dreamed you.'

'I'm real, Eli, and I won't break.' She sent him a sultry smile. 'Just love me.'

'That,' he replied with a wicked smile, 'will be no hardship whatsoever.'

His lips worked their way down her neck, nipping and kissing, filling her with such selfish longing that it relieved her anxiety about her ability to satisfy him.

'The first thing we must do is to rid you of this awful gown,' he said softly. 'Have you any idea how much I dislike it? It simply isn't good enough for you. We can do a lot better, and as soon I have replenished your wardrobe, I never wish to see this one again.'

'Yes, your grace,' she replied meekly, biting her lip to prevent herself from smiling. 'Are you always this dominant?'

'You think this is me being dominant?' He raised a brow and then swooped to kiss the end of her nose. 'My darling, you have a lot to learn about me. Now, sit up and let me at the ties.'

This was it, Athena thought through a haze of passion, the point of no return. She sat up and Eli found the ties that held her gown up without difficultly. Clearly ladies' apparel held no mysteries for him. The bodice fell away, and she quickly lay back down, her breasts now covered just by her thin cotton chemise. He looked down at her, an awed expression on his face, and then blew softly on each nipple in turn. She felt them harden almost painfully.

'So responsive,' he said softly as one hand moved to caress a breast. 'And a perfect fit for my hands, just as I knew you would be.'

The firm touch of his fingers on her sensitive flesh made it seem as though she was floating outside of herself. It was a wonderful, sensual feeling, and she squirmed in an effort to push herself more firmly into his hand.

'So eager,' he said for a second time.

His hand went to her other breast while his lips came down to capture her opposite nipple. The pleasure was so intense Athena cried out. This was beyond her wildest expectations, and she revelled in the feel of his fingers and lips, sucking and moulding until she was in a frenzy of desire.

'Lift your hips,' he said softly.

She did so and felt her gown slide down her legs. He threw it on the floor and smiled when he saw her wearing one of the petticoats he had bought her.

'At least I don't have to be ashamed of that,' she said.

'You don't have to be ashamed of anything, angel, and nor will you be from this point on. I guarantee it.'

He knelt at the end of the bed, removed her shoes and then slowly worked his fingers up her legs, rolling her stockings down, one at a time. Little mewing noises slipped past her lips. It was impossible to remain silent, or passive, in the face of such provocation. She was encouraged when Eli didn't seem to think there was anything unusual about her reaction. With her stockings gone, he picked up one of her feet and sucked each toe in turn, tugging at them gently with his teeth before applying his magical tongue to her instep. The pleasure was so intense that Athena's body elevated from the bed.

'Shush! Stay still or I shall have to tie you down.'

'You wouldn't!'

His rich, throaty chuckle echoed off the walls of the room. 'I'm in charge, angel. Never forget that.'

She harrumphed. 'As if I could.'

'Lift your hips again, darling. I need to look at you as nature intended.'

Eager now rather than embarrassed, Athena did as he asked, glad she wasn't expected to do anything other than lie there and allow him to take control. She looked up at him, expecting at any moment for her reservations to return. When he had rendered her naked, and she saw an expression of wonder and appreciation settle upon his features, she felt empowered. Eli could probably select women at his whim, and she wasn't quite so naïve as to imagine many had not preceded her. And yet she, with her complete lack of experience, could hold him in her thrall. It was what gave her confidence a timely boost as the love she felt for her complex, highly intelligent, and domineering duke swamped her senses.

'You are so beautiful!'

He spoke in a tone of reverent awe, his eyes dark and intense as he stood back and simply stared at her. He reached down and ran a finger gently down the middle of her body, starting between her breasts, ending in the tangle of curly hair between her legs. Athena shuddered as a kernel of sensation, unfamiliar and primitive, flooded her body.

'You like to be touched?'

'Yes.'

Eli muttered an oath beneath his breath and shed his clothes in seconds.

'I wanted to take more time, but you make it impossible.'

Oh my! His cock was enormous. It jutted aggressively from the juncture of his tapering hips and strong thighs, looking angry, twitching as though impatient to be inside her. Athena seriously doubted it would fit. She would disappoint him, he would decide against her, and her appointment to the position of duke's mistress would be over before it had begun.

Eli joined her on the bed, and she reached out a hand to touch his chest. The last time she had seen it he had been chopping logs at the cottage, and she had been filled with the same urgent need to touch him then, never imagining it would happen. Her fingers tangled with the hairs on it, and she tugged gently.

'I must have you now,' he said, an urgent edge to his voice.

His large, hot body covered hers as he took his weight on his arms and nudged her legs apart with his knee. His lips covered hers as his fingers parted her creamy folds, slick and yielding to his touch. She tensed when she felt the tip of his cock replace his fingers, then went with her instincts and lifted her hips to welcome him inside. He deepened the kiss as he moved slowly into her — and hit the barrier that was her virginity. Athena tensed, wondering if he would notice. Well of course he would! She sensed his confusion as he tried again, with the same result.

Abruptly he stopped kissing her and withdrew. Her eyes flew open and stared directly into his very angry ones.

'You've never done this before?'

15

Eli ran a hand through his hair, broadsided by this totally unexpected turn of events. He stared at Athena with a mixture of anger and confusion clouding his thoughts. What the devil was going on? Was this some elaborate ruse to trap him? He wouldn't have thought Athena capable of such behaviour but, still in the grips of the most desperate passion, he couldn't come up with any other explanation.

He stood up, pulled his breeches back on and threw her chemise at her.

'Get dressed,' he said curtly.

'Eli, let me explain.'

'Oh, you'll explain all right, madam, but you will do it fully dressed.'

He turned away from her as he pulled on his shirt, stockings, and boots, clumsy in his anger and disappointment. He had thought she was different, but it transpired she was no better than all the rest. As soon as she noticed his interest in her, she exploited it, using it to get him into a compromising position. He was willing to wager some aggrieved relative would have burst through the door as soon as the deed was done, demanding that he pay dearly for his passion.

Eli's disillusionment was absolute.

He heard her struggling with her gown, but made no move to help her. Right now, he could barely look at her and didn't trust himself to touch her. In spite of what she had tried to do to him, he still wanted her with a desperate passion that rid him of both common sense and the ability to think in a rational manner.

'Eli.' She was dressed and moved in front of him, forcing him to look her way. 'Why are you so angry with me?'

Could she really be that naïve? 'There is no Mr. Defoe,' he said starkly.

'No, obviously not.'

'Then why the devil did you pretend otherwise?'

'I needed somewhere to live. Would your steward have rented the cottage to a single woman? Besides, I would not have been left in peace, even if he could have been persuaded to do so.'

Eli grunted. 'But you have not yet told me why you were so desperate.'

'I wanted to . . . er, consummate our agreement before telling you my life story,' she replied, turning away from him, her face flaming. 'Had you not found me to your liking, I didn't want you to feel you owed me anything.'

Was he supposed to believe such flim-flam? 'You imagined I would take your virginity without a second thought?' He was filled with virulent rage. 'What sort of man do you take me for?'

She shrugged. 'It's what men do.'

'Not honourable men.' He sent her a damning glare. 'What precisely did you expect to get in return for your sacrifice, Athena?'

'Nothing. I merely . . . just a minute.' The colour left her face, a visible tremor swept through her body, and he seriously thought she might strike him. 'You think I came here, deliberately to . . . to exploit you in some way?'

'What else am I supposed to think? You're a beautiful woman, and I doubt I'm the first man who's wanted to do . . . to do what we almost just did.' She couldn't expect marriage, but she must have been sure of a very handsome pay day. 'Why me? Why now? That's what I would give much to know.'

She cast him a look of bitter contempt through eyes shimmering with unshed tears. Eli refused to be taken in by her genuine-seeming anger. She had much to be angry about since he had managed to resist her charms and ruined her conniving scheme.

'Take me home,' she said, turning away

from him again. 'I was wrong about you, and we have nothing more to say to one another.'

Eli flexed his jaw. 'It seems we both made a mistake.'

She walked with great dignity towards the door, her spine rigidly upright, head held high. Through the blinding mist of his rage and regret, niggling little doubts crept into Eli's mind, and he wondered if he had misjudged her in some way. He wanted to call her back and make her tell him what had really happened to bring her here. There was definitely something. She couldn't have known their paths would cross and would not have rented his cottage with the expectation of their doing so. But he was still too angry to give her the benefit of the doubt and strode to the door ahead of her, threw it open, and offered her a sarcastic bow as she walked through it.

Walters was nowhere to be seen. Eli collected Byron himself, replaced his saddle and climbed aboard. He took Athena's hands and pulled her up behind him. She pulled hers free as soon as she settled and didn't wrap her arms around him this time. Instead, she must have held on to the back of the saddle. Eli told himself it was just as well, he didn't want to touch her any more than absolutely necessary and rode back to the

Hollow as fast as he safely could. As soon as they arrived, she slid from behind him before he could dismount to help her and strode off in the direction of the cottage without saying a word.

'Just a moment,' he said, going after her. 'I'll walk with you.'

'There's no need,' she replied without turning around. 'I'm quite familiar with the way.'

'You didn't answer my question, Athena.'

'What question?'

'Why me? Why now?'

She paused, and this time did turn to face him, fixing him with a disillusioned look. 'Because I wanted you to be the one,' she said softly.

And then, she was gone, slipping through the trees like a shadow.

He followed her, watching from a distance until he saw her disappear inside. He then turned back to Byron, rode back to the Park at breakneck speed, wondering why he felt so guilty when he was the injured party. Wondering why he missed Athena so desperately already when it was obvious she had used their accidental meeting to her advantage and tried to trick him.

He entered the house by the usual side door and ran up the stairs. His mother was leaving her apartment as he walked past it.

'Ah, Eli, there you are. A word, if you please.'

'Not now, Mother,' he replied, not breaking stride as he headed for his study, conscious of his mother's startled *oh* and her gaze boring into his back.

He sat behind his desk for several minutes, willing himself to calm down and think the matter through rationally. Was Athena really out to gull him? Just because most people were, it didn't mean she was amongst their number. Damn it, he should have insisted she tell him who she was so afraid of, then he would have been in a better position to judge. He had been too angry at the time to listen, and probably wouldn't have believed her anyway, but he still should have made her talk. He thumped the surface of his desk in frustration, barely conscious of the resulting pain that throbbed through his fist. Why was he so quick to judge her? Why did he find it so hard to think coherently when he was anywhere near her?

If the fear she had shown the previous day at the harvest dance had been fabricated then he ought to refer her to the manager of the Savoy Theatre. She would make a fortune treading the boards.

Eli continued to fester, feeling ill-used and yet bereft since he could no longer look

278

forward to Athena's engaging company. He sat bolt upright when he realised why he felt so uneasy. She was in danger in that cottage. She would either run, or live in fear of being attacked. He must guard her against both possibilities. He wasn't ready to let her go, at least until they had spoken again, and the thought of anyone harming her filled him with a murderous rage beyond anything he had ever known before.

Eli yanked the bell pull, tapping his fingers as he waited for Jessop to respond. Her words whirled around inside his brain as he did so, stark in their honesty.

Because I wanted you to be the one.

Athena, Oh, what I would give to make that possible! But you lied to me.

'Your grace.' His secretary entered the room and stood in front of his desk.

'Arrange around the clock watch on Mrs. Defoe's cottage,' he said curtly. 'She must be protected at all costs and not permitted to leave. Don't allow her to see the men keeping guard. The workers will be there during the day, but your men must watch for strangers who have no business being there.'

'Do we know whom those strangers might be, your grace?'

'No. Just tell them to be alert and not take any chances.'

'I will see to it at once, your grace.'

'Any news from Nottingham?'

'No, your grace.'

'Dammit, what's taking so long?'

Eli knew he was being unreasonable. It would have taken Jessop's man at least two days to get there, and then he would have had to establish contacts. Even so, he became more uneasy with each hour that passed.

'Let me know as soon as you hear anything. And send Salter to me. I have an errand for him to run in Portsmouth.'

★ ★ ★

'You look like you've lost a shilling and found a farthing, lamb.' Millie looked up from her baking and frowned when Athena stormed into the cottage. 'Was it so very bad?'

Athena flapped her arms around, still feeling his rejection like an arrow to the heart. Still smarting from his harsh, unjust words. 'It went horribly wrong.'

'Tell me everything.' Millie wiped her hands, and guided Athena to a chair beside the fire. 'I'm sure it can't have been that bad.'

'No, it was worse than bad. It was a disaster.'

Athena, angry and upset, related the entire humiliating event.

'I didn't realise you intended to go through with it today,' Millie said, sending Athena an appraising look. 'I thought you would wait for the contract.'

'Yes, that's what I should have done. I can quite see that now.' Athena managed a ghost of a smile. 'Would I have been in breach of contract for not telling him beforehand I was a virgin, do you suppose?'

'What made you suggest lying with him immediately?'

Athena sighed. 'I wanted to, Millie. All those years of waiting, never even being tempted, and then suddenly, it was all I could think about.' She impatiently brushed away an errant tear. 'I thought he felt the same way.'

'He did, lamb. I'm sure of it.'

'No, Millie. He was so cold, so angry with me. It was a side of him I've never seen before. He thought I had done it deliberately to exploit him in some way, you see. He wouldn't even look at me once he knew.'

'Well, I suppose you can't blame him for that.'

'Whose side are you on?' Athena demanded hotly.

'Put yourself in his position. He told you himself when you first met that people always want something from him.'

'I suppose, but I thought I meant more to him than that.'

'You do, never doubt it. I've seen the way he looks at you. When he's had a chance to calm down and consider the matter, I'm sure he will want to apologise. It's just a shame you didn't get to tell him what we're running from. That would have convinced him, if anything could, especially since the facts would be easy enough to verify.'

'I was going to . . . afterwards.' She shook her head. 'Oh well, it's too late now. The trust is gone. Shame, the house was lovely,' she added, trying to sound casual and failing dismally.

'What shall we do then?'

'Move, I suppose.' Athena sighed, wearied by the thought. 'But we'll wait until the duke's house party is over and his guests have left. If Blake has found out, or even suspects we're here, he will appear sometime today. You know how he never learned to be patient, so we must be vigilant. We shall simply remain hidden away for two more days, and that will give us a chance to lay proper plans.' She flashed a wry grin, even though her heart broke anew each time she considered Eli's cold reaction to her situation. Surely, a woman he admired offering him the gift of her virginity was a cause for celebration, not

282

censure? 'I hear Scotland is quite beautiful,' she added whimsically.

'If you want to go gallivanting north of the border, you can go without me, miss.' Millie puffed out her ample chest. 'Those Celts are barbarians. We would never be safe in our beds.'

Athena flashed a brief smile, thinking she at least would be perfectly safe since her virginity clearly didn't have a value beyond rubies. 'No, Millie, not Scotland. I shall think of somewhere easier to reach.'

'There's no rush, lamb. If Blake leaves Winsdale again without finding us, surely we'll be safer here than anywhere?'

That was true, except Athena couldn't possible remain anywhere near Winsdale Park and have daily reminders of the man she loved. And who had rejected her.

Millie lumbered to her feet when the workmen came in to continue renewing the staircase. At least the cottage now smelled of freshly sawn wood rather than mould, even if they wouldn't be here long enough to enjoy the new interior.

'I'd best go and sit with the girls,' she said.

'Have something to eat first.'

'No, Millie. I'm not hungry. Anything I attempted to eat would only stick in my throat.'

Millie tutted, but one of the workmen distracted her, and Athena took the opportunity to slip into the other room and join the twins. Their bright chatter helped to distract her, as did the calming normality of making lace.

'Are you all right, Athena?' Selene asked at once point. 'You're very quiet.'

'And very pale,' Lyssa added.

'Oh, it's nothing. I'm just tired and have a slight headache.'

'You're not ill?' they asked together.

Their anxious faces brought her to her senses, and she summoned up a genuine smile of reassurance. They had suffered so much with the loss of their mother and father within a year of one another, and then all the unpleasantness that had followed. Athena had been their only constant throughout it all. They were still very vulnerable and would be devastated if anything happened to her.

'I'm really quite well, girls,' she said. 'Now, you have yet to tell me everything that happened to you at the dance yesterday. I want to hear it all. Whom did you each dance with? Did you enjoy it as much as you thought you would?'

Suitably distracted, the girls were soon chatting away again and seemed not to notice when Athena fell into gloomy contemplation and sometimes forgot to respond to them.

The workmen left at dusk, and the cottage was theirs again. Millie was about to serve supper when Boris sat up and let forth with a volley of barks.

'Someone is outside,' Athena said tersely.

'One of the men probably forgot something,' Selene said, heading for the door.

'Stay where you are!' Athena's sharp voice stopped her sister in her tracks. 'Let me go.'

Athena peeped through the window, unsure if she was more relieved or distressed when she saw Eli's curricle outside. He wasn't driving it, though, and that was a disappointment. The man who alighted from the conveyance was the same one she had encountered on the track on the day Eli had his accident. He came up to the door and Athena opened it before he could knock, stepping outside to speak to him in private.

'Good evening, madam,' he said, doffing his hat. 'I am Salter, his grace's valet.'

'Good evening, Mr. Salter,' Athena replied cautiously. 'Are you lost?'

'No, I come with a message from his grace.'

'I see.'

He probably wants us to leave his property, Athena thought, accepting the note the man handed her with a heavy heart. He certainly hadn't wasted any time getting over his brief interest in her. Her fingers trembled — a combination of worry and anger — as she broke the seal.

Athena, she read. *We didn't finish our conversation this morning, for which I hold myself responsible. I can't get away for the next two days, but we have a masquerade ball at the Park tomorrow evening. Please come. My man will collect you, and we will be at leisure to resolve our differences then. Eli*

Athena paced about in front of the cottage, unsure what to make of the note and it's rather cold wording. That he wanted to speak to her at all implied he no longer thought her a fortune hunter, or worse, but he hadn't actually apologised.

'His grace sent a gown and mask for you to wear, if you agree to come,' Mr. Salter said, looking rather bored, indicating a package on the seat of the curricle, as though her acceptance was a foregone conclusion. Presumably, he acted as the duke's go-between in such matters on a regular basis and never met with any opposition. Just for the hell of it, Athena was severely tempted to send him packing, but something stronger than her own determination prevented her.

'Just a moment.'

Athena went back inside and told Millie and the astonished twins about the invitation.

'What should I do?' she asked Millie.

'You should go,' Millie replied without hesitation.

'He should have apologised.'

'About what?' Selene asked.

'This *is* an apology,' Millie replied, ignoring Selene's question. 'He has a lot on his mind at the moment, and you will never forgive yourself if we leave here without clearing the air.'

'Are we leaving again?' Lyssa asked.

'Oh, but we like it here.'

'How can we talk at a masquerade when he will have four women vying for his attention the entire time?'

'Easily, you will all be masked, and therefore unrecognisable,' Millie said. 'It makes a big difference to the way people behave, so I'm told. Besides, you will also get to see how the land lays with our other, er friend.'

She was referring to Blake, and it *did* make sense, Athena supposed. But dare she be in the same room with her hated foe? The thought of being unidentifiable held a certain allure. And the prospect of seeing Eli again, even if it was just to give him a piece of her mind, set her pulses racing.

'It's not like you to back down from a challenge, lamb,' Millie said mildly. No, it was not. Athena elevated her chin. She was no coward. She would do this and emerge from it with her dignity intact, even if it left her heart in smithereens.

'And nor shall I from this one,' she replied with determination.

Athena returned outside and told Mr. Salter she agreed. He smiled, as though he had always known she would and insisted upon carrying the gown and mask into the cottage himself.

'I shall be here tomorrow evening at ten to collect you myself.'

'So late?'

'There is to be a dinner for the party guests, and then other attendees will arrive from all over the area. There will be over a hundred in total.'

Meaning Athena would pass unnoticed in such a crowd.

'Very well. I look forward to seeing you tomorrow, Mr. Salter.'

'Oh, Athena,' Selene said the moment Salter had left, and she and Lyssa eagerly unwrapped the gown. 'Just look at this.'

'It must have cost a fortune, Athena,' Lyssa added. 'The duke must be violently in love with you.'

'Dukes don't fall in love with lace-makers, Lyssa.'

'Well then, they should,' Selene replied

stoutly. 'You are at least as good as those stuffy women up at the Park who want to marry him. And far prettier.'

'You haven't looked at your gown, Athena,' Lyssa said impatiently.

Athena did look, and gasped. The magnificent gown Eli had sent for her to wear was of shimmering pale blue silk, with a silver spangled overskirt. The bodice was sewn with exquisite silver beads, as was the flounce. There were petticoats of the finest quality to go with it. What was it about Eli and petticoats, she wondered, unable to suppress a smile. The matching slippers would, she was sure, be a perfect fit. The half-mask was trimmed with silver beads and extravagant plumes. It was a perfect, confidence-giving disguise, meaning for once she could face Eli on equal terms, if only in terms of her apparel.

'He must have sent to Portsmouth for it,' she said, almost to herself. 'Where else would he have found such a beautiful garment at such short notice?'

16

She was coming. Eli had been in torment until Salter returned from the cottage and told him she had agreed to attend the masquerade. He knew he had upset her, hadn't thought she would want to know him anymore, and couldn't altogether blame her for that. Her disinterest in his influential position was one of the many things that attracted him to her. But, in spite of her fears, in a few short hours Eli would see her again.

He was more nervous than he had been on his first day at his preparatory school, which was saying a lot. As a young boy of eight, he had been left to his own devices amongst a sea of older boys. They all seemed to know each other and looked upon the new intake, nervously huddled together in one corner of the cavernous hall, with speculative interest. Eli had rightly assumed his induction into school life would be brutal, teaching him hard lessons about life that were not on the curriculum.

He stood stock still as Salter brushed imaginary specs from his immaculate coat, trying to anticipate what he would say to her, and she to him. That he owed her an apology was beyond question. He had over-reacted and knew without her having to convince him she hadn't been trying to manipulate him for her own ends. It disgusted him that he could have entertained such a thought about his goddess and knew he thoroughly deserved her derision. When it came to Athena, he lost all sense of proportion because he wanted so badly for her to be what she appeared to be. He wanted even more for her to place her trust in him and allow him to slay all her dragons for her. By his stupid reaction to the precious gift she had offered him, he had made that task ten times harder to achieve.

But, he reminded himself, she was coming. She was actually coming, so there must be some small hope for him still. Now, the rest was up to him.

'Still nothing from Jessop's man in Nottingham?' he asked Salter.

'No, your grace, but Jessop lives in expectation of hearing something any hour now.'

'Interrupt me if he does. I don't care what I'm doing.'

'As your grace wishes.'

For once, the prospect of the dinner to come didn't fill him with dread. He could fend off his would-be brides easily enough, and would get through it by separating his mind from his body — another skill he had learned at school. Masks wouldn't be donned until the meal was completed and the rest of the guests had arrived. Eli planned to behave charmingly to his devoted followers until that happened, if only to put his mother at her ease. He had been able to avoid the conversation she'd wished to have with him when he returned from his assignation with Athena. She had arranged so many entertainments for her guests, all of which required his participation, and there had been no time for private talks. But still, he had been conscious of her watching him speculatively, as though she understood his turmoil. All the time they didn't actually discuss it, he could avoid the serious disagreement that was bound to ensue.

His mother might think she understood him, but she never could. She didn't believe in love, only duty and responsibility. She had made that very plain, and he almost felt sorry for her.

Almost.

If he hadn't fallen headlong for Athena, then he wouldn't be suffering such torment now. *Love goes by haps; Some Cupid kills with arrows, some with traps*, Eli thought, borrowing Athena's habit of quoting the great bard.

'Right, Salter, that will suffice. Remember to find me if there's any news.'

'Your grace.'

Eli went down and was swallowed up by the throng of waiting guests. Men and women alike appeared to have something of import to say to him. Eli listened without absorbing a word. The ladies had outdone themselves in their efforts to shine, as if they knew this evening would be the defining moment in their respective campaigns to win his favour. Tonight Eli would have to make a decision about which lady to propose to and, although the information hadn't been made public, everyone here appeared aware of it. There was an air of expectation about the gathering, and Eli felt himself under close scrutiny the whole time, his every word and action noticed by ambitious mothers, his own included. He longed for the dinner to be over, at which time everyone would don their masks, the rest of their guests would arrive . . . Athena would arrive.

At last, the ballroom was full, and he and his mother had greeted all the arriving guests personally. The musicians struck up, the dance floor began to fill, but could never be as full as Eli's heart. There was still an hour to go before he could expect her to arrive. It felt more like a year. To allay his mother's anxieties, Eli danced one cotillion with Lady Caroline, and a country dance with Lady Cynthia. Then he retired to the back of the ballroom, from where he would be able to see her the moment she entered. He couldn't risk her being waylaid by any other men before she reached his side. In his current frame of mind, he would call out any other men who so much as looked at her for too long.

He sensed her presence even before he turned and saw her walking towards him, a vision in blue and silver, half of her face covered by her mask, her hips swaying to the accompaniment of softly rustling silk. Her beauty took Eli's breath away, momentarily rooting him to the spot, too enthralled to move. This is how she should always be dressed, and would be if he could find a way to salvage himself in her eyes. He sent her a devastating smile as she reached his side and paused, clearly recognising him in spite of his plain black mask. He took her gloved hand and kissed the back of it, his eyes not once leaving her face. There was tension in the air between them as he reacted in the time-honoured fashion to the mere contact with her hand. Her eyes were enormous through the slits in the mask, her attitude guarded as she dropped a curtsey.

'Your grace,' she said in a neutral tone.

'You wished to speak with me?'

'Yes, I . . . ' The musicians struck up the first waltz of the evening. It would be sheer folly to take to the floor with her, but Eli was taken over by a reckless desire to behave . . . well, recklessly. He had had more than enough of being sensible. 'My dance, I believe, Mrs. Defoe,' he said, holding out his hand.

She hesitated. 'We should not. People will notice.'

'This is a masquerade. We are supposed to be anonymous.'

'You believe that?'

'Not for a minute, but I would still waltz with you.' He caressed her with his eyes. 'Come, sweet mysterious lady, where is your courage?'

Her eyes burned with an unfathomable emotion as a smile flirted with her lips and she placed her hand in his. He led her to the floor and swung her into his arms, leading her assuredly into the steps. He was vaguely aware of his four would-be brides, all watching from the edge of the dance with varying degrees of curiosity and annoyance. He was aware, too, of his mother's countenance, from which she hadn't troubled to remove a frown. He ignored them all and concentrated on his goddess, who was as light as air in his arms, her feet hardly appearing to touch the ground as they followed his lead.

'I'm so very sorry,' he said, conscious of other couples swirling past them and so keeping his voice to a low, gravelly whisper.

'Are you?'

'You bring out the worst in me, Athena. I overreacted.'

'I didn't think being untouched was such a very bad thing.'

He swept her into a turn. 'It is the most precious gift a woman can bestow upon a man, but it took me by surprise. I believed you were married.'

'Yes, I suppose you did. You must forgive me, but I've never found myself in such a situation before and was unsure how to react.'

'No man has been crass enough to invite you to be his mistress,' Eli said with a self-depreciating grin. 'Other than me.'

'I have received my share of propositions. None of them have tempted me.'

'Then I am honoured, but even more ashamed of myself for handling it all wrong.'

'Shush, people will hear us. We shouldn't talk of this here, on a dance floor. We shouldn't talk of it at all when you're supposed to be . . . well, concentrating on other matters.'

'Damn the other matters!' he cried passionately. 'I only care about you.'

She swallowed. 'But I offered myself to

you, and you made it very plain you don't want me.'

'Can you have any idea how comprehensively wrong you are? I have never wanted anything more in my entire life.'

'Oh, Eli.' She shook her head. 'I wonder why you asked me to come at all. I wanted to be your mistress. Now I know it would be a mistake.' She met his gaze and held it as they swirled around the floor. 'It would never be enough for me, you see.'

He tightened the arm circling her waist. 'Yes,' he replied desolately. 'I do see, only too well, because I feel the exact same way.'

The dance came to an end. 'Come this way,' he said. 'We will slip out the back of the ballroom and go somewhere private where we can at least talk to one another.'

'All right. I will come with you.'

With Athena's hand on his arm, Eli led her away. He had almost reached the back of the room when Salter appeared at his side.

'Forgive the intrusion, your grace, but you asked to be informed when Jessop had news for you.'

Damn it, so he had. Of all the wretched timing. He briefly considered leaving Jessop to stew, but he still wasn't entirely sure Athena would tell him the truth about her circumstances, and he was equally determined she would. Whatever else they could or could not be to one another, at least he could give her back her freedom, so she didn't have to hide away from the world. Jessop's news must be significant, or he wouldn't have interrupted Eli in the middle of a ball. Yes, he would see him immediately. It would only take a moment or two. But what to do with Athena in the meantime? In whose care could he safely leave her? Harry obliging stepped up to them at that moment, resolving the problem.

'Harry, I entrust Mrs. Defoe to your care for five minutes while I attend to an important matter. Guard her well or I'll know the reason why.'

'Oh, you can rely on me, big brother,' Harry replied with an irrepressible grin. 'I shall take the greatest possible care of her, never doubt it.'

'Hmm.' He sent a warning frown to Harry, and a heated smile to Athena. 'I shall be just a few minutes,' he said softly to her.

'Take all the time you need. I shall be perfectly content with Lord Shelton's company.'

Eli rolled her eyes. 'That's what worries me.'

★   ★   ★

Athena watched Eli go, wondering what could be so urgent that he must leave her almost as soon as she got here. He had seemed so determined to talk to her. Was his life always like this, and he had to put other interests ahead of his own? It was evident he was torn between whatever duty it was that distracted him and remaining with her. So she forgave him. It was so exhausting being in his presence, she almost welcomed this respite, and yet, also missed him already. Lord Shelton was a very adequate substitute, but no more than that.

'You look exquisite,' Lord Shelton said, bright eyes shining from behind his mask.

'Thank you. And I rejoice in seeing you looking so well. Are the inhalations still working?'

'Yes. I've cut them down to one a day and feel better by the minute.' He shook his head, sending a shock of dark hair cascading across his brow. 'It really is remarkable.'

'Then I am glad.'

'Would you like to dance?'

'No, thank you. Not unless you wish to. I'm rather enjoying watching everyone. It's not very often I attend such gatherings, you see.'

'You're a student of human nature?'

'No, Lord Shelton. I'm merely inquisitive.'

He laughed. 'Come, let's take a stroll instead then.'

He offered her his arm and she placed her hand upon it. 'Has the duke decided upon a bride yet?' Athena forced herself to ask.

'Oh,' Lord Shelton replied, fixing her with a candid gaze. 'I rather think he has.'

'Then he ought to be kind to all four ladies and put them out of their misery.'

'All five, don't you mean?'

Athena blinked. 'I beg your pardon.'

'Oh, don't mind me. I expect — '

A footman approached them and handed a note to Athena. 'I was asked by a gentleman to give this to you, madam.'

'To me?' Athena assumed it must be Eli, playing some sort of game. 'Are you sure?'

'Quite sure.'

'Oh, all right, thank you.'

'Aren't you going to open it?' Lord Shelton asked. 'It looks as though Eli has frightened off some ardent admirer who has been reduced to the written word.'

'Really, Lord Shelton, you do have the most active imagination.'

'I beg to differ. You see, I saw the expressions on the gentlemen's faces when you were dancing with Eli. Every single one of them envied Eli his good fortune, including me. As to the ladies, I fear your popularity doesn't extend to their ranks. That, of course, means you are an unmitigated success.'

'Lord Shelton!' She laughed. 'Just to prove you wrong, I shall open the note straight away and allow you to read it.'

But Athena was gripped by the most dreadful premonition. She knew it wasn't from Eli and was equally sure it couldn't bring good news. She had been so taken up by Eli, and now Lord Shelton, that she hadn't even thought to look for Blake amongst the masked gentlemen thronging the room. How could she have forgotten herself to such an extent? Dear God, had she been recognised? She was foolish to have come at all. She had allowed her heart to rule her head, and she was now paying a heavy price for her momentary lapse.

Someone touched Lord Shelton's arm, taking his attention away from her. It was now or never. She had to know. Athena steeled herself to open the note and gasped, her worst fears realised. Inside were two silver crucifixes on chains — the ones Selene and Lyssa had received on their tenth birthday as gifts from their parents and always wore.

Blake, it had to be Blake.

He had known she was here all along and had been playing her as masterfully as the orchestra was playing *La Boulangere.* Something had happened to the twins — the worst possible thing.

Blake had them.

Quickly, Athena scanned the note.

Come to the nest you visited yesterday with your lover. Come alone. Tell no one. If you are not here within the hour I will have them instead of you.

The note wasn't signed, but then it didn't need to be. Blake had the twins and Athena didn't doubt for a moment he would harm them, despoil them, if she didn't offer herself to him instead. This time he held the winning hand, and she couldn't afford to call his bluff. He had taken them to Amulet House, obviously, but how the devil did he know about that? Had he followed them there? No, they would have noticed someone, surely. Athena had spotted a lone horseman on the common land when she glanced out of the bedroom window, but Eli had told her people rode there so she thought nothing more about it. Yea gods, how could she have been so careless?

Lord Shelton turned back to her and frowned.

'Are you all right, Mrs. Defoe? You have gone deathly pale.'

'Just a little overheated,' she replied,

quickly pushing the note and necklaces into her tiny reticule, hoping he wouldn't point out that overheated people didn't pale. 'It is so crowded in here.'

'Then let us walk on the terrace.'

'If you don't mind,' she replied, frantically trying to think of the best, the quickest, way to get away from there, 'I first need to visit the withdrawing room.'

'By all means. I will show you where it is.'

Promising to join Lord Shelton on the terrace in a short while, Athena waited a moment for him to clear the area and then dashed back down the corridor leading directly to the stables. The beautiful silver-grey cloak with midnight blue lining that Eli had given her to wear with the gown was where Salter had left it, draped in solitary splendour across a chair by the door. Not many guests arrived at such events by the side entrance, it seemed.

She hastily put it on and covered her head with the hood, her mind working fast as she tried to decide how to get back to the cottage in a hurry. She must go there first. It was on her way to Amulet House anyway, since she had no idea how to reach it if she went through the village. She needed to satisfy herself that Millie was all right. Dear God, don't let him have harmed dear, faithful

Millie. She would satisfy herself on that score and learn anything she could from her about Blake's state of mind. Not that there was much she didn't already know. She was well aware what he wanted — what he had always wanted.

Her.

And this time there was nothing she could do to stop him because the alternative was unthinkable.

A violent rage consumed Athena and with it came a deathly calm. This thing would be over, one way or another, by the end of the night. No more running, no more hiding. No matter the cost to her, the twins would be safe. Blake could take her virtue, but he could never take her heart or own her in the way he had wished to for so long. He would know it, and it would infuriate him. He craved her total obedience and adoration. He was used to captivating women with his charm, money, and good looks, and his failure to impress Athena had resulted in this wretched obsession of his. If Athena had pretended to be taken in by him, perhaps they wouldn't have reached this sorry state of affairs. But Athena wasn't good at pretence. She knew what he was really capable of, what depraved depths he regularly trawled in pursuit of his pleasures, without caring about the lives he ruined in the process. Given that knowledge, she was incapable of treating him with anything other than total disdain.

Now the time had come, as she supposed she had always known it would, Athena would do whatever was necessary to save the twins. Then she would wait for Blake to lower his guard and kill him the first opportunity she got. She would use her knowledge of herbs to poison him. No one would ever guess.

Thus resolved, Athena walked sedately into the stable yard, forcing herself not to break into a run, even though Blake had given her little time and every second could be vital. She saw the curricle that had transported her there, the horse still between the shafts. She also recognised the groom who had taken care of Meg and walked up to him with a confident smile on her lips.

'I'm ready to return to the cottage now,' she said. 'His grace said you would be kind enough to drive me.'

The groom looked surprised by the request, but didn't question it. 'Very good, ma'am.'

'Oh botheration. I've left my reticule on the table outside the withdrawing room,' she said, ensuring the reticule in question was well concealed beneath the folds of her cloak. 'How very careless of me. Would you be kind enough to fetch it for me?' *Please go yourself and don't send someone else.* 'I shall just sit in the curricle and wait.'

'Of course. I shall be but a minute.'

Please take longer than that. The yard was alive with activity, which worked in Athena's favour. All the grooms attending the carriages of the visiting guests were gathered together, chatting amongst themselves and completely ignoring Athena. As soon as Eli's man disappeared inside the house she sprang into action. Picking up the reins, she encouraged the horse forward by slapping them sharply on its rump. With Meg this would have resulted in a reluctant step forward. Startled, this horse sprang from a standstill into a fast trot, almost knocking Athena backwards off the seat. She steadied herself and guided the horse down the driveway as fast as she dared to drive it.

Her path was well lit with an extravagant number of flambeaux, but that wouldn't be the case once she reached the track to the cottage. Still, one problem at a time. First of all, she needed to get out of the grounds without being challenged. She glanced up at the star-studded sky. It was a fine, clear night, the moon almost full, lending additional light. At least the elements were on her side.

She turned out of the gates to Winsdale Park without mishap and set the horse to a steady trot on the track that led to her cottage, wishing she could go faster, and knowing it would be folly to try it. The track was full of potholes and divots. Meg's sturdy hooves could cope with them, but this fine animal was altogether another matter, and laming one of Eli's horses would achieve nothing but additional delay. The mask obscured her vision. She untied it and left it where it fell, her heart palpitating as she drew steadily closer to the cottage, and she wondered what she would find there.

She pulled the curricle to a stop outside and jumped down. Catching her toe in the hem of her lovely gown in her haste, she heard it rip. With a strangled oath, she picked up her skirts and ran into the cottage. She found Millie stretched full length on the floor, groaning. Athena's blood ran cold as she dashed up to her and felt her forehead.

'Millie, talk to me. Are you all right? Where does it hurt?'

'Millie blinked up at her, tears in her eyes. 'Blake,' she gasped. 'He came. Took the twins. Couldn't stop him. I tried.'

'Shush, it's all right. I'll get them back. Can you stand?'

Athena helped Millie up, and saw a large lump forming on the side of her head. She touched it gently and Millie winced.

'I tried to bash him with a frying pan. His man grabbed it and bashed me right back.' Millie looked furious at her failure. 'He knocked me clean out, and when I opened my eyes the twins were gone. I couldn't . . . couldn't seem to get up.'

'Come and sit down.'

Athena helped Millie into a chair, then grabbed a cool cloth for her to hold against her head. 'I don't have time to linger,' she explained, untying her gown and stepping out of it, dropping it carelessly on the floor. 'He sent me a note. The twins are at Amulet House. I have to go there, or . . . well, you don't need me to tell you what he will do to them.'

Tears spilled down Millie's face. 'I'm so sorry, lamb. I let you down.'

'Nonsense. Blake's been one step ahead of us all the time. I'm just glad you, at least, are okay. And so will the twins be. I shall make sure of that.'

'Aye, but at what cost to you?'

'Never mind that.' Athena suddenly realised something was missing. 'Where's Boris? Why didn't he warn you?'

'He was outside, doing his business. I heard him bark once, then Blake and his man burst in, and I didn't have time to think about him.'

'Oh no!'

Athena dragged breeches and a shirt out of her valise, thrust her feet into her trusty half-boots and went outside, calling to Boris. A pathetic whimper reached her from the outhouse. She opened the door and Boris slunk out on his belly, as though he knew he had failed in his duty. She stroked his head, and he winced, filling Athena with another wave of lethal rage. Of all the cowardly, dastardly . . . the ogre had struck Boris with something. Hard. It explained why he hadn't come to the twins' aid.

'Come on, Boris, if you can walk you can come with me and get your revenge.'

Still subdued, Boris licked her hand and followed her into the cottage.

'I have to leave you now, Millie, time's a-wasting. Will you be all right?'

'I'm fine. It's you I'm worried about. I just wish I could come, too.'

'Don't worry, I'll take Boris, and a few other little surprises with me.'

Athena took the dagger she always carried from her valise and stuck it in the back of her breeches. She also selected a couple of other, less obvious, weapons before donning her lovely velvet cloak again.

Back outside, Athena swiftly released Eli's horse from the curricle, removed all of its harness except for its bridle and leapt onto it, bareback. The driving reins were far too long for riding, so she knotted them to the appropriate length, waved to Millie and pushed the horse forward. Boris loped along beside her, and then took the lead, as if knowing the horse needed help to see the track. Athena wished she had taken more note of the route Eli had followed, instead of enjoying the feel of his solid back and daydreaming about surrendering to him. Fortunately, there was only one spot in which she had to make a choice. Since common sense told her the left hand track would have led her straight back to the village it was an easy decision to make.

The horse stumbled on several occasions, almost tipping Athena over its head. Fortunately, she was a competent rider and they both survived. Their pace, by necessity, was frustratingly slow. Moonlight filtered through the thick canopy of leaves in places, but without Boris trotting assuredly in front of them, she never would have been able to see the path.

Surely, it had been more than an hour since she left the ball? Even if it was, Athena had to believe Blake wouldn't actually harm the twins. If he did then he would no longer have any hold over her. That chilling thought brought her some comfort, and she pushed on through trees that seemed sinister, their shapes distorted, in the near-darkness. Branches brushed against her arms, scratching her, impairing her progress, but not halting it. Nothing would prevent her from reaching the twins, who must be truly terrified and wondering what was keeping her.

She was starting to think she must have missed a turn somewhere, when she finally saw dim light in the distance. Amulet House. They had made it. Seeing no point in stealth, Athena made her way to the stable yard and put the horse in the first vacant stall she came to. There was a curricle in the yard, the horses still harnessed to it, and a riding horse, still saddled. She wondered what had happened to Mr. and Mrs. Walters. She hoped no harm had come to them, but couldn't pause to look for them, not quite yet.

'Right, Boris,' she said, carefully touching the dog's head. 'Let's go and find the girls.'

She walked up to the front door and saw light spilling from behind the drawing room curtains, as well as from the master bedroom she had briefly shared with Eli. How long ago that seemed now. Her instinct was to go charging in with Boris and order him to attack. But they had somehow got the better of Boris once already, and her dog was weak from the injury he had incurred in that skirmish. It would be better to exercise caution.

'Stay.' She spoke firmly and pointed to a spot immediately outside the front door. Boris whimpered in protest, but obediently went down on his belly. 'Good boy. Don't worry. You will get your chance if I have any say in the matter.'

Athena took a deep breath and walked straight in, careful to leave the door ajar so Boris could respond when she summoned him. She pushed the door to the drawing room open and was confronted by the sight of the twins, gagged and tied to wooden chairs, but otherwise seemingly unharmed. Their eyes widened with a combination of alarm and relief when they saw Athena. Blake's valet was standing directly behind them, looking impassive, and very large. Blake himself stood in front of the fireplace, an impossibly smug smile gracing his vile features.

'Ah, there you are, Athena,' he said. 'How nice of you to join us.'

17

Eli strode into his study. Jessop and a man whose attire bore the dust and grime of travel awaited him there.

'Close the door and stay with us, Salter,' Eli pulled off his mask and sat behind his desk. When he looked more closely at the man with Jessop, he noticed both his eyes were blackened, and he had a deep cut on the side of his chin. He stood awkwardly as though further damage had been inflicted upon his body. 'Good heavens, whatever happened to you?'

'This is Manning, your grace,' Jessop replied before the man could speak. 'He is the person I sent to Nottingham on your behalf.'

'I didn't send him to go brawling. Sit down both of you. Manning looks as though he's about to fall down. First compose yourself, and then tell me what you have discovered for me.'

'I know the identity of the lady you sent me to make enquires about, your grace,' Manning said without preamble.

'Good man.' Eli looked at him expectantly. 'Well, don't keep it to yourself.'

'Have you ever heard of Cunningham lace?'

Eli shook his head. 'Can't say as I have.'

'It's handmade lace, your grace. Very fine handmade lace, produced as a cottage industry in Nottingham. It was started by Miss Athena's grandmother.'

'Athena is actually Miss Cunningham?'

'No, she's a Moncrieff. Her father was Lord Moncrieff's youngest son.'

'Moncrieff?' This was starting to make sense. Athena's ladylike qualities, her education, everything. 'The Marquess of Worcester. That Moncrieff?'

'Yes, your grace. He fell for Miss Cunningham, and married her against his father's wishes. The father cut off all relations with him, and the oldest brother didn't want to know him, either. His wife's lace saved them from ruin. Mrs. Moncrieff made the patterns and employed the workers, who made the lace in their own homes. Moncrieff found markets for it. It was, and still would be, much sought after. Mrs. Moncrieff taught her daughters to follow in her footsteps, and Miss Athena took over responsibility for production when her mother became unwell two years ago.'

'Is she still alive?'

'No, your grace. She fell victim to consumption, but survived longer than people expected

314

her to. The mother was knowledgeable about herbal remedies, another skill she passed down to her eldest daughter. Those remedies eased her suffering and prolonged her life. She died a little more than a year ago. The father, by all accounts, was bereft, lost the will to carry on, and Miss Athena had to look after him as well as keeping the coffers full. Anyway, six months after the mother died, the father was also found dead, murdered — '

'Murdered?' Eli sat up and scowled. 'Are you sure?'

'Quite sure. It created a scandal locally. Mr. Moncrieff was found in a derelict part of town and no one could understand what business would have taken him there. His throat was cut, and he was robbed of all his valuables, but the culprits were never caught.'

Eli leaned his chin in his head as he listened, feeling great sympathy for Athena and her sisters. 'Why didn't Athena . . . Miss Moncrieff, carry on making Cunningham lace? It sounds as though there was a good living to be had from it.'

'So there was, your grace. It was the father's will that caused the problem. He still kept in touch with his middle brother. Joseph Moncrieff has a small estate just outside of Nottingham, where the estranged family were welcomed on a regular basis.'

Hmm, this Joseph Moncrieff presumably traded on his connection to the Moncrieff marquisate to assure his place in local society. It would account for Athena's high standard of education, social mores, and so much else about her character besides. His mother had remarked upon her poise and self-assurance after Athena had taken luncheon with her and Susan. Even ladies accustomed to the ways of society were generally struck dumb in the duchess's presence. A ghost of a smile flirted with Eli's lips. His Athena had, apparently, been an exception to the rule. It hadn't particularly surprised Eli at the time. Now he better understood why.

'The uncle became the girls' guardian under the terms of the will, I take it.'

'Exactly so, your grace.'

'But Miss Moncrieff was of age by then,' Eli said sharply. 'He could wield no influence over her.'

'Yes, your grace, but her twin sisters were not.'

'Ah, I see, and the uncle could keep them apart, if he so chose.' Eli was filled with a blinding rage at the thought of it. He knew how close Athena was to her sisters, which was hardly surprising since they only had each other now. It also made sense of Athena's comment about Eli not being above the law. She was in hiding because she was protecting her sisters from their guardian. But why? 'What purpose would it serve to separate them?' he asked aloud.

'Everyone I spoke to agreed there was profit in Cunningham lace, but the uncle didn't agree. He felt improper control was wielded over the workers because they were scattered all over the district, and were trusted with the materials given to them, no proper accounts being kept of them. He fixed on the idea of the new lacemaking machinery, convinced it would eclipse the far more time consuming handmade version. Apparently, he had tried to convince his brother to go down that route when he was still alive, but Miss Moncrieff's father would have none of it. Anyway, the uncle stopped paying the outworkers and laid out a large sum of money on machinery.'

'The fool!'

'Quite so, your grace. He and Miss Moncrieff argued quite violently about his methods, apparently. The uncle seemed to think they could replicate the unique Cunningham lace by machine. It has a large 'C' worked into each piece,' Manning added in response to Eli's quizzical look. 'Miss Moncrieff argued that no one would be fooled, which proved to be the case.'

'So, let me guess, Moncrieff found himself in dun territory.'

'Indeed. And in the meantime, Miss Moncrieff and her sisters defiantly continued to produce handmade lace, although they couldn't pay any of the ladies who had previously worked for them, and so new supplies of the lace gradually dwindled.'

'And became more sought-after in the process, I shouldn't wonder.'

'Most likely so, your grace. But Miss Moncrieff was very distressed about the ladies, whom she looked upon as friends, no longer being in a position to earn the money they relied upon to feed their families.'

Eli could see the hypocrisy. Athena had been running the business with her father as a figurehead, and no one thought anything of it. But with her father gone and her uncle unwilling to put his support behind the hand-made lace, as a single woman, she couldn't continue alone.

'Her uncle became very unpopular in Nottingham when he was unmoved by the women's plight.'

'Good!'

'Unfortunately for him, he hadn't done proper research into machine lace. He was late into a market that was already overcrowded. When the machine-made Cunningham lace failed to take, he couldn't find buyers for his products. Still, he had to pay for his machines, so he needed a partner.'

Eli didn't like the sound of that. 'Did he find one, Manning?'

'Yes, your grace, but the man was only prepared to invest under certain conditions?'

'Which were?'

'Miss Moncrieff's hand in marriage.'

Eli half rose from his chair. 'The devil he did!'

'Miss Moncrieff adamantly refused. She hated the man and all he stood for. Apparently, he had an appalling reputation locally and, even though he was rich and well-connected, she wanted nothing to do with him. Her uncle, desperate for the man's patronage, tried everything to persuade her, by all accounts. Threats, bribery, guilt.' Eli snorted. 'None of it worked, so he separated her from the twins, telling her she would never see them again unless she remembered the duty she owed to her uncle and did as she was told. They somehow escaped and have been on the run ever since.'

'You've done well, Manning,' Eli said, understanding Athena so much better now. 'How did you come by all the bruises?'

He winced, presumably at the memory. 'I must have asked one too many questions, your grace. Certain people asked me, very forcibly, why I was asking them and who had sent me. I did not reveal your grace's name.'

'Thank you, Manning. You will be rewarded for your loyalty. Presumably your attackers worked for Miss Moncrieff's admirer.'

'No, your grace, for the uncle. I heard his name and the name of his estate mentioned when they thought I was insensible.'

'My God, he must be desperate.'

'He stands to lose everything and blames Miss Moncrieff for his misfortunes.'

'Does he indeed?' Eli would be having a not-so-friendly discussion with Joseph Moncrieff in the very near future, he decided, grinding his jaw. 'But you haven't yet told me the name of the blaggard who was so insistent upon Miss Moncrieff's hand.'

'Oh, I beg your pardon, your grace. It was a Mr. Blake.'

'Blake!'

Perdition, now it all made sense! Blake had been beside Baintree at the harvest dance when Athena had gone so pale. Eli had always known there was something off about the man. He jumped from his chair. Athena would be safe at this moment with Harry, but he had foolishly invited her to the house at the same time her worst enemy was in residence. Why the devil had she come? Why take the risk of showing herself, even if she was masked? *Oh, Athena, you little fool, don't you realise how recognisable you are? No one who knows you could doubt your identity.* And where was Blake now? Eli wanted the satisfaction of planting him a facer. Well, several actually.

The door burst open and Harry stood there, wheezing, deathly pale.

'What the devil's happened?' Eli asked, jumping out of his chair.

'It's Athena,' he gasped. 'She's gone.'

★ ★ ★

Athena looked at her sisters, checking for signs of physical injury. If he had harmed so much as a hair on either of their heads, Athena would make him pay dearly. He would pay anyway. It was all a matter of degree.

'I think I preferred you in the blue ball gown.' Blake ran his gaze down the length of her body in an insolently speculative manner and smacked his lips together. 'But those breeches have a certain allure, too. They cling rather enticingly to certain parts of your person. I hope you don't make a habit of going out dressed in such a fashion. Not that I will permit it in future. I don't want others seeing what's mine.'

'Kidnapping children,' Athena replied indolently. 'That's a low blow, even by your own standards. I really had no idea you were quite that desperate.'

'Ah, but they are no longer children.' Blake's gaze rested upon the twins in a way that made Athena's skin crawl.

'Of course.' Athena flapped a hand. If she showed how frightened she actually was it would give him the upper hand. He already had it, of course, but she had no plans to make matters easy for him. Would he really take her against her will? The answer was as obvious as the question was futile. He would hardly have gone to all this trouble just to prove a point. 'Men like you wouldn't bother to make the distinction.'

'There's nothing I wouldn't do to get your attention, my dear. You ought to know that much by now.' He shook a finger at her. 'You really shouldn't have run away. You only have yourself to blame for your sisters' discomfort.'

'Is it really necessary to restrain and gag them? I am here, that's what you wanted, and you've made your point. There can be no profit in restraining them.'

'They kick like the very devil.'

'What did you expect? Quiet capitulation?' Athena forced a laugh past her lips. 'They are my sisters, after all.'

'Remove their gags,' Blake said to his man. 'But if either of them utters a sound they will go back on, tighter still.' He sent Athena a sickly-sweet smile. 'There, you see how reasonable I can be when you do as I ask.'

Reasonable wasn't a word Athena would use in the same sentence as Blake's name, but refrained from saying so. There was a fine line to be trod between appeasement and goading this dangerously unbalanced individual.

'Thank you,' she said curtly.

As soon as the gags were removed, the twins flexed their jaws. Athena was furious to see lines etched in their cheeks where the gags had been tied so tightly. That was cruel and unnecessary, another reason for Blake to pay dearly.

'Are you all right?' Athena asked, crouching in front of them. 'Did they harm you?'

'No, but we harmed them,' Selene said with considerable satisfaction.

'We kicked them both,' Lyssa explained. 'Hard. Just like you said we should.'

'And I scratched *him*,' Selene added, pointing a defiant finger at Blake. Athena, who had avoided looking directly at him until that point, noticed a long scratch, coated with dried blood, down the side of his face.

'You did well, girls.' She turned to Blake. 'So what happens now?' She saw hunger in his eye when he looked at her, and she thought she probably knew the answer to that. 'I still refuse to marry you, if that's what you're hoping for, and you can't seriously expect to get away with kidnapping all three of us.'

'Marriage? Who said anything about marriage?' Blake's greedy expression gave way to a jealous glare. 'I saw you at the harvest dance, down the side of that barn with Winsdale, acting no better than a whore. You with all your haughty disdain.' His eyes blazed with resentment. 'You've done nothing but sneer at me, pretending I'm beneath your notice, when the reverse is actually true. But still, I was willing to lower myself and marry you. I was prepared to give you a life of comfort, and the protection of my name, when I could just as easily have taken what I wanted by force.'

'You could have tried,' Athena replied, taken aback by his violently passionate tirade.

'And I would have succeeded. Perhaps that's what I should have done, and then I would have recovered from . . . well, from whatever it is about you that holds me captive.' Blake shook his head as though his feelings still mystified him. 'Your uncle wouldn't have protected you. He was far too anxious for my help to care what happened to you. And yet, I respected your standards, only to see you give yourself to a man who hasn't the slightest interest in matrimony. Which begs the question, why would I be interested in marrying a duke's doxy?'

'Why indeed?' Athena's tone was caustic. She added a careless shrug for good measure. 'You're wasting everyone's time. I most emphatically don't want anything to do with you, and you now feel the same way about me, apparently, so why this charade?'

'Nobody takes what's mine and expects to get away with it!' Blake was falling apart in front of her eyes, which made him both unpredictable and dangerous. She had known there was a spoiled, depraved side to his character, which was the main reason why she hadn't saved her family by marrying the man. He had always kept his debauched nature hidden from her — until now. 'You still fascinate me, sweet Athena, in spite of everything. I do so enjoy a challenge, you see, and you are *the* most challenging woman in all of England. You've led me a merry dance, but that will make the prize all the sweeter.'

'You're deluded if you think I'll willingly surrender to you.'

'Oh, I hope you will not. I would so much prefer it if you fought me every step of the way.'

Athena sent him a damning glance. 'Be careful what you wish for.'

'You gave yourself to him. Now I want the same. You owe it to me after all the trouble you've put me to.'

Athena tossed her head. 'I owe you nothing.'

'If you please me, I shall marry you anyway and save your uncle's miserable hide into the bargain. If not, I shall keep the three of you somewhere, and enjoy myself. So, too, will my friends when I've had my fill.'

Athena hid her alarm by laughing in his face. 'How long do you suppose it will be before Millie raises the alarm?'

'The old hag is dead.'

'No!' Selene and Lyssa cried together, looking devastated.

'Sorry to disappoint you, but you didn't hit her hard enough.' She quirked a brow. 'Out of practise at attacking old ladies, are you?'

'What?' Blake's gaze swung accusingly to his henchman, who merely shrugged. 'It doesn't matter. There's nothing she can do until morning, and we will all be long gone by then.'

Fear trickled down Athena's spine. Why, oh why, hadn't she let Eli know where she would be? Because she had known Blake really was depraved enough to harm the twins if she failed to arrive within the prescribed timescale, or if she didn't come alone. Even so, she ought to have told him, and her failure to think rationally left her with no option but to delay Blake here until help could arrive. If not, he would spirit them all away to God alone knew where and no one would ever find them.

Harry and the groom would have missed her by now, and Eli would come after her. She had to believe that. His first port of call would be the cottage, and Millie would tell him where she was. All she had to do was keep Blake bragging about how clever he was to have found her, and buy herself some time that way. The only alternative was to whistle to Boris. He would come at once, but he couldn't tackle Blake and his man at the same time because they were standing in different parts of the room. His man had a knife in his hand and the twins right in front of him, helplessly bound to chairs.

No, she couldn't risk any harm coming to her defenceless sisters.

She had one final weapon in her armoury. If necessary, she would go upstairs with Blake and allow him to do his worst. Bile rose in her throat at the thought of his hands pawing at her. But she would go through with it if she had to — anything to save the girls from a similar ordeal — but only if she couldn't outwit him by playing upon his vanity.

'How did you know where we were?' she asked.

'Oh, that was pure chance. I can't take any credit for it really. I just happened to be in Brighton, playing cards with Baintree. He was complaining like the devil about having to come down here and watch Winsdale choose a bride. Terrible bore, he said it would be. Then he went on to mention Winsdale had almost killed himself, falling from his horse. He had heard all about it in a letter from his doting wife. Seems he was rescued by a woman who knew all about herbs.' He cocked an indolent brow at Athena. 'Does that sound like anyone you know?'

'Do go on. I'm intrigued.'

'Well, it just got better and better after that. Seems this paragon had also helped Shelton with his wheezy chest.' Blake put his hand on his own chest and mimicked loud, exaggerated breathing. He appeared to think he was amusing, but he was the only person in the room to laugh. 'Not only that, but Baintree's wife was green with envy over a lace ribbon this miracle-worker had given to her sister. It was as though you were sending me a direct message, sweet Athena.' He blew her a kiss. 'Come and get me. I want you to really,

Blake, but I don't know how to reach you. And so, I simply wangled an invitation out of Baintree. He's not the brightest spark in the tinderbox, so that was easily achieved since he treats the duke's place as though it was his own.'

Damnation, Athena had always known it would be a risk selling their lace. That's why they had avoided putting the distinctive 'C' anywhere in the finished products, reducing their value, but helping to hide their identity. Choosing an area to settle where there were so many grand houses meant there was more likely to be customers for their wares, but the chances of being recognised increased exponentially. It was all Eli's fault. If he hadn't been disobliging enough to fall from his horse, practically beneath her nose, they would have been safe still.

'You must be very proud,' she said scathingly. 'But how did you know about this place?'

'Oh, I thought you saw me riding across the common when you were here with Winsdale.' His eyes darkened with anger. 'Or were you too taken up with what he was doing to you to notice?'

'You didn't follow us here through the woods, so how — '

'The servants' hall,' he replied succinctly.

329

'An endless source of useful information, I always find. My man simply asked if there was anywhere on the estate used for, er . . . shall we say, ducal assignations. You're not his first, of course, my dear. Sorry if that knowledge oversets you, but there it is. They all knew about this place. It's quite a family tradition dating back several generations, apparently. Having seen your wanton behaviour at the side of the barn, I knew the duke would be back for more.' His eyes glistened with hostility. 'It was simply a case of figuring out when. His mother had his daylight and evening hours accounted for. And so, I went to the trouble of rousing myself early and watching to see if he left the stables at first light. When he did, I knew where he would be. I wanted to believe you would not but, of course, I was wrong about that.'

'Why would I not be?' she asked, knowing it was dangerous to provoke him when he was clearly so jealous. But the alternative — having him run out of words and drag her upstairs — was even more unpalatable. 'The duke is everything you are not.'

He reached out and slapped the side of her face so hard that her head snapped back. The twins cried out, but Blake's man flashed his knife at them and they quieted. Athena rubbed the side of her face, conscious of the tangy taste of blood on her tongue. He had split her lip open. Hot tears pricked her eyes, but she kept them in check. It absolutely wouldn't do to show the slightest signs of weakness in front of this bombastic bully.

'There, now you've made me hurt you. Why did you have to do that?'

The feel of his fingertips gently brushing against her sore face was almost worse than his violence. The man's moods were as unpredictable as they were mercurial, which is what made him so dangerous. He was obsessive, and completely unstable. She thought of the knife, tucked into the back of her breeches, and the urge to use it had never been greater. But, of course, she couldn't. The twins would pay dearly for her actions if she did.

'When I saw you arrive at the dance tonight, I knew my opportunity had arisen. Otherwise, I would have been put to the inconvenience of leaving here at the end of the party, allowing you to think you were safe, and then coming back again to fetch you. So much better this way.'

'And we wouldn't wish to inconvenience you,' Athena replied scathingly.

'Enough words!' he said in another abrupt mood swing.

Without warning, he reached forward and

grabbed her forearm so tightly he was bound to leave bruises. She almost laughed as the thought flashed through her mind. A few insignificant bruises would be the least of her problems. He unfastened her cloak and threw it at the twins to hold. His free hand moved behind her waist. He laughed as he withdrew the dagger from where he was supposed to find it and slipped it into his coat pocket.

'So predictable, Athena. You almost disappoint me. Come.'

His hold on her was so tight she had no choice but to follow him towards the door, her heart plummeting at the thought of what would soon follow.

'Athena!' the twins cried her name in unison, their eyes huge with fear.

'It will be all right,' she said, knowing it was very much not all right. 'I shall be back directly.'

One glance at their stricken faces, and she knew she couldn't just give in like a wilting violet. She had to do something to gain the upper hand. In the vestibule, she noticed the front door still ajar. She had forgotten all about Boris. Dare she?

Yes! Blake's man wouldn't really harm two innocent children, would he? She was about to whistle to her dog when Blake noticed the open door and kicked it closed. The sound of it slamming echoed through her head, an audible reminder of just how badly she had mishandled everything. Blake dragged her towards the stairs, telling her he was quite prepared to carry her up if she wasn't willing to walk.

Athena walked.

18

Eli forced his brother to sit before he collapsed through lack of breath.

'Tell me what happened,' he said, striving to remain calm.

'Someone delivered a note to her in the ballroom. She thought it was from you.'

Eli shook his head, fear trickling through him. Blake! 'Why would I send her a note?' he asked no one in particular.

'I have no idea,' Harry replied. 'Anyway, I was distracted by someone while she read it. When I looked back her face was the colour of chalk, but she said nothing was wrong. It was just that she was hot.'

'Hot people don't go pale, Harry,' Eli said in a tone of mild rebuke.

'No, sorry, I didn't think. I offered to take her outside for some air, but she said she needed the withdrawing room. I conducted her there, but could hardly go inside with her. I walked down the corridor, waiting. Next thing I knew a footman came up looking for her reticule.'

'Her what?'

'It would be easier if Blackmore explains.'

Eli's head groom came into the room, looking shamefaced. It transpired that Athena had duped everyone, and taken off in one of Eli's curricles.

'How long ago did she leave?' Eli asked.

'She must have at least a twenty minute start,' Blackmore said, shuffling his feet uneasily. 'I couldn't come up here to look for her reticule, so had to find a footman to do it. He took some time looking, couldn't find it, and well — '

If Eli hadn't been so worried about Athena, he might almost have applauded her cunning. Why, oh why, hadn't she come to him as soon as she received Blake's note? What had he done to make her take off in such a tearing hurry? He must have the twins. It was the only explanation. Then he recalled the men he'd set to guard the cottage and his fears subsided.

'If Blake tried to get to the twins, your men would have intercepted him, Jessop?'

'Er no, your grace.' Jessop lowered his eyes. 'They are no longer there.'

'No longer there?' Eli bellowed the words. 'I gave strict instructions that a watch was to be kept on Mrs. Defoe and her family.'

'Begging your pardon, your grace, but you asked for a watch to be kept on Mrs. Defoe. Since she was here this evening, I didn't see

335

any reason to keep the men there. They were needed here.' Jessop looked shamefaced. 'I apologise.'

Eli wanted to separate the man's head from his shoulders, even though he had done nothing more than follow Eli's instructions — a little too literally.

'So we must assume he has the twins,' Eli muttered to himself. 'Salter, see if you can find Blake in the ballroom, although I suspect you will be unsuccessful. If he does happen to be here still, detain him, by force if necessary. Then arrange somewhere for Manning here to sleep. Have someone attend his wounds and give him something to eat. Jessop, you're with me.'

'Where are we going, your grace?'

'To Whispers' Hollow to see if we can find out what's happened to Miss Moncrieff.'

'I want to come,' Harry said.

'No, Harry, you're in no fit state.' Eli placed a hand on his shoulder. 'Stay here and keep Mother happy. If she wants to know where I am, stall her.'

'What shall I tell her?'

'Anything you like, just so long as it isn't the truth.'

Eli and Jessop pushed through the throng, Eli ignoring anyone who tried to waylay him. He saddled Byron while Jessop sought out his own mount and they were cantering down the driveway within five minutes of Harry's devastating news. Eli was furious with himself for putting her in danger, but more angry and disappointed with Athena for not running to him in her hour of need. Surely, by now, she knew he was at her service. Eli shook the thought away, accepting she must have had her reasons. Besides, getting angry would do no good. Angry people seldom made rational decisions, and so he forced himself to breathe deeply and calm down. What was done was done. They weren't far behind her and would hopefully get to her before any harm came to her.

They arrived at Whispers' Hollow to find his curricle in front of the cottage, without the horse. He banged on the door and was greeted by Millie, looking decidedly wobbly on her legs, brandishing a frying pan. She lowered it when she saw who it was and sank into the nearest chair. She had a very large lump on the side of her head. Someone had hit her with considerable force, and Eli knew precisely who that someone had to be.

Millie related all that had happened with commendable lack of emotion but great urgency, showing him the note that had started it all. Eli read it, curling his upper lip in disgust. At least now, he understood why she hadn't come to him.

'She took Boris with her,' Millie said.

'Ah, so she did one sensible thing.' Eli prepared to leave again. 'We will get them back, Millie, never fear. Remain here and we'll send word as soon as we can.'

'Don't let her do anything rash, your grace. She's like a tigress protecting her cubs when it comes to her sisters.' Millie choked on a sob. 'I dread to think what she would be prepared to sacrifice in order to save them. Blake is a deviant. He likes young girls, the younger the better. That's why Athena wanted nothing to do with him and was so worried when she learned he had the twins.'

Eli ground his jaw. 'The only sacrifice being made this night will be Blake's liberty. Come, Jessop, there's not a moment to lose.'

★   ★   ★

Blake dragged Athena into the master bedroom, where the curtains were closed and candles already burned. He had set his stage, fully expecting her to come. She had been hoping for darkness, but presumably he either wanted to look at her or didn't trust her if he couldn't see her. That was rather wise of him, since it definitely wouldn't be sensible to trust Athena in her present frame of mind. She was angry, frightened, and determined, rather like a wild animal backed into a corner with no option left to it, other than to fight its way out. Eli hadn't wanted her virginity when she gladly offered it to him. She was damned if she would sacrifice it to anyone else — especially not to Blake.

She tried not to think about how differently she had felt the last time she had been in this room with Eli. On that occasion, she had desperately wanted to be seduced but had failed in that ambition. She wasn't such an optimist as to expect a second failure, but she absolutely wouldn't be subdued without a fight.

Blake released his hold on her arm so he could push her with considerable force onto the bed. She fell there winded, temporarily unable to move. The pins holding her hair in place scattered, and it fell in a tangled profusion around her face. He looked down at her with a lustful expression as he threw off his coat and undid his neckcloth, casting that aside also. His waistcoat followed. Then he slowly unfastened his breeches. Oh God, this was really about to happen! She had to do something to slow him down.

Where the devil was Eli? Would he actually come, or had he become caught up in his mother's entertainments and word of her difficulties hadn't yet reached him? She hadn't stopped to consider that possibility and tried not to dwell upon it. He had invited her to the ball, so he was hardly likely to neglect her for long. But such were the demands upon his time that he *had* left her to deal with an emergency, which apparently surmounted his need to be with her.

Suddenly, Athena was no longer quite so confident he *would* come — at least not in time to save her virtue.

She was on her own.

'Do you have any idea how long I've waited to see you in such a position?' Blake asked, looking down at her through smouldering eyes. 'On your back, compliant, willing, ready for me.'

'You have anticipated forcing me then, since it's the only way for you to achieve that ambition. Even you can't be so deluded as to imagine I am here willingly.'

'Oh, you will soon change your tune.' He smirked at her. 'Once you discover what I have to offer you, you will be back for more. You're a very sensual woman, Athena. That's part of the attraction.'

'Does it make you happy to use your superior strength to subdue a woman, or are you so used to having to do so, you no longer think about it?'

He had the temerity to laugh at her. 'You make me happy, Athena. You're mine,' he added aggressively. 'I don't care what Winsdale did to you. I forgive you for your lapse. He turned your head, I dare say, but will never touch you again. If you want your sisters to be protected, then no one will ever touch you except me.'

'I don't trust you to keep your word.'

'You have no one to blame for that but yourself. I offered to do this the right way around. I was prepared to marry you against my family's wishes and make generous provision for your sisters, but you laughed in my face.' He wagged a finger beneath her nose, enjoying himself at her expense. 'You should not have laughed at me, Athena. I shall punish you for that at a more appropriate juncture. But for now, you will just have to trust me when I say I *will* do right by the twins.' He shrugged. 'What other choice do you have?'

'Your version of right and mine are two very different concepts.'

'You are delightful when you're roused.' He shook his head. 'Women nowadays are so compliant, whereas you . . .'

Without warning, he swooped. Grabbing a handful of her shirt, he ripped it open, leaving her chest exposed, just the thin fabric of her chemise covering her breasts. She gasped, unprepared for the violence and speed of his assault, although she ought to have anticipated it. The cool air in the room caused her nipples to pucker. God forbid he should think it had happened because she desired him.

'Ah, so beautiful.' She flinched when he reached down and touched one of her breasts. 'Did Winsdale take you? You might as well tell me. If he did not, then I shall be gentle, so it's in your best interests to be honest.'

Athena sent him a look of pure vitriol. 'He did not.'

Blake's eyes glowed like molten lava. 'I thought he wouldn't go that far.'

'I very much wanted him to,' Athena replied defiantly. 'Almost as much as I wish you would not.'

'Why did he bring you here then?'

'I'm sure he will tell you himself when he arrives.'

Blake laughed. 'He can't leave the Park. This is his night to shine. Everyone knows it's the evening when he will decide whom he wishes to marry. The whole place is alive with speculation, the candidates on the point of scratching one another's eyes out in order to gain an advantage. It was dreadfully amusing to watch. Anyway, I don't wish to overset you, my dear, but you are not so important to him that he will defy his mother's wishes and walk out on his own party.'

Athena very much feared Blake was right about that.

'Now come.' He sat beside her and, in another abrupt change of mood, caressed her sore face again. 'Be nice to me and I will return the favour.'

He bent to kiss her, his breathing short and excited as his lips touched hers. Athena bit his tongue when he tried to force it into her mouth. He howled and slapped her face again even harder. Her head exploded with the pain, bringing tears to her eyes. Far from deterring him, the bite appeared to spur him on, and his eyes glistened with anticipation as he lowered his body over hers.

'Just so you are aware, I enjoy giving and receiving pain. So if you mean to deter me by your actions, they are actually having the reverse effect. I like a woman with spirit, Athena, and I've known since I first saw you that you have it in abundance.'

He had lowered his breeches to his knees, and she felt his cock, thick and heavy, pulsating against her thigh. Perhaps she should bite that, too. Surely, that would deter him? The thought of having it anywhere near her mouth revolted and disgusted her, putting paid to that plan, but her resistance was far from over. He reached between them and fiddled with the placket to her breeches, easily popping the buttons free.

'Lift your hips.'

He presumably expected her to demur and couldn't hide his surprise when she obediently did so.

'Ah, so you do want me after all.'

She yearned to wipe the smug smile from his face but contented herself with a brief shrug. 'What's the point of resistance? You're far too strong for me. Let's just get it over with.'

'By all means.'

'You promise to care for the twins?'

'You have my word.' His breathing was hot and heavy as he struggled to pull her breeches down.

Athena let him get them so far, distracting him with her words while she desperately sought with the fingers of one hand for the vicious bobbin — one of the sharp wooden ones they used in lace-making — she had concealed in the waistband. Did she fix it to the right hand side, or to the left? She was sure it was on the right, but she couldn't feel it anywhere. She panicked, worried she hadn't secured it firmly enough and it had fallen out during her ride here. She had known he would expect her to arrive armed, which is why she had made it so easy for him to find the dagger. He was too foolish to think beyond a man's choice of weapons.

'Oh, my beautiful girl!' He gazed in awe at her near-naked body, the candlelight flickering, casting it in light and shadow. 'You are a prize so worth the winning. I promise to be gentle, my dear.'

Eli wasn't coming. If he was, he would have been here by now. She listened for the sound of horses, for men's voices. All she heard were the sounds of the night — an owl hooting, the leaves on the trees immediately beyond the window rustling in the breeze — nothing more encouraging than that. Well, that settled it. She was on her own and couldn't wait another second. He could force his vile member into her at any moment, and the sacrifice was too much to ask of her. Just when she had given up hope, her fingers closed around the bobbin and she drove it into his groin area with considerable force. He howled, hopped off the bed and jumped about the room, breeches around his ankles, both hands clutching his genitalia.

'You bitch, you'll pay for that!'

He pulled the bobbin out and headed for her, but by then Athena was on her feet and had the advantage of her breeches being back where they belonged, not hampering her movement. She blew out the nearest candle and picked up the heavy stick, brandishing it as a weapon.

'Put it down,' he said, fixing her with a murderous look. 'Or it will be worse for the girls.'

Only if he could go downstairs and give the order, and Athena would do whatever it took to ensure that didn't happen. He had miscalculated in separating himself from his man. Even if he shouted, it was unlikely he would be heard, especially if the girls had discovered the tiny knife she had hidden in the pocket of her cloak. She had schooled them often enough for this very situation, and warned them always to look for weapons in the most unlikely places. It was a piece of good fortune that Blake had so obligingly thrown her cloak at them. She trusted them to do the rest. If they could free their hands without Blake's man noticing, that would be something. Failing that, they could at least stab him in the thigh, if he got within striking range.

'No,' she said succinctly, stalking around him in a wide circle, her gaze fixed on his face. 'You will never bend me to your will, and there's an end to it.'

He pulled up his breeches without looking down, matching his movements to hers. 'Your spirit never fails to move me.'

Damnation, he was enjoying this! He sprang like an agile cat and caught her unawares, pulling her against him with considerable force. She was too close to be able to use the candlestick as a weapon, but her knee would do just as well. She drove it between his legs as hard as she could, but he moved at the last moment and her blow merely caught his thigh.

'Nice try.' He actually laughed. 'I told you already. I like it rough.'

Frantic barking and a loud crash interrupted them both. Thank God, Boris had found a way inside. An open window perhaps? Athena could only hope he had subdued Blake's man and the twins would have the good sense to remain downstairs until she could do the same thing to Blake. Her aggressor obviously heard the noise as well, but appeared too intent upon her to worry about it.

'That useless hound obviously escaped,' he said carelessly. 'Which is more than you will manage to do, my sweet.'

'I disagree.'

They both turned to see Eli standing in the doorway, filling the aperture with his imposing musculature, looking disturbingly poised. Only the stormy glitter of rage in his eyes gave away just how angry he actually was. Athena's body sagged with relief.

'Let her go,' he said in a mordant tone.

'Why would I do that when I've gone to so much trouble to find her?' He wound a strong arm around Athena's waist and held her in front of him, her back to his front. 'She's a troublesome minx, Winsdale, but I'll tame her eventually. I've spent many a long hour planning precisely how to go about it.'

'He actually believes that.' Athena shrugged. 'He's quite delusional.'

Eli flexed a brow. 'Evidently.'

'The twins?' she asked anxiously.

'Are unharmed.'

'Thank you,' she said, briefly closing her eyes.

'My pleasure.' He turned his attention to Blake. 'You're out of bargaining tools. Give it up now, let Miss Moncrieff go and face me like a man.'

Miss Moncrieff? He knows who I really am?

'You'd fight for the little doxy?' Blake sounded as surprised as he looked. 'She really has made an impression upon you, just as she has me. I wonder what it is about her.' Without telling Athena to expect it, he pushed her aside. She landed heavily on her backside beside the bed, winded but unharmed. 'Come along then, Winsdale. This ought to be amusing. Are you armed?'

348

Eli held up his hands. 'I don't need weapons to best you.'

Blake laughed as he turned his back on Eli and reached for his jacket. In a flash, Athena knew what he planned.

'Eli, be careful, he has a dagger!'

The dagger he had confiscated from her earlier, to be precise. It was too late for Eli to react to the threat. Blake again moved with surprising speed and agility and held the lethal blade to Eli's throat with a grip that didn't waver. Oh no! She had to do something. She was quite sure Blake really was sufficiently unbalanced to kill a duke without a second's thought. Madness was reflected in his eye. Madness and determination. He pressed the tip of the knife against Eli's throat, drawing blood.

Athena's brain stalled, inertia occasioned by fear for the man she loved. The two of them stood, facing one another, tantalisingly just out of her reach. If she tried to stand and intervene, Blake would strike at Eli and laugh while he did it, no doubt blaming her for forcing his hand. That was a risk she couldn't afford to take. There had to be another way.

Her sluggish mind was working at a frantic speed, logic no longer hampered by anxiety. If she was to somehow save Eli, she must set her own fears aside and think only of him. No wonder Blake hadn't demurred at facing him, she thought disgustedly. Forget gentlemanly conduct. He had never planned to fight fair. Knowing him as well as she did, how could Athena ever have supposed he would?

A young man appeared in the doorway. She recognised him from the Park, and was fairly sure he was Eli's secretary. He took the scene in at a glance and paled, fisting his hands at his side impotently. He glanced at Athena. She shook her head at him. There was nothing he could do without endangering Eli. Blake was facing him and would see the moment he made a move.

Athena, on the other hand, was directly behind Blake. Out the corner of her eye, she noticed the candlestick, and knew what she must do. Blake had his back to her, and was still standing stock still, holding the knife to Eli's throat, presumably waiting for him to admit defeat. Eli's eyes were pools of hostility, and Athena knew he would never concede. She also knew she would never get a better chance. Blake and Eli were staring at one another, neither of them taking any notice of her. In one fluid movement she rose to her knees, grabbed the candlestick, and threw it with as much strength as she could muster, aiming directly for the back of Blake's head. At such close quarters, she couldn't miss. Her blood pounded through her ears as she put all the pent up resentment she felt at the turn her life had taken into her aim. She hit him squarely on the back of his neck, not hard enough to do any damage, but sufficient to make his dagger hand slip.

Two things happened very quickly after that. Blake turned with a look of surprise on his face, as though he had only just remembered she was there, and kicked her viciously in the head. She cried out as her vision blurred and a pain beyond imagination exploded inside her brain. At the exact same moment, she heard a masculine roar of anger, a heavy blow being landed, and the sound of bone cracking. She smelt the tang of fresh blood and was dimly aware of Blake's colourful cursing as he crumpled to the floor beside her.

Then the world lost focus, and Athena fainted clean away.

19

Eli's heart stalled when he saw Athena lying motionless on the floor. The kick Blake had delivered to her head had made it snap backwards and might well have broken her neck. His body seized at the thought. He absolutely couldn't lose her. Not now. He crouched beside her, calling her name, anxiously feeling for a pulse. It was there thank the Lord, steady and regular. But Athena — his beautiful, courageous, spirited Athena, who had just saved his life for a second time — was deathly pale, and showed no signs of regaining consciousness.

He scooped her into his arms and gently laid her on the bed. When she still didn't stir, he removed her shoes, pulled back the covers, lifted her again, and placed her between the sheets. He didn't know what else to do for her, other than to brush the hair away from her brow and talk softly to her, willing her to open her eyes. What a fool he had been not to suppose Blake would pull a weapon on him and come suitably prepared. That miscalculation had possibly cost the life of the woman he loved to distraction.

He heard a sound behind him. The twins

had joined Jessop in the doorway, their eyes round with fear.

'Is she dead?' Selene asked, her lips trembling.

'She can't be dead.' Tears streamed down Lyssa's face.

'No,' Eli replied, his tone gently reassuring, 'she isn't dead.'

Boris barged into the room, went straight up to the bed and snuffled Athena's cold hand, pushing his nose beneath it. Then he whined, as though he too felt he had let her down and settled on the rug beside the bed. He rested his large head on his outstretched front paws, making it very plain he didn't plan to budge.

'Did you secure Blake's man?' Eli asked Jessop.

'Aye, your grace. The dog bit him, and he's bleeding pretty badly from his shin. I tied him up, just in case.'

'Tie this one up, too.' Eli indicated Blake, who had just sat up and was attempting to stem the flow of blood from his broken nose. 'Put them both in the cellar for the time being.'

'You can't put me in a cellar,' Blake protested, his voice a nasal whine. 'I need a doctor's services.'

'Count yourself fortunate I don't put you in the ground,' Eli replied in a glacial tone. 'I still might do that.'

'Miss Moncrieff and her sisters are my responsibility. I have her uncle's agreement on that score. You have no right to interfere.'

Eli ignored Blake and returned his attention to Jessop. 'You'll need to rouse Walters. You will find him in the apartment above the stables. Get him to help you with these two, and send Mrs. Walters to me. She might know what to do to help Miss Moncrieff.' There had to be something. 'When you've done all that, take the horse Miss Moncrieff rode here, the one from my curricle, and go back to Whispers' Hollow as fast as you can. Make sure Millie's safe and comfortable, and reassure her about Miss Moncrieff and the twins. As soon as it gets light, harness the horse to the curricle again and bring Millie back here with you. She will want to see her charges. Don't try and drive here until you can see. It's hard enough on horseback. You'll break your neck if you attempt it in a curricle in the dark.'

'I will see to all of that at once, your grace.'

Jessop detached a cord designed to hold the curtains back and bound Blake's hands tightly behind his back. With Blake still cursing and promising dire retribution, Jessop encouraged him down the stairs with considerable-sounding force. Presumably, he then locked him in the drawing room with his valet while he went to

354

fetch reinforcements in the shape of Walters.

The twins planted themselves on the bed beside Athena. Eli wasn't sure if they should get so close to her, but knew better than to try and remove them.

'She will wake up soon,' Eli said.

'She must,' Selene said bleakly. 'She's all we have left.'

'We would be nothing without her.'

'Things will be different now,' Eli promised them. 'You will never have to worry about Blake again.'

'Will we have to live with our uncle?' Lyssa asked, wrinkling her nose.

'Not if you don't want to.'

'We don't,' they replied in unison.

'You could live in this house, if you think you might prefer it.'

'Here?' Again they spoke together.

'It's very grand,' Selene said dubiously.

'I expect Athena will say we can't afford it.'

'The cottage is going to be very nice once the work is finished. That would do just as well.'

'But this is better.'

'I suppose we could make proper Cunningham lace again if we no longer have to worry about Mr. Blake.'

'That would make a big difference to our income.'

Eli listened in dazed fascination to their seamless communication, glad to have temporarily taken their minds off their unconscious sister. Her condition seemed unchanged, and Eli persuaded himself that was a good thing. He had heard somewhere the brain often shut itself down as a means of protection in times of extreme anxiety. This situation certainly qualified. He could only pray it would wake up again, none the worse for the experience.

Mrs. Walters interrupted them. 'Your grace.' She curtsied, looking utterly astonished by the scene that greeted her.

'Are you and Walters unharmed?' Eli asked.

'Yes, your grace. We had no idea what was happening. We heard horses earlier, my husband went to see who it was, but we had been locked into our apartment from the outside. There was nothing we could do.'

'I'm glad you weren't harmed. But now, is there anything you can do to help Miss Moncrieff? She has received a blow to the head. Should we send for a physician?'

'I don't see what he can do to help her that we can't. Just give me a moment.'

Mrs. Walters returned quickly with a bowl of water and cool cloth, which she pressed to Athena's forehead.

'She's very warm, your grace. We ought to get her out of these clothes.'

Eli refused to leave the room, contenting himself with turning his back while Mrs. Walters and the twins between them stripped off Athena's breeches and the remains of her tattered shirt, leaving her in just her chemise.

'There, she will be more comfortable now.'

Eli turned back again in time to see Mrs. Walters pulling the covers up to Athena's chin.

'I'll get this cleaned up.' Mrs. Walters wrinkled her nose as she pointed to the rug stained by Blake's blood. She bent to roll it up and threw it onto the landing. 'I'm sure Miss Moncrieff would prefer not to see it when she opens her eyes.'

'Quite, and find a room for these two young ladies, if you please, Mrs. Walters. They are all done in.'

'We want to stay with Athena.'

'You will be no good to her if you're too tired to keep your eyes open.' Eli shooed them from the bed. They had the same stubborn set to their chins as Athena adopted when she was displeased about something and looked ready to argue. In the end they didn't and went off with Mrs. Walters.

'You will call us if she opens her eyes, won't you, your grace?' Selene popped her head back around the door to ask the question.

'She will be worried about us, you see.'

Lyssa's head joined her sister's.

'You may depend upon it.'

'You will stay with her until Millie gets here?'

'You won't leave her?'

'I can safely promise you I won't leave her for a second.' Were all the females in the Moncrieff family so argumentative?

'Don't you have ducal duties that will take you away?'

'No. Now go!'

Left alone with Athena, Eli kissed her brow, sending thanks to anyone who could hear his thoughts for her safe deliverance.

And for his.

Without the twins' chatter, only Athena's shallow breathing and Boris's snores intruded upon the silence. Eli drank in the sight of his precious Athena, his feelings of fierce, protective love so strong they almost frightened him. Her features were so delicate, so pale, so heartbreakingly lovely, that Eli died a little more inside each time he looked at her and knew she could never be his. His courageous little firebrand's quick thinking had saved his life, at the possible cost of her own, and the only way he could repay her was to offer her and the twins this house and his protection. What he would give to be able to offer her the protection of his name, too.

He wanted Athena for his duchess, but that could never be — not unless he turned against his mother and everything she had strived to do to build the duchy into what it was today. What a farrago! He rested his head in his cupped hand and shook it from side to side. A vicious pain twisted and tore at his insides, and a leaden weight in the vicinity of his heart dragged him down to the depths of despair.

He felt bereft, an empty, hollow shell of a man. How the devil was he supposed to go back to the Park and choose a bride from the silly girls assembled there as though nothing had happened? And yet, that was precisely what he must do, and his duty, the weight of responsibility he carried on his shoulders, had never felt more onerous.

Eli would do his duty, but he wasn't going anywhere until Athena regained her wits. He didn't care whom he offended with his absence.

Incredibly, he must have dozed. He jerked awake in the chair beside Athena's bed, conscious of the first fingers of dawn light creeping through the gaps in the curtains. The sound of wheels and a horse whinnying had roused him. He immediately checked on Athena, feeling her forehead for signs of fever, relieved not to find any. But her eyes were still firmly closed. He hadn't had time to decide if that was a good or bad thing when the door opened and Millie waddled slowly in, looking battered and anxious.

'How is she, your grace?'

'The same.' He turned a bleak expression upon Athena's loyal retainer. 'I'm so glad you are here. I just don't know what else to do for her.'

Millie checked her for herself. 'There's not much else you can do. If the blaggard kicked her in the head, then she will either recover or she will not.' Millie wiped a tear from her wrinkled cheek. 'To have come all this way, only to stumble at the last hurdle.'

'She wouldn't have been kicked if she hadn't been trying to save me,' Eli said bleakly, because he needed someone to know the truth. 'Blake had a knife to my throat.' He indicated the spot of dried blood on his neck. 'I am absolutely convinced he would have used it, too, but for Athena.' He clenched his fist and thumped it against his thigh. 'Damn it, I should be the unconscious one, not her.'

Millie patted his hand, something only his mother had ever done before today. It didn't seem to occur to her that he was a duke, she a servant, because their love for Athena put them on equal terms.

'Don't think that way. Athena would prefer

to be the way she is than submit to Blake, you just take my word for that. She could have been living in luxury as his wife long since, but she preferred the existence we've been reduced to this past six months to that and wanted nothing to do with the blaggard.' Millie squared her shoulders. 'No, just so long as she knows the twins are unharmed, she will be content. She's been mother, father, and sister all rolled into one for those two since her parents' passing.' Millie paused and fixed Eli with a speaking look. 'No, she will be glad to have done what she did, especially since it was your life she saved, your grace.'

Eli dropped his head, too emotionally charged to speak for a moment. 'How about you, Millie?' he asked, when he recovered himself. 'You were brutally attacked, too.'

'Aye, Blake has never liked me. He blames me for turning Athena against him.'

'Why would he feel that way?'

'Because I opened her eyes to his true character. When he first came sniffing around Athena, he seemed charming and gracious. Well, he can be that way when he puts his mind to it, and she briefly considered accepting him. She has received no end of attention from men of all ranks, as you can probably imagine.'

Eli ground his jaw, consumed with a jealousy he had no right to feel. 'Indeed I can.'

'She takes after her mother, you see. She was a rare beauty, too. I was her mother's childhood friend. We grew up together in the same village. I used to make lace, too, before my fingers got too stiff for the delicate work. Anyway, when Athena's mother married, I went along with her and became a sort of maid-of-all-work, companion to Mrs. Moncrieff, and nursemaid to the girls.' She shrugged. 'I was treated as a member of the family and still am.'

'It shows,' Eli said softly. 'Athena and the twins hold you in great affection.'

'Mr. and Mrs. Moncrieff were quite modern in their outlook. They knew Athena could make a living with her lace and didn't insist she accept any of the men who applied for her hand, unless she was truly in love. They married for love, you see, and didn't want anything less for their daughter.'

'I do see.' And it explained a lot. 'But she considered Blake?'

'At first. He noticed her before her father died, but I didn't trust him even then. There was just something about him that didn't seem right.'

'I've always felt that way about him, too.'

362

'I found I had good reason not to like or trust him. One of my tasks was to go around the women who made lace for Athena, collecting it and making payments. One lady I called upon was in a terrible state. Her daughter had been brutally attacked, you see, and she subsequently died from her injuries.'

Eli scowled. 'Blake?'

'Aye, and that's not the worst part of it.' Millie paused. 'The child was just twelve years old.'

'My God!' Eli closed his eyes, waiting for the violent proclivities this intelligence engendered inside him to subside. 'No wonder Athena was so worried about the twins.'

'Exactly. I heard more stories about his tastes for young girls but, of course, no one could touch him because of his money and position. He seemed to think it was his God given right to have any child he fixed his interest upon, and that's pretty much what he did all over Nottingham.'

'But he wanted to marry Athena. Isn't she a little old for his tastes.'

'She is Athena,' Millie replied, as though that explained everything. And to Eli, it did. 'He was bewitched by her. Her father was still alive at the time. I told him what I'd heard about Blake, and he agreed Athena shouldn't have to see him again. Then, shortly after, her

363

father was murdered. I've often wondered about that but, of course, I have no way of proving Blake was behind it.'

'Extraordinary. To think he got away with so much.'

'He was indulged by his mother, could do no wrong in her eyes.' Millie shrugged. 'No good ever comes of such treatment.'

'What I fail to comprehend,' Eli said thoughtfully, 'is why the uncle was so determined to destroy a successful business.'

'To understand that, you need to know a little more about the interaction between the two families, Athena's and her uncle's. Athena's father was an educated man, and he took delight in teaching his daughters.'

'Ah, that would explain Athena's love of books, the Greek names — '

'Yes, he was a Greek scholar. Athena has an enquiring mind and absorbed everything her father could teach her, while at the same time learning about lace and herbs from her mother. The family spent a lot of time with the uncle, and Athena was thrown into local society from the age of fifteen. That's where she learned to dance and how to behave in company. Her cousin was besotted with Athena, and his father actively encouraged him to pursue her. I think that was because he knew the lace production would eventually fall to Athena, and he could see how profitable it was.'

'And, let me guess, Athena rejected the young cove, and the uncle took exception to that.'

'Precisely. He reminded his brother, in no uncertain terms, that if it weren't for him, Athena would never have been admitted to society in the first place. He all but ordered Athena's father to force her into the union, which of course he refused to do. He placated his brother by making him the executor of his will and the girls' guardian, never assuming it would be necessary for him to act in that capacity.' Millie looked wistful. 'I've often wondered if that was what got him killed.'

'And explains why the uncle wouldn't listen to Athena's advice when he took control of the business.'

'Yes, I've always thought so. He's one of those men who thinks a mere female couldn't possibly have a head for these things.'

Eli snorted. 'The fool!'

'Even before her father died, once Athena heard the stories of Blake's activities, she wanted nothing more to do with him anyway. It wasn't necessary for her father to ban him. Perhaps if he had not . . . but anyway, she was terrified for the twins as much as for herself. And after she sent him packing, her father wasn't cold in his grave before he was back again. He thought he had her this time, since her uncle needed Blake's money to bail himself out of the trouble he'd made for himself. Unfortunately for him, he failed to take into account Athena's strength of character.' Millie paused. 'Blake blames me for encouraging her to run away, and told his man to kill me when they found me at the cottage. Athena doesn't know that. There was no point in telling her, upsetting her even more. I survived, and that's all that counts.'

'How did you?'

'Pure luck. I don't think his man had the stomach for murder. He bashed me hard, and I had the good sense to stay down and play dead. He knew I wasn't, but did nothing about it, and I live to tell the tale.'

Eli shook his head. 'You've been through a lot.'

'And I'm blessed with a thick skull.' She touched the lump on the side of her head and offered him the ghost of a smile. 'That helps. I used some of Athena's herbs on it, and I'll be as right as rain in no time.' Her smile faded. 'It's our lamb I'm more concerned about.'

'You and me both, Millie,' Eli replied with feeling.

Millie struggled to her feet and straightened Athena's bedding. 'I'd best go and check on the twins,' she said. 'They tend to rise early and will be anxious about Athena.'

'I'm sure they will be glad to see you.'

Before Millie could leave the room, the door opened and the twins burst in.

'Millie!'

They threw themselves at her, and Millie opened her arms to embrace them both at once, even though Eli could see it hurt her battered body to do so.

'How are you?'

'We were so worried.'

'How is Athena?'

'Has she not woken at all?'

'There must be something we can do for her.'

Eli said little, sitting back instead and watching the scene unfold, now seriously concerned about Athena. She had been unconscious for eight hours — too long, surely? Boris stirred, sniffed her hand again and whined.

'He needs to go out,' Eli said to no one in particular.

Before anyone could do anything about it, there was the sound of voices on the landing directly outside the bedroom.

'I must see for myself.'

Eli's heart sank. It was his mother.

Harry stuck his head round the door.

'Sorry,' he mouthed to Eli. 'She insisted knowing what was going on.'

'And you told her?'

'Have you tried resisting her when she makes her mind up about something?'

Eli shrugged. His brother had a point.

'Certainly I required to know.'

The duchess sailed into the room as though she owned the place. In a manner of speaking, Eli thought with a wry twist of his lips, he supposed she did. Millie stood up and managed a creaky curtsey. The twins, struck dumb for once, did the same thing.

'This is the Duchess of Winsdale,' Eli told them. 'Mother, these are Miss Moncrieff's sisters, Selene and Lyssa, but don't ask me which is which.'

'I am Selene, your grace.'

'And I am Lyssa.'

'It's very nice to make your acquaintance, girls, but now, if you will excuse me, I require a word in private with the duke.'

Eli didn't doubt it.

Everyone obediently trouped from the room, including Boris. Eli vacated his chair so his mother could occupy it, and perched one buttock on the edge of Athena's bed, absently brushing a stray strand of hair away from her face.

'How is she?'

'Before you say anything more, Mother, she saved my life.' He paused, in no mood for a parental lecture. 'Again.'

'I'm sure we're much obliged to her, Eli. But it wouldn't have been necessary if you had remained where you were supposed to be.'

'Am I to take it you're happy for one of our tenants to be attacked by a guest staying in our house and have me do nothing about it?'

20

Discounting the throbbing pain in her head, Athena couldn't remember the last time she had felt so comfortable. She drifted just outside of consciousness, aware of voices and activity around her, but remaining apart from it. People were concerned about her, and she wanted to assure them she was all right, but her eyes refused to open. Cocooned between crisp cotton sheets, she craved the touch of Eli's soothing hand on her brow.

It *was* Eli's hand. She recognised his touch, sensed his flowing masculine power, and fed from his strength. She heard Millie. She heard the twins, excited about living in this house, yet subdued because of her condition. What house? Had Blake got them again? No, they wouldn't be excited about that. Lord above, was that the duchess she could hear? What was she doing here? Presumably, she had come to remind her son of his duty and forcibly remove him from her side.

Don't go, Eli. I need you, my love.

'I won't leave until she opens her eyes, Mother, and nothing you can say will change that decision.'

More words were exchanged. She couldn't make them out, but the duchess finally left. Eli did not. The twins came back. She had no real sense of time. How long had she been here? An hour, a day, a week? What had happened to Blake? It was all confusion inside her head, which ached from the accumulation of so many months of responsibility and worry. She was tired, so very tired.

They were alone again, just her and Eli. She could sense his sculpted torso and absorbed his unique masculine smell as he leaned over and kissed her brow. His hand gripped hers and squeezed.

'Wake up, my love. We need you to come back to us.'

Athena tried, really tried, to force her eyes open. She had rested for long enough, and Eli sounded so desolate. She thought she had heard him sobbing at one stage. Surely not because of her? The thought of such a strong man reduced to tears revived her. This time her eyelids did as they were told and opened when she asked them to. Bright sunlight hurt her eyes, and so she closed them again, but remained conscious.

'Eli?'

'Athena?' He leaned over her again. 'Oh my love, you're awake!'

His dear face, stubbled with a day's worth of beard and creased with concern, was the first thing she saw when she opened her eyes again. This time they remained open. He placed a hand on her brow and a gentle kiss on her lips.

'How do you feel?'

She smiled weakly. 'Alive. Is Blake under guard?'

'Don't worry about him. He will never hurt you again.'

'Good.'

'Does your head still hurt?'

'Not too badly.'

'Don't lie to me, sweetheart?'

'Is Millie here?'

'Yes, she's with the twins, and much as I would like to keep you to myself, they need to know you are awake. They can do far more for you than I can.'

He's anxious to go already. Athena's heart now ached worse than her head. 'How long have I been here?'

'More than twelve hours.'

'No wonder I feel so rested.' She reached for his hand, and he grasped hers gently yet firmly, raised it to his mouth and brushed her knuckles with his lips.

'I thought I had lost you.' His voice shook with emotion. 'You saved me again, but almost paid for it with your own life.'

'And I would do it again, in a heartbeat.'

'Oh, my love.' He placed a gentle kiss on her lips. 'You're too weak to talk right now. I shall send Millie and the girls to you. I must go back to the Park, but I will be back in the morning.'

Don't say it unless you mean it. I don't need false promises.

'Promise me you will rest until then.'

'Yes, I will rest.'

She said it to make him feel better, so he could leave her with a clear conscience. And leaving appeared to be uppermost in his mind. Athena's heart broke at the prospect, but she reminded herself her life was now her own. She no longer had anything to be afraid of and tried to count her blessings.

'Make sure you do.' He ran his index finger gently along the line of her lips. 'I shall know if you break your word.'

'I doubt I will be allowed to do anything but rest.'

'Good.'

He bent to kiss her again, and then pulled the bell rope. The twins exploded into the room almost immediately, whooping with delight when they saw she was awake. Millie followed more slowly, as did another lady who introduced herself as Mrs. Walters.

Athena was smothered with affection and spent some time reassuring her sisters she really was all right. Mrs. Walters spoke of broth, and Athena agreed she would try some, even though she wasn't hungry. Amidst all the attention she received, Athena still noticed Eli as he slipped from the room. He paused at the door, caught her looking at him, and sent her a smouldering smile that melted her insides. Then he was gone, and shortly thereafter she heard the sound of a horse cantering away.

I wonder if I *will* actually see him again, she thought. A hand painfully squeezed her heart when she realised she most likely would not, despite his promises. His mother didn't approve of her, would almost certainly try to prevent it, and perhaps that would be for the best.

Athena did manage to eat a little and enjoyed being washed and having her hair brushed by Millie as she listened to the twins' non-stop chatter. It seemed the ordeal they had suffered at Blake's hands had had no lasting effect. Ah, the resilience of youth! But then, they were not aware just what a narrow escape they had all had and what would eventually have happened to them if they had lived beneath Blake's roof. Athena vowed they would never learn the complete truth. At least she could protect them from that.

'His grace says we can live in this house for as long as we like,' Selene said. 'Just imagine that.'

'It's so much more comfortable than the cottage,' Lyssa added.

'We shall have to see about that.'

Athena didn't think she could live so close to him and yet not actually be with him. She couldn't bear the thought of seeing him with his bride-to-be. He had made it plain he didn't want her as a mistress, and what else was there for them?

'Come along you two,' Millie said when daylight faded and Athena felt her eyes droop. 'Your sister needs to sleep. We'd best leave her in peace.'

The twins complained, but Millie wasn't in the mood to let them argue. Only Boris refused to leave her, settling down on the rug he had apparently occupied all the time she had been out of her senses. She was glad of his undemanding company and reached down to scratch his ears.

Athena didn't think she would sleep because her head was still sore, her brain full of images of Eli. Millie said he had refused to budge from her side all the time she was unconscious. Well, she *had* saved his life, so she supposed he felt obliged to do something in return. Even so, he'd left her with a speed that was almost insulting the moment she had woken up.

Athena did sleep and woke feeling restored and thoroughly rested. Mrs. Walters came in with her breakfast.

'How do you feel, ma'am?' she asked.

Ma'am? 'Much better, thank you.'

'Would you like a bath?'

'Oh, yes please, if it's not too much trouble.'

'None at all.'

A bath was brought up by Mr. Walters. He then trudged up and down with kettles of boiling water, and Athena soon had the luxury of sinking into the hot, fragrant water. It soothed her aching bones, even if there was nothing it could do to cleanse her broken heart. Millie helped her wash her hair, and by the time she forced herself to leave the bath, she felt quite like her old self again.

'Here we are, lamb.' Millie held out the bronze gown Athena had worn to the harvest dance.

'How did that get here?' she asked, surprised.

'All of our things are here. His grace had them sent over.'

'Oh, well I suppose we can stay here until the work on the cottage is completed. But we must also consider our future. We can do as we please now, although I suppose my uncle will still try to interfere with the twins.'

'Don't you worry about that now.' Millie brushed the tangles out of Athena's wet hair. 'Do you want to come down and sit in the drawing room for a change? We have a nice fire going there.'

'Yes, I think I would like that.'

The twins greeted her with great enthusiasm. The identical pinched looks of concern they had worn for so long were gone, and they were behaving like children should, laughing, playing with the dog, bickering amicably, and allowing their personalities to shine. Athena glowed with sisterly pride.

They took luncheon together, after which Athena dozed in front of the fire. When she awoke again she was alone, the twins nowhere in sight.

'The duke sent a carriage for them,' Mrs. Walters explained in response to Athena's concerned enquiries. It would be a while before she stopped worrying when she didn't know where they were. 'Millie went with them. Lady Susan invited them to spend the afternoon at the Park.'

'Did she indeed.' Athena creased her brow. 'How very extraordinary.'

'Would you like something to read? There

is a small collection of books in the study.'

'Is there?'

Athena brightened. How long had it been since she had enjoyed the luxury of whiling away her time with a book? She ran her finger along their spines, choosing one at random, and settled back in front of the drawing room fire. The words blurred before her eyes, and she nodded off to sleep again, only to be woken by a presence looming over her. Half awake, she panicked, worrying that Blake had broken free and found her again.

She knew at once it wasn't Blake, even before she looked up and saw Eli standing there, all lithe muscle and graceful co-ordination. He was dressed, not in ducal splendour, but as she preferred to see him, in breeches, hessians dusty from the ride over, and an open-necked shirt.

'How do you feel?' he asked softly.

'Much better, thank you.'

'You look it.' He sat beside her. 'Should you be out of bed?'

'Certainly I should.'

'I'm vexed with you. Why did you come to the masquerade, putting yourself in danger when you knew Blake was in the house?'

She shrugged. 'I've asked myself that question many times. I suppose part of me wanted it over with once and for all. I'd started to realise I couldn't run indefinitely, and if he had seen me, it was better to get it over with.' She paused, knowing she hadn't told him the complete truth. 'Besides, I wanted to see you.'

'Oh, Athena!' Eli shook his head, sending his thick hair cascading across his brow. 'You should have told me.'

'I was going to, here in this house, after . . . well, after what I wanted to do and you did not. Then we fell to arguing, and the moment to reveal my secrets was lost.'

'Yes, put like that, I suppose — '

'I was going to tell you at the masquerade then I received that note — '

'Which is when you should have definitely involved me,' he said severely.

'I couldn't take the chance.' Athena stared at the flames flickering in the grate, wondering how she could make him understand her fears. 'I didn't imagine you could leave your own masquerade, even if you were prepared to help me, especially since you were supposed to be making your final choice.'

Eli shook a finger at her. 'When will you begin to understand I can do as I please?'

'And yet you left me to deal with something important.'

'That was to do with you, you goose.'

'Oh!'

'I knew you were reluctant to tell me your secrets, so I sent someone to Nottingham to make enquires. He arrived back during the masquerade.'

'Ah, so that's how you knew my name. I thought Millie had told you.'

'I would have known it a lot sooner if you had told me yourself, and my man wouldn't have been beaten by your uncle's oafs.'

'Oh dear, will he be all right?'

'Yes, I don't think any bones are broken.'

'That's good.' Athena paused, conscious of the atmosphere that seemed to vibrate with his presence. 'What are you doing here?' she asked, not looking at him.

'What sort of welcome is that?' He sent her a tender smile that melted her vulnerable heart.

'Your Mama will not be pleased. You are supposed to be dancing attendance upon your would-be brides.'

'I am.'

Athena blinked. 'I beg your pardon.'

He removed the book from the lap and put it aside. Then he took her hand and turned it over so he could again place a kiss on the centre of her palm.

'I had to come,' he said quietly. 'I told you I would.'

'Yes, I remember.' A torrent of conflicting

emotions wrought havoc with her equilibrium as he continued to softly caress her palm with his thumb. 'But you shouldn't be here. I've already caused you enough problems.'

The corners of his mouth lifted. 'There's nowhere else I would rather be.'

'Thank you for allowing us to live here temporarily. As soon as I can make plans, we shall move away, and you can have your house back.'

'You will certainly move away,' he replied.

'There was no need for you to say that,' she replied, miffed. 'I've already told you we will go as soon as we can.'

'Do be quiet, Athena, and let me tell you what I meant. You will be moving, very soon I hope, into the Park.'

Athena was astounded. She couldn't possibly have heard him right, surely? 'You want to employ us in some manner?' She frowned. 'I hardly think — '

'No, you goose. I'm making a very bad job of this, but what I'm asking you . . . the reason why I found a way to get the twins out of the way, is that I came here to ask you if you would do me the very great honour of becoming my duchess.'

'What! Have you taken complete leave of your senses?' She canted her head and scrutinised his face, furious with him for toying with her. 'Please don't joke about impossibilities.'

'It's no joke, my love.'

'Are you sure you didn't receive a bump on the head, too?'

He had the nerve to laugh at her reaction. 'Perfectly sure.'

'Eli, be serious. I can't marry you.'

'Why ever not? I thought you returned my feelings.'

'That's as may be, but your mother requires you to marry someone *suitable*. She went to considerable trouble to assemble suitable candidates for your inspection at the Park. It would be a sorry way indeed to repay her if you were to marry a lace-maker.'

'My mother's suitable candidates have all gone home disappointed.'

Athena blinked. 'They have?'

'Indeed.'

'Then your mother must be very vexed.'

'Oh no, she sent them off herself.'

'Eli, you're talking in riddles. Have the goodness to explain yourself.'

'My mother came here when you were unconscious.'

'You know, I think I heard her. You told her I had saved your life, and said it wouldn't have been necessary if you hadn't come here after me.' Athena suppressed a persistent giggle. 'She did not sound pleased.'

Eli elevated both brows. 'You were awake?'

'Not precisely, but I was aware, on some level, what was going on. It was most peculiar, almost like a dream. I had convinced myself it was, and that the duchess had never been here.'

'Did you hear what else my mother had to say?'

'No, I heard you say you were going to stay until I woke up, I think, but I don't remember anything else.'

'My mother is not romantic. Duty is her byword, and she was convinced I would be happier if I married a suitable woman, rather than one I entertained feelings for. She had her suspicions about us when I endorsed your lace and then had the cottage renovated. She saw us dancing together at the harvest party — '

'Everyone seemed to,' Athena replied with a wry smile. 'Including Blake.'

Eli frowned. 'Don't mention that blaggard to me.'

'What's happened to him?'

'He and his man are currently enjoying a long voyage to the Indies,' Eli replied, setting his jaw. 'It was either that or have them up on charges of kidnap and rape. For your sake, I decided not to go down that route. Besides, being banished from these shores and good society will almost be a worse punishment for Blake. He knows if he sets foot back in England he will be arrested.'

Athena shook her head, marvelling at how effortlessly he made things happen. 'I think you did the right thing. I fully intended to kill him the first chance I got, rather than risk him anywhere near the twins, so he ought to be grateful to you.'

Eli elevated a brow. 'You would have gone that far?'

'Certainly I would. Herbs don't just *cure* maladies, you know. They can create them, too.'

Eli chuckled. 'Remind me never to overset you, Miss Moncrieff. And kindly refrain from changing the subject. It's a very disconcerting thing to do to a man when he's trying to propose to the woman he loves.'

He loves me? 'I beg your pardon. Pray, continue with your proposition. I am quite at leisure to hear it.'

'Proposal, Athena. One does not proposition the woman one intends to marry.' He raised their joined hands and kissed the inside of her wrist this time. 'However, we were speaking of my mother's disinclination to believe in romantic love, or that it could endure even if it did exist.'

'She ought to have met my parents,' Athena said wistfully. 'When they were in the same room together, right up until the end, it was as though no one else in it existed. I think that's why I have never been tempted to marry. If I couldn't have that, then I would prefer not to have a man dominating me.'

'But you can have it, sweet Athena, if only you will accept me.'

'You're actually serious.' She blinked at him, still convinced she must be dreaming. 'Your mother has had a change of heart?'

'Yes, that's what she came over here specifically to tell me. You have saved both of her sons' lives, mine twice, and she has seen for herself just how we feel about one another. She was quite overcome with emotion, actually. I never thought to see her so affected. Anyway, she said the matter was sealed for her when she saw us waltzing at the masquerade . . . oh, and when Susan introduced you to her at luncheon, and you stood up to her cross-questioning.'

'I suppose she did seem rather surprised by my forthright views.' This time there was nothing Athena could do to quell her giggle. 'I couldn't afford to satisfy her curiosity about my circumstances, you see.'

'Oh yes, very clearly.'

'My uncle,' she said, shaking her head. 'He

385

is the twins' legal guardian. He bears me a grudge and will probably insist they live with him, just to spite me.'

Eli laughed. 'He's certainly welcome to try, but it won't serve. Just leave your uncle to me. The twins will live with us, and want for nothing.'

'Even if you manage to get the better of him, there is still my lineage to consider. I am not duchess material.'

'You are connected to the Moncrieff's. That is enough for my mother. That and the fact she really does want me to be happy.'

Athena absorbed his words, at a loss to know how to respond at first, even if this was what, subconsciously, she had wanted since first meeting Eli. People might raise their eyebrows, but if Eli and his mother didn't mind, why should she?

'I love you, Eli,' she said simply, lifting her free hand to gently stroke his face. 'And if you're really serious about marrying me, then I accept your proposal with gladness in my heart.'

'Oh my sweet love!'

Eli pulled her into his arms and kissed her witless.

'I have just one condition of my own. Well two, actually,' she told him when he finally released her.

'Name them.'

'Firstly, I can't stop thinking about the women who used to make Cunningham lace in Nottingham. Many of their husbands returned from the war, expecting to find gainful employment after serving king and country so diligently, but none was available. Others didn't come back at all.' Athena sighed. 'In both sets of circumstances, the women needed the money they made from the lace to keep food on their tables, but my uncle took that away from them without a thought for their welfare.'

'You would like to resurrect your Cunningham lace production?'

'Yes. The twins and I could supply new patterns, and I know a lady who could keep control of it all in Nottingham. I wouldn't need to actually be there.'

'I had assumed you would want to do that.'

She blinked. 'And you don't mind your wife working?'

'Not in the least. And my name . . . our name, endorsing the product will ensure its success.'

'Thank you!' She clutched his face in her hands and planted a soft kiss squarely on his lips. 'One of the reasons I didn't wish to marry was because I feared the loss of my freedom. I can see that won't be a difficulty where you are concerned.'

'Provided you don't keep anything from me ever again.' He pulled her into his lap and settled his chin on top of her head. 'What's your second condition?'

'Well.' She looked down at her lap, colour flooding her face. 'When I offered myself to you before as your mistress, you rejected me.'

'Athena, I didn't — '

'What if we don't suit?'

He chuckled and flashed a devastatingly wicked grin. 'Oh, trust me, angel, we'll suit.'

'Then prove it to me. I'm four-and-twenty. I've waited quite long enough, don't you think.'

'Why, Miss Moncrieff, I do believe you're no better than you ought to be.'

She fluttered her lashes, repeatedly. 'I am what you made me, your grace.'

'Angel, I haven't started with you yet.'

'Then may I humbly suggest you stop talking and let your actions speak for you.'

With a roar of laughter, Eli stood up, swept her from his lap into his arms, and carried her up the stairs, taking them two at a time. 'It's fortunate the twins will be gone for several hours,' he said, kissing her as he kicked open her bedroom door.

As it was, several hours wasn't long

enough. But, as Eli pointed out when he heard the sound of the twins returning and hastily removed himself from Athena's bed, they had the rest of their lives to make up for lost time.

A BITTERSWEET PROPOSAL

Wendy Soliman

When Marcus Rothwell, Earl of Broadstairs, is forced to spend the night alone with Harriet Aston he willingly does the honourable thing. In this marriage of convenience, Harriet determines to engage Marc's affections. However, she is brutally attacked, and whilst suspicion falls upon the dowager countess, who disapproves of Harriet, there's the village beadle's unaccountable behaviour to be considered, as well as Marc's Machiavellian steward. Wanting to protect Harriet, Marc delves into the mystery surrounding her attack. Now he must examine his feelings for the woman he married on a whim. But he too is in mortal danger . . .

THE CARSTAIRS CONSPIRACY

Wendy Soliman

As sole heir to the late Duke of Penrith's estate, Abigail Carstairs suspects that someone is trying to kill her for her fortune. In desperation she turns to the notorious Lord Sebastian Denver. Unable to deny a lady in distress, Sebastian inveigles his way into Abby's hunting lodge where all the prime suspects are gathered. However, distracted by his growing attraction towards Abby, he is unprepared when a further attempt is made on her life. As Sebastian lays a daring trap for her aggressors, he's in a race against time to keep her safe . . .

THE SOCIAL OUTCAST

Wendy Soliman

Eloise Hamilton, the illegitimate daughter of a wealthy banker, knows that society will never open its doors to the likes of her. So when Lord Richard Craven, heir to the dukedom, singles her out, she harbours no false illusions about the outcome. Her neighbour, the formidable rakehell Harry Benson-Smythe, is not only suspicious of her high-born admirer but inexplicably jealous too. It is only as Eloise and Harry work together to solve the mysterious abductions of local girls that Richard's true purpose becomes apparent. As do Harry's feelings for Eloise, which go beyond the merely neighbourly . . .

DUTY'S DESTINY

Wendy Soliman

When Felix, Viscount Western, discovers his father's shipping line is being used to smuggle ex-sla_____ ____ ied to put a stop to th_____ _____ man masterminding th_____ ____augh-ter, Saskia Eden, ____ ___ ___ ____ted of being involved. F__ _____ __ ___est at her aunt's house ___ __ _____ __ find Saskia running th_ _____ _____ ingle-handed. Felix sc___ realizes tha_ _askia knows nothing o_ ___ estrange_ _____ther's business and relu_____ly accepts __r help to get to the tru__ ___ ____ ___ d not plan on was fallin_____